RISE AND FALL

KRISTA COOPER-SCHMIDT

CRIMSON AETHER PRESS

RISE AND FALL

To the bright-eyed little girl who endured unbearable weight, and the resilient woman who finally put it down. May this be your catharsis.

ACT I

CHAPTER I
DANI

Consciousness comes to Dani in a slow kind of startle. Like when you found yourself being shaken from a nightmare, only to find there were still shadows of it creeping at the edge of your vision. Was this a nightmare?

Dani really hopes it is.

Her eyes are open, but her environment is pitch-dark. The only audible sound is Dani's labored breathing as she tries to sit up and a pain rattles her skull, pushing her back down.

She takes a breath, feels around. A box. A wooden box. She's in a –

Fuck. She's fucked.

Dani's throat burns as a scream rips itself from it, while the vaguest thoughts remind her the action won't work in her favor. It's only after she breaks a nail from clawing into the coffin lid that Dani forces herself to calm.

Right. Buried alive. Well, she's gotten out of worse, right? Right? She could do this. She could totally do this.

Dani feels around, searches for anything that might be of use. There's nothing. No phone, no pockets – all she has is the black lace dress on her back. She does remember the dress. Remembers wearing it all of once to her foster parent's funeral before being shuffled back to the group home with Matt.

A chill grips her spine.

She can't do this. Oh, god. Oh, god. She was going to die down here! Had she already died? Oh, god.

What had even happened? If Nickie and Matt –

Dani freezes. Can feel her mind stutter and scratch, the previous record of panic thrown off the player.

Nickie. Matt. She could do this for them. She had to try. And anyway, what was the alternative? Wait down here to die? Again?

And so, Dani rips the lower part of the fabric from her dress, covers her face with it, and takes a generous breath before maneuvering the coffin lid off.

The panic returns and it is all Dani can register. Her vision is spotting and her lungs are screaming by the time she finally breaks the surface of the graveyard, proceeding to collapse on its surface.

Her gravestone mocks her through blurred vision and pained gasps. *Danielle Olivia Argent,* the inscription reads, *Beloved sister and friend. Heaven is lucky to have gained such a bright angel.*

Dani frowns, coughs, and frowns again. Neither Nickie nor Matt would have come up with an inscription like that. Which meant they were either too busy fighting to reach a verdict or didn't have much to do with the planning of her funeral at all. Neither of which sits well with Dani.

Thoughts of her brother and best friend eventually motivate Dani enough to reach a standing position. The action takes her longer than she'd like. Longer still, to limp over to the adjacent church.

It's nighttime, probably heading towards dawn, and that foreboding sense of urgency pushes her adrenaline into higher gear.

The backdoor of the church opens without complaint and Dani limps inside. Her feet follow her mind's scream for 'water!' to a nearby water fountain, her bloody and dirt-covered hands shaking as they fumble for the button.

Dani drinks and the movement feels so foreign she has to double-check she's doing it right. Water. Mouth. Swallow. Right? *Right?*

Dani shudders. She catches a glimpse of her reflection in the steel of the water fountain and shudders again. She looks half-dead.

A dread washes over her that she works desperately to force down, along with another few mouthfuls of water. Finally, and with only the fuzziest sense of her surroundings, Dani hobbles back towards the entrance. She is about to look for a phone when her eyes catch sight of a calendar on the wall.

Time slows then, or at least, more so than it already was. For a long time, Dani stares at the calendar, as if by doing so she might will the date to change.

A year. An entire year she's been –

A shooting pain in Dani's skull forces her to her knees as the memories begin to resurface.

It was her birthday. Dani and Nickie had been celebrating (see: getting shitfaced) with drinks all night. After stumbling through most of downtown, they end up in a park. It's a nice park; one of Dani's favorites. Littered with fruit-bearing trees and surprisingly upkept pathways.

There's an apple tree almost in the dead center. When Nickie sees it, she spaces out for a moment before erupting into a fit of giggles. She asks Dani to grab a few so they can make some

3

appletinis. Of course, Dani's alcohol-ridden brain thought it was a hilarious idea.

Except there are no apples within reach, so Nickie hoists her up. Dani is laughing as she reaches for one. Nickie wobbles, curses under her, and then Dani is falling.

She can feel the impact, the sharp and then numbing pain that paralyzes her neck and spine. Gasped breaths that refuse to let any oxygen in. Her vision blurs, seeing only a silhouette of her best friend and then –

A bile rises in Dani's throat that scatters the previously drank water, along with what she can only assume is embalming fluid, over the pristine tiled church floor. Panicked gasps follow, as her feet give way underneath her.

Was it too late to crawl back into her grave?

"Miss? Miss! Are you alright?"

Lifting her head to see the wild-eyed expression of the pastor feels like more than Dani can manage. *Get a grip!* Her mind shouts at her, livid in its attempts to get her to her feet. *Just get a grip now and you can deal with the fall-out later.*

"Miss, can you tell me your name? Do you need me to call an ambulance?"

"No," Dani says a little too quickly as she makes her way to a standing position. "I just need a phone."

"Miss...."

"Dani."

"Dani," he repeats, along with a forced smile leaking of sympathy. Dani hates it. "I can help you. There are people that can help you, whatever your situation might be."

Dani stifles a laugh. Who the hell was this guy going to call? *Ghostbusters?*

"Listen, ugh, Father – "

"Neil is fine, Dani." The pastor corrects her softly,

4

kindly. As if begging Dani to allow him to help her. Dani only wishes he could.

"Neil," Dani says. "I appreciate the concern. Really. It's... nice. But I just need a phone, okay?"

Neil looks hesitant and Dani can't say she blames him. After a few uncomfortable moments, the pastor leads her to a nearby desk. Dani finds herself dialing her brother's number on instinct, but her finger stills at the last moment before pressing the 'call' button.

She hadn't seen Matt in over two years. Doesn't know what he was doing with his life or if he ever finished that degree in Political Science. The only exchanges Dani ever got from him were 'Happy Birthday' texts, and those were more for her benefit, so she at least knew he was alive.

And wasn't it something that even after crawling out of her own grave, she was still more worried about her brother than herself?

"Dani?"

Dani startles, gives Neil a shaky nod, and dials Nickie's number. Her best friend answers on the third ring.

"Heyo," Nickie greets, and the warm familiarity has Dani nearly crying with relief.

"Nickie. It's Dani. I'm −" Not dead? Half-dead? What was she supposed to say? Would Nickie even believe her?

The call drops and Dani curses.

Frantically, Dani redials. And when she gets the voicemail, dials again. And again, and *again*. All while Neil looks on with an expression that has Dani wanting to punch something.

"Listen. I don't know who the hell you think you are but this is *so* not funny," Nickie spits into the line after the twelfth ring and Dani doesn't waste any time.

"Nickie, listen to me. I need you to listen to me, okay?

It's *me*. It's Dani. You're my best friend. We met in foster care when I was ten and you were eight. You were sitting alone in the dining hall, and when I came to sit next to you with Matt, you told me I looked sad and asked if I wanted to be best friends. You had a crush on me in tenth grade, which you –"

"*Everyone* had a crush on you, you jerk. You and your cool leather jacket and combat boots and broody – OH, MY GOD. Dani? Holy fuck. Holy shit. What the fuck?"

"Nickie, I need you to stay calm, okay?"

"*Stay*....are you fucking kidding me?!" Dani can only put some space between her poor eardrums and the phone. Finally, Dani screams back, "If you're freaking out, how the hell do you think *I* feel?! Can you just tell me where you are, or better yet, pick me up?"

Silence. Dani is very close to screaming into the line again when Nickie says, "I'll send a cab for you."

"A cab? Seriously?"

"Listen," Nickie bites back, but even through the line Dani can hear the fear in her voice. "This is kind of, no scratch that, this is *definitely* how every bad horror movie in the history of forever begins. So, excuse me if I'm taking some precautionary measures here, Miss I'm Back From the Dead and Very Well Might Try and Eat My Best Friend's Face."

"I'm not a zombie!" Though as soon as the words leave her mouth, even Dani can't be sure.

"Well, you're something," Nickie says. "And I quite like my face attached to my body, thank you very much." A beat. "Where are you?"

Neil thankfully pushes one of the church's pamphlets her way, though not without giving her a look that said the man was very concerned for the state of her mental health.

Join the club, buddy.

"It's the First Congregational Church. 1284 Hillside Road. Still in Roselake."

There's another few beats of silence before Nickie says, "Okay. I'll call them right now," and promptly hangs up.

Dani stares at the receiver, lets out a breath, and slams it back down. Still, she likes to think that conversation could have gone a lot worse.

Pastor Neil walks her out, providing a much-appreciated bottle of water and blanket, and thankfully makes no further comments. She shifts the blanket from shoulder to shoulder as she waits for her ride. Waits for something else, too, that she can't place a name to yet. All while Nickie's horror movie reference tickles coldly at the back of her neck.

The cab arrives and the sight of Neil is enough to allow her into the backseat without much complaint. Though not before said pastor reiterates that he is here should she ever want any help and that 'God is always with her'.

Dani gives him a tight smile as she shuffles into the backseat.

"So, ugh, rough night?" The driver says awkwardly as they are well on their way to her destination.

Dani does allow herself to laugh then, though it comes out far less manic than she was expecting. The sound reverberates painfully into her chest.

"*Rough year.*"

When Dani steps out of her cab to be met with the sight of a run-down new age shop called A New Dawn, she is certain Nickie must have sent her to the wrong address. Which would figure, wouldn't it? Turning back toward the curb, she finds her driver, unsurprisingly, long gone.

She tugs her blanket tighter against her body and pushes forward into the shop.

It's far bigger than she expected it to be, with numerous rows of books adjoining tables filled with crystals, herbs, and figurines. There's a reading area off to the far left and beside that, a mini café. Dani is greeted with the smell of espresso intermingled with an incense she can't care to place.

She is a few steps into the shop and getting ready to call Nickie's name when a splash of liquid against her face startles her back.

"Exorcizamus te, omnis immundus spiritus, omnis satanica potestas, omnis – uhm, omnis, omnis legio? Shit."

Dani smiles despite herself. Nickie tries and fails a few more times with her chanting and Dani is more than welcome to let her.

Nickie looked good; better than Dani had seen her in a while. The bags under her eyes aren't so prominent and she's put on some much-needed weight. It looks good on her short frame, as does the choppy, braided strawberry hair.

The relief of her visage is so overwhelming that Dani doesn't notice when Nickie has stopped her exorcism in favor of a comically large gape.

"I guess there isn't an exorcism for zombies?" Dani tries. "*Dani?*"

Dani was tempted to say her best friend looked as if she's seen a ghost, but well, the statement seemed a bit too morbidly on the nose, given the circumstances.

Nickie reaches out a shaky hand and jerks back when she finds Dani is an actual physical object she can touch.

Just as Dani begins to think she might bolt, her best friend surprises her by bringing her into a crushing hug.

"Jesus Christ, Dani. Are you okay? What the actual hell? I thought you were dead!"

"I was." Just as the words leave her mouth does Nickie start taking in Dani's appearance. Her expression pales further.

"Please don't tell me you just crawled out of your own grave, Dani. *Please.*"

The look on Dani's face is answer enough.

"Dani. Oh, god. Oh shit. Shouldn't we be in a hospital right now?"

"And tell them *what* exactly, Nickie?" Dani says. "That I've inexplicably risen from the dead and need medical attention for the injuries I sustained while crawling out of my grave?"

Nickie gives her a nasty look. After a few moments of massaging her temples, she throws her hands up in some kind of vague acceptance before ushering Dani out the back towards her red sedan.

"Nope. Don't mind us. Just a zombie and her best bud going for a drive. Nothing strange to see here, folks."

"Who are you even talking to?" Dani asks, as she carefully maneuvers herself into the passenger side, Nickie joining her at the wheel. "This part of town has always been a dead zone. How did you end up working here? You always hated woo-woo stuff like this."

It's a futile attempt, trying to force any kind of casual conversation, but Dani is desperate for a distraction. Of course, Nickie is in no state of mind to placate her.

"I am talking to myself." Nickie starts the engine with far more force than necessary. "I am desperately attempting to hang onto some shred of sanity and just for the record,

9

you using words like 'dead zone' isn't exactly helping the cause!"

Dani elects to remain silent as Nickie begins their drive. The neighborhood passes by in a blur of parks, apartment buildings, and small businesses. Of which Dani realizes that she's never taken the time to pay much attention to until now.

"I'm glad you're here, just so you know," Nickie says, some ten minutes later. "I – I really fucking missed you, dude."

"Yeah. Me too."

It's not a lot, but it's enough to keep Dani grounded. She places her hand on Nickie's shoulder and watches as her grip on the wheel relaxes. Feels herself relax the slightest bit too. It's enough for now.

They arrive back at Nickie's apartment and she quickly goes to work assessing the extent of Dani's injuries. Which is to say, she gives Dani a half-hearted once over, shrugs, and hands her a bottle of morphine.

Dani frowns at the unlabeled prescription bottle but knows now isn't the time to comment on it. It never is with Nickie, but well, it's Nickie. Instead, she pops two pills, forces herself into the shower, slips on the provided PJ's and joins Nickie back at the couch.

"How are you, Nickie?" Because despite her apparent enthusiasm at the current leftover pizza on the coffee table, her friend looked very unwell.

Nickie takes her place across from Dani on the opposite couch. Gravely. Silently.

"I'm managing. That's all I've been doing, really, since

you –" She gives a vague wave. "Been doing better though, I think, at least for my standards."

"Yeah?"

"Yeah," Nickie says, a little surer. "Getting there, at least. Though I'm pretty sure I'm the one that's supposed to be asking you that."

"I'm managing," Dani says, picking at a piece of pizza that she wonders if she would throw up too.

"Try to eat something," Nickie says, giving her a suspicious side-eye. "Something that preferably isn't my flesh."

Dani lets out a snort before picking up her slice of pizza and forcing down a bite.

"You know," Dani says. "I'm pretty sure if I was going to eat your face, I would have done it already."

"Horror rule numero uno," Nickie says. "Can't be sure of anything."

A chill grips Dani's spine. *Was* she sure of anything? Even her own sanity?

The possibility is startling in a way that Dani isn't prepared for. It's not like she was any stranger to uncertainty. Dani had become intimately familiar with the emotion before her sixth birthday. But this? This wasn't grieving her parents, or navigating foster care, or taking care of her brother. This was a literal horror movie and Dani was playing the starring role.

That is, of course, if her role wasn't already designated to the inside of a mental hospital.

Dani drops her current slice of pizza back to the plate. Her mind is reeling, and reality is sinking in far, far too fast. *Come on* – find something to ground yourself with. *Anything!*

"Where's Matt?" Dani's brilliant brain decides on. And

regrets it the moment she sees the look that crosses Nickie's face at the name.

"Don't know, don't care," Nickie says as she drops her own slice of pizza back down to the plate and wipes her hands off on her jeans. "Dickwad didn't even come to your funeral. Doesn't call, doesn't write. Honestly, Dani. Why do you still bother with him?"

"Why do you?"

Nickie purses her lips. "Look. All I'm saying is worry about yourself. For one god-damned time, alright? I'm sure your little brother is, as always, faring just fine."

Knowing she wasn't going to get much further with this conversation, Dani eventually nods. Not that she could make the attempt, what with how fuzzy her head was getting.

"Hallelujah!" Nickie cheers with a clap, and it's only a little bit sarcastic. "Progress is progress. But ugh, hey –" The grip of her best friend's hand on her shoulder is faint as she begins to lead Dani to the guest bedroom. "Looks like the pain meds are starting to kick in, so why don't you try and get some rest, yeah?"

Not being in any state to disagree, Dani allows her body to *'plop'* headfirst onto the mattress. Nickie brings her a glass of water and assures Dani everything was going to be fine. Dani can't take comfort in the words, but she can, at least, in approaching unconsciousness.

After all, tomorrow can't possibly be any worse, right?

CHAPTER 2
DANI

There's fire. At first, it's a small flame. As if someone's lit a match in the very far distance. She's not aware of any surroundings besides that single, barely visible flame. Not sure, really, if any other surroundings exist. Nothing exists except Dani and the flame.

And then someone drops the match.

She's six years old again. The smell of smoke chokes her awake and she frantically searches for her parents. They aren't waking up, even as Dani screams for them. Her eyes burn as she searches for Matt. But this time, he too, lies lifeless in his bedroom.

Dani screams again. It's all she's able to do, until the flames begin to lick her paralyzed skin and silence her.

~

There's fire.

At first, it's a small flame. As if someone's lit a match in the very far distance. She's not aware of any surroundings besides *that single, barely visible flame. Not sure, really, if any other surroundings exist. Nothing exists except Dani and the –*

Dani is jolted awake by the sound of her own scream. The previous day's memories return to her slowly and even then, appear through a haze of smoke. God – she can still *taste it.*

Nickie's grip is like a vise on her arm. She looks terrified and with good reason. Dani is more afraid now than she thinks she's ever been.

The connection is made quickly. A visceral kind of knowing that evaporates all previous suspicion of insanity on sight. Dani can feel her reply to Nickie dry on her tongue and in its place another scream threatens to erupt.

Dani pushes Nickie off her and sprints to the guest bathroom. The door slams behind her and Dani knows she won't have long before Nickie comes banging on it, demanding answers that Dani doesn't have.

Though that was the entire problem, wasn't it? She had the answers, but they were ones she couldn't believe.

Dani raises her head to look at her reflection – slowly, very slowly. Almost afraid of what she might see.

Dani blinks and the reflection of her chestnut eyes follow suit. Turns her head and watches as her dark, gnarled curls fall against her shoulder. She looks the same, but the usual connection of 'oh, hey, that's me' is long gone.

Maybe she left it in Hell.

Organized religion was never Dani's thing, for obvious reasons. It seemed childish, at best. Like a fairytale for grown-ups that couldn't cope with the idea of their life at face value. And Dani had never gotten to be much of a child to begin with.

Not to say Dani didn't believe or have faith in something greater than herself. She doubts she would have lasted these twenty-four years of her life if she didn't.

Now...now, what? What was there to believe in? What would make a difference? What even mattered?

Right on cue, Nickie is assaulting the bathroom door, begging Dani to tell her something. But where would Dani even begin in formulating a believable lie? Her normal defense mechanisms are failing her; failing her like they failed her in Hell.

Suddenly Nickie's presence is not so comforting.

Dani's blood runs cold as she scans the bathroom, searching for any signs of deceit. She's not sure what she's looking for exactly, but she just needs proof that she's not still –

The bathroom door breaks off its hinges with a *'BANG'* as Nickie comes barreling in, expression drawn back in a pleasant surprise at her handiwork. A unique kind of pain settles in Dani's chest at the possibility of this not being her Nickie.

"Dude, what the hell?" Nickie demands, quickly making her way beside Dani on the bathroom floor. When had she sunk down to the floor? "Are you okay? What happened back there?"

Dani shakes her head and Nickie's arms are around her in an instant. It doesn't help, not like it should and not like Dani needs it to.

Still, they remain like that for a while until Nickie suggests that Dani try to eat something. She had been asleep for over twenty hours apparently, and already Dani can see the faint outline of the morning sun glimmer through the bathroom window.

A single nod later and Nickie hurries off to make them some breakfast. Dani forces herself to a standing position, splashes some cold water on her face, and avoids her reflection at all costs.

It doesn't help, but Dani doubts much would at this point. There is not much more to do, Dani thinks, than choke down any 'what ifs' of her current reality with Nickie's signature pancakes.

They don't talk about it. Or well, Dani doesn't talk about it. And Nickie, for all her suspicious and concerned glances, doesn't press for answers.

Answers. Boy, would those be nice to have.

Time feels sinister now. With each bite of her pancake, Dani wonders if it will be the bite she chokes on. Because it's only a matter of time, right? Her brain screams at her to 'run!' and Dani wants to laugh. Where was there to go but down?

"Am I bad person?" Dani is unaware the words have left her mouth before Nickie sets her fork down slowly to stare.

"You're a god-damned saint," Nickie says. "Which sucks, yeah? Seems to be a rule of the universe or something. Bad shit happening to good people. But we're going to figure this out, okay? Maybe's there something at A New Dawn that will help."

Maybe. "You never told me how you ended up working there."

"The lady who owns it was a sponsor of mine. Lily. Cool lady. And yeah, it's all a bit 'woo-woo', sure. Lily even claims to be psychic. But it helped, you know? Having something to believe in. Especially after you, well, you know."

Dani swallows. "So, there's books on religion? And the afterlife?"

Nickie takes her unfinished plate back to the sink, attention never leaving Dani's. "Sure. Got books on a lot of stuff," she says. "Religion, the occult, meditation, mythology, etcetera. Though specifics do help with any kind of inquiry, you know."

Dani does know. But the idea of burdening Nickie with 'specifics' isn't one she's willing to entertain right now. Especially not after everything her best friend has already done for her.

That is, if it *was* her best friend.

"Mind if I join you? At the shop? I don't know what I'm looking for yet either."

"Need to get back to work anyway," Nickie says tersely, already grabbing for her keys. "Something, something, capitalism, something."

"You're angry," Dani says without meaning to. That's twice now. She'd have to watch that.

Nickie turns to her. She looks exhausted. Exhausted and
—

"I'm *scared*, Dani."

Yeah. That was it. Though it's a truly alien expression to see on Nickie's face. When was the last time her best friend was genuinely afraid of anything?

"But whatever. Benefit of the doubt and all that," Nickie says before motioning to what Dani can only assume is her still very disheveled appearance. "Are you ready to go or did you want to change?"

Dani stands, places her plate in the sink beside Nickie's, and the two make their exit. The drive feels longer this time around, and the silence that falls between them more deafening.

～

The books are mocking her, they must be.

Numerous rows and obscure titles that all seem to scream 'fool's errand'. She feels small; so impossibly small among them. And more than a bit fitting of the Fool card as she saunters along the spines, still donning Nickie's ridiculous superhero pajamas.

Still, if it was the only reprieve Dani could get from the current dumpster fire that was her psyche, she'd gladly take it.

It doesn't take Dani long to find the Judeo-Christian section. A single bookcase of titles that Dani struggles to find the significance of. The store is silent aside from the faint sounds of Nickie's current organizing and the pounding of Dani's own heart in her ears.

Her hands trail along the spines before freezing over the only title she recognized. Dani stares at the little black book and it seems to stare back. Her hand jerks forward to pick it up, half expecting to be burnt on contact.

She isn't. It's not as comforting a revelation as Dani expected.

Dani stares at the bible, turns it over in her hands, and stares some more before flipping open to a random page. Genesis 1:4. And God divided the –

"That probably won't be of much help."

The voice is soft, almost melodic, but it might as well have been a gunshot taking place over Dani's shoulder. She reacts accordingly, spinning around and knocking over a nearby cluster of angel figurines. Two of which fall to the ground, each one shattering on impact.

Dani's heart feels about ready to leap out of her throat

as she meets the gaze of a woman who only looks down at the figurines in vague amusement.

Nickie comes barreling onto the scene then, the opposite of amusement as her eyes trail angrily between the woman and the scattered glass now lining the floor.

"I apologize for startling you, Danielle."

There's that voice screaming at her to 'run!' again but her entire body is paralyzed. Vaguely, Dani can hear Nickie yelling before there's a soft brush of fingertips against her temple and her mind quiets.

The relief nearly knocks her off her feet.

"My name is Hanael," The woman says. Dani looks up at her.

'Hanael' looks like the kind of person who might frequent shops like these. Bookish, feminine, maybe trying a bit too hard. Beautiful, undoubtedly. Though there's something that rests under the surface that gives Dani the distinct impression that she was not, in fact, here on a patchouli run.

"I am the angel assigned to your case," Hanael says. "My job is to help your transition back to Earth be as seamless as possible." She takes a step back and Dani mirrors her, only now realizing how close they had been standing. "Though you weren't supposed to remember your time in Hell. It's...miraculous you're conscious right now."

Dani has a lot of questions. More questions, apparently, than her brain knows how to put into words. All she can manage is a choked stutter.

"I'm sorry. Did you just say *Hell*?" Nickie's eyes are begging Dani to tell her it was a lie. Dani only wishes she could.

Nickie charges over to Hanael in the next moment, teeth

19

bared and fists clenched. Dani hopes she doesn't try and land a punch.

"What kind of upper management are you running, huh? Dani? Hell? That's a fuck up if I've ever heard one!"

Hanael takes several steps back, looking thoroughly startled.

"I...do realize that," the angel says, though her words do nothing for Nickie. Her next ones don't do much for Dani either, as the blonde turns to her and says, "You were sent to Hell due to what was, in simplest terms, a clerical error. I'm so sorry, Danielle. You didn't deserve what happened to you."

A clerical error.

A *clerical* error?

"Is that a fucking joke?" Nickie bursts out again. "She was in Hell for over a year!"

'No' Dani wants to say, 'I was in Hell for over three hundred years'. Though by the look on the angel's face, she already knows.

Where were you? Where were you? Where were you? Dani wants to scream at her – bang her over the head with the words – but they too, remain lodged in her throat.

The words she does end up saying are not the ones she intends, but they do the job well enough.

"Go to Hell, Hanael."

Her chest burns, only inches away from Hanael's again. The angel looks distressed, and Dani wishes it meant anything at all.

"If you need me, you can pray to me." With an echo of wing flaps, Hanael disappears. So too, does any remaining energy for anger on Dani's part, as her body collapses to the shop floor.

Nickie tries desperately to get her attention, but Dani

doesn't have the energy for her either. God – she can't believe she's managed to drag Nickie into this, this, whatever this was. Clerical error! What a joke.

Just one big cosmic joke.

Nickie has turned her attention to the shattered angels that Dani had previously knocked over. She sweeps and Dani stares. This is what she wanted, wasn't it? Answers. Reassurance that she wasn't going to be sent back to Hell. That she wasn't still *in* Hell.

Wasn't she, though?

"I need some air," Dani says, getting up too quickly for Nickie to stop her. "I'll be back. I just need to take a walk." Just need to stew in my existential dread for a while.

"Dani, are you sure that's a good idea?"

The look Dani gives Nickie silences her. Then she's marathoning it out of A New Dawn, only slightly relieved that her best friend doesn't follow.

Dani walks for a while, thinks, and then walks faster when her mind threatens to turn in on itself. It's not a great neighborhood she's in, but the concept of fearing such mundane things is laughable now. Hell was not empty, oh no, not at all.

Dani only stops when the ache of her feet forces her to.

It's the only thing that still hurts, Dani realizes. Hanael must have healed everything else.

Dani startles. Had she really just told an angel of the literal Lord to go to hell? And here she was worried *Nickie* would do something reckless.

When Dani finally begins to survey her surroundings, she realizes she has no idea what part of town she's in. There's a run-down apartment complex to her immediate right, and the scent of an overly chlorinated pool somewhere to the back. Across the street, an abandoned car garage. And next to that, a dollar store. How is it that she recognizes *nothing*?

"Hey!"

Dani spins around, panic at least partly subsiding at the sight of Nickie.

"You know, usually it's me that's dazing around bad neighborhoods in nothing but my PJ's," Nickie says through her now rolled down window. "Listen, you don't have to talk to me, alright? But at least let me give you a ride back to my apartment. A few more blocks and you'll be sorry if I don't."

Wordlessly, Dani gets into the passenger side. She doesn't end up remembering the drive back to Nickie's at all.

"Hey, I got some stuff of yours that I saved, did I tell you that?" Nickie says, once they're through the threshold. "Might help. Seeing something familiar."

At Dani's lack of reply, Nickie brings out the box, unseals it, and places it on the couch beside her. Dani peers inside – clothes mainly. Nestled among a photo album and that hideous stuffed beaver Nickie had won for her at that carnival in seventh grade.

"I can't believe you kept this stupid thing," Dani says, running her hands along the toy's gnarled fur, desperately waiting for an emotion – any emotion – to surface.

It doesn't.

"Fred? Of course I kept Fred! That was a proud moment for me, you know. And a great inspiration for my dart-hustling."

"Oh, I know."

They both exchange a barely-there smile before Nickie says, "Listen, I'll call Lily, okay? Tell her I need to take more time off work."

Dani shakes her head. "Nickie, you've already done plenty. Really. Go. I'll be fine."

"Are you sure?"

Was she?

"Yeah."

The look Nickie wears is strained but relieved as she swipes her phone from her back pocket and hands it to Dani.

"The shop's number is in there. Anything at all and I'll be here, alright?"

"Thanks, Nickie."

"'Course. 'Course. No problem at all."

Dani frowns, but before she can ask Nickie if she's alright, her best friend is already making her exit. Instead, she turns her attention back to her box of belongings.

The photo album feels heavy in her hands. It's falling apart by now, worn and torn from years of over-use and transport between foster homes. Dani doesn't open it. She tries, but she can't manage it.

She barely manages to change into one of her old outfits.

The leather jacket gives her particular trouble. Dani spends an inordinate amount of time adjusting, squirming, and readjusting before settling in front of the guest bedroom mirror.

It's ill-fitting. Dani doesn't know how, but it is.

She forces herself to keep it on. Forces herself further, to go back to the living room and flip through the photo album. Fake it till' you make it, right?

At least that's a concept that rings familiar.

CHAPTER 3
HANAEL

H anael has always loved gardens. She helped create the first one, studiously studying the botany until finally, and after so many failed attempts, the first roots began to take hold. The apple tree was still a particular point of pride for her, but that's another story.

Yes, gardens were wonderful places for contemplation. However, the scenery doesn't seem to be helping her much now.

Kagoshima, Japan. The Kanoya Rose Garden. Massive, beautiful, but does nothing to quell the growing unease the confrontation with Danielle had left her with.

It was unheard of for a human to be able to fathom the nature of Hell, much less have any memory of it. And if they did, well, they certainly wouldn't be coherent enough to have an opinion.

Danielle's anger is perfectly justified, though. Hanael is angry. Though Hanael is rarely anything else where the Heavenly Host's mishaps were concerned. They couldn't make her job easy, could they?

Not that they would, even if they could.

Letting out a sigh, Hanael takes a seat on a nearby bench to watch the bystanders. Couples, mainly. All meeting up to enjoy the lush landscape of red, pink, and purple rose hues. Hanael envies their naivety.

It's been two days now since she's talked to Danielle. Two days of mulling over her limited options. Two days of wordlessly cursing Heaven to Timbuktu and back.

When she receives Danielle's prayer, it is almost a welcome reprieve.

"*One chance. You have one chance, Hanael. I deserve a real explanation. You owe me that much.*"

An explanation. Now, wouldn't that be nice?

Hanael supposes she should be happy the woman was speaking to her at all. It's more than Hanael thinks she could manage, were their situations reversed.

It only takes Hanael a moment to hone in on Danielle's energetic signature, less than that to fly to her current location. Of which, does nothing to raise Hanael's confidence in the conversation ahead.

Hanael disliked graveyards greatly. Always too much stagnant energy bouncing around. Even now, as she approaches Danielle, she can feel a bitter taste begin to form at the base of her throat.

Danielle's body stiffens at Hanael's presence, eyes never leaving her own gravestone. She looks a bit more put-together this time around – dressed in jeans, sneakers, and a heavily worn leather jacket – though no less angry.

"You couldn't have cleared the dirt?" Danielle says.

"I'm sorry?"

She spins around, eyes blazing. "I had to claw my way out of my own grave! How is that making my 'transition back to Earth as seamless as possible'?"

The bitter taste in Hanael's throat turns to full-blown nausea. Why was she not surprised?

"Did you...not know about that?"

"Of course not!" Hanael fumes. "Danielle, I am so *very* sorry. I know it probably doesn't mean much after having to deal with such incompetent –"

Danielle snorts. Hanael stops to look at her and Danielle mirrors her action.

Danielle's soul was incredibly vibrant. The effects of Hell are minimal; practically non-existent. Hanael finds herself wondering, not for the first time, how a soul like that could have been sorted into Hell to begin with.

Danielle clears her throat and Hanael averts her gaze, cheeks growing hot.

"So, what level of Heavenly incompetence are we talking about here?" Danielle asks. "Is 'clerical error' just a fancy word for you guys screwed up?"

"More or less."

"Well. Thanks for being honest, at least." Danielle grimaces, shoving her hands into her pockets.

The air of the graveyard has grown thick, waves of fog beginning to roll over the hills. Hanael narrows her eyes at it.

"Here," Hanael says as she materializes a folder of documents and a new cellphone. Danielle accepts them wearily. "Your updated identifying documents, bank account information, and a new phone to get you started. Though if you need anything else, please don't hesitate to ask."

Danielle's eyes widen as she flips through the pages, though collects herself quickly before saying, "Well, it's the least you can do."

"I know."

"It's a colossal screw-up. Unforgivable. I mean, I was –" Danielle closes her eyes and forces a breath. Hanael's chest tightens.

"I know," Hanael says, softer. "Danielle, I –"

"Dani," she says. "It's Dani."

"Dani," Hanael says, already liking the sound of it more. "If you need anything at all, I'll be here. Okay? For as long as you need."

"Sure."

Hanael is about to turn around when she notices Dani hesitate. She seems to be struggling with something a moment before blurting out, "If you could just...check on my brother for me. Matt. Matthew Argent. Make sure he's okay. I'd appreciate that."

"Of course." That could be her next stop. Hanael does wonder why Dani would struggle so much with the ask, but then again, she wasn't exactly in a place to hold judgment toward anyone's relationship with their brother, now was she?

Hanael takes flight, relieved to leave the weight of the graveyard behind her. Though something else sinks in its place that Hanael isn't sure was much better.

It doesn't take long for Hanael to locate Dani's brother and confirm his safety. The twenty-two-year-old seemed to be flourishing in some sort of assistant legislative position for a town a few hours outside of Roselake. Far more so, in Hanael's opinion, than might be expected for someone who lost their sister to a tragic accident only a year prior.

Then again, what does Hanael know?

Still, she elects to follow him. Partly out of lack of anything better to do and partly because she was genuinely interested in learning more about Dani's brother.

Matthew exits a rather large government building and Hanael needn't even cloak herself, the packed sidewalks providing concealment plenty as she follows in pursuit. They both weave themselves through the crowds, Hanael trailing a few yards behind, until the man enters a coffee shop a few blocks down the road.

Hanael enters the establishment and is immediately hit with the scent of espresso and pastries. She smiles; breathes it in. No, certainly not a waste of a trip.

Still keeping an eye on Matthew, Hanael orders a macchiato for herself and takes a seat in the corner. There wasn't anything remarkable about the man. He seemed rather familiar, what with how many features he shared with Dani, but aside from that?

Hanael relaxes her shoulders, taking a sip from her macchiato. There's a handful of magazines stacked in the corner of the table that the angel begins to busy herself with. Celebrity gossip, fashion, pets, oh! Interior decorating.

Hanael flips through the pages as she thinks back to the vacation rental she had just secured. How long would she be stationed on Earth? Surely Dani would require her assistance for a little longer? This bookcase would look lovely in her foyer.

Hanael takes another sip of her drink as she turns her attention back to Dani's brother, only to find the previously occupied barstool now empty. Hanael frowns, setting her drink down. She scans the coffee shop for any sign of his presence and comes up short.

When had he left?

Hanael doesn't have long to mull as her attention is drawn again to an incoming prayer.

"Listen, Hanael. I don't know how this works, but you better get your angelic ass down here and tell me where my best friend is or I will find something that can hurt you. I got a whole shop full of weird-ass occult shit and nothing but time!"

Letting out a tired sigh, Hanael stands to order another coffee and muffin to go before flying back to A New Dawn.

Hanael materializes to find Nickie aggressively pacing the floor of the shop. The angel eyes the woman for a few moments, still sipping her coffee, before Nickie notices her presence.

"Here," Hanael tries, offering Nickie the plain dark roast and muffin. "A peace offering."

"First of all – wait, is that chocolate chip?" Nickie eyes the pastry in growing interest before snapping back, "No! Where the hell is Dani and why the hell was she in Hell?"

Hanael really wishes people would stop asking her that.

She places the muffin and coffee on the nearby checkout counter before turning back to face Nickie.

"Dani is safe," Hanael says. "We just spoke. I provided her a new identity, paperwork, funds – I'm sure she'll be in touch when she's feeling more herself."

"More herself? Is that a joke?" Nickie spits out. "She was in Hell! Now, you want to tell me –"

"I don't know!" Hanael snaps. Silence settles over the shop. Hanael tosses her coffee into a nearby trashcan, the nausea from earlier returning full force.

"I don't know," Hanael says again. "I know that Dani didn't deserve what happened to her. I know that it's unfair and it's cruel and it's unjust. Believe me, *I know*. But besides that? All I know is what I already told you."

"What?" Nickie says. "That this is all some celestial 'clerical error'? You don't seriously believe that, do you?"

"It doesn't matter what I believe," Hanael says. "I'm just following orders."

"Just following orders, huh? Yeah, never heard that one before."

A chill grips Hanael. She aims a glare at Nickie that she hopes is just as icy but fails miserably.

Nickie looks her up and down a moment before asking, "Do you even care? About what happens to Dani? About what happens to any of us?"

"Of course I do," Hanael says, and it is the truth. More of the truth than Hanael wishes at times.

"Does Heaven?" Nickie prods further. "Do the other angels? And what about God?"

Hanael says nothing. Nickie's expression sinks to indifference as she approaches the checkout counter to pick up her coffee and muffin.

"So, we're all just puppets to an uncaring puppeteer of a universe," Nickie says through a bite of her muffin. "Hah. Should have stuck with the nihilism. So, why keep helping them?"

"Excuse me?"

"Why stay on Heaven's payroll if they're all a bunch of dicks? Can't you just, I dunno. Leave? You got powers, right?"

Hanael stifles a laugh. "My powers are connected to Heaven. If I leave, I'm powerless." Hanael doesn't say that she wouldn't even make it that far, but Nickie seems to get the gist regardless.

"That, ugh, kinda blows, actually. I'm sorry."

Hanael shifts under her gaze. The bookshop feels far smaller than it was when she first entered.

"This doesn't mean I trust you," Nickie continues. "Or like you. But if you're here to help Dani, and I mean *really* help her, then I will admit to having a common goal." She raises her muffin. "So, we're good. For now."

"Is that all?"

"Listen," Nickie says, tone turning grave. "All I care about is Dani staying safe and sane and out of Hell. You manage that much and you won't make my shit list. Got it?"

Hanael has to admit she admires the girl's nerve. "We have a deal."

The jingling of the shop door behind Hanael alerts them both to an arriving customer. Nickie smiles at the older woman unconvincingly while Hanael slips past her and makes her exit. The exhale that leaves her chest as she steps back onto the sidewalk does nothing for the tightness that had made its home there.

Still, Hanael supposes the interaction could have gone worse.

It's a lovely rental. A quaint little cottage nestled at the very outskirts of town, surrounded by endless forest. Hanael walks up the pathway and is at least partly soothed by the faint trickle of a stream in the distance.

She enters from the porch into the foyer, smiling as she sees the new bookcase. A snap of her fingers later and it is filled with the works from some of her favorite authors. Steinbeck, Woolf, Vonnegut, and Orwell to name a few. Her expression falls when she wonders if time will permit her to pick a single one up. Hanael never did stay in one place long.

She supposes she and Dani have that much in common.

Her heart truly does ache for Dani. Hanael had read her Life Review shortly before coming down here. It's what had made her so motivated to take this case to begin with. She truly was an incredible, resilient woman.

Hanael enters into the living room and takes off her purse, hanging it on the coat rack. Though not before slipping her hand in to retrieve her smartphone. It still amazes her how fast technology was advancing; every time she was down here there was something new.

Knowing Dani might not appreciate her popping in again so soon, Hanael sends her a text to confirm Matthew's safety. She then tosses the device aside on the couch before settling in. Or at least, attempting to settle in.

What a mess this all was.

Hanael shifts in her seat, thinking back to her conversation with Nickie. What a coward she must have come across as. All this power and what is it good for? She couldn't help people, not really. Not in the way she wants to.

Hanael does enjoy breathing, though. Enjoys not being a bloodied smear on Heaven's wall. Or Hell's, for that matter. She doubts her brother's favor would get her very far now.

So, as it always is, the train of thought is stomped out as quick as a lit cigarette under Hanael's shoe. Though perhaps not as hard this time. Perhaps just enough smoke filters upward for Hanael to choke on.

Perhaps she would do well to have an actual cigarette.

One is in Hanael's hand the next moment, lit and just strong enough to be worth the effort. Her thoughts trail back to Dani as she breathes out.

Hanael still feels undeterred. If she goes a little above and beyond in her efforts to help Dani, well, that was her business, wasn't it? She was still following orders, after all. Still doing exactly what they sent her down here to do.

Hanael finishes her cigarette in an unrestful silence.

CHAPTER 4
DANI

'Y'our brother is fine. He is healthy, safe, and doing well for
himself. - H' Dani has lost track of how many times
she's re-read the text message. She's done little else this
past week besides stare at Hanael and Nickie's messages
and mope around one of Roselake's signature hole-in-the-
wall motels.

A little alone time, her mind had encouraged her. *Just
until she started feeling like herself again.* Except the more
time that passed, the more Dani begins to question if she
still knew who that was. Or if it even mattered.

Her existence feels heavy. Not a depression kind of
heavy but more 'I am but a fly to an indifferent swatter'
kind of heavy. There is not much, Dani realizes, that she
knows to be true. And the answers she does have come
from an angel that is as clueless as her.

Hanael does seem to be trying, Dani will give her that
much. Nickie is too, of course, but Nickie still has her own
demons to contend with.

Dani sits up and can hear the spring of the motel
mattress under her. The bright green numbers of the

bedside clock flash 3:32 p.m. as Dani wonders, yet again, how badly sleep will elude her tonight. Perhaps she should have snagged a few more of Nickie's morphine when she had the chance.

The first few steps towards the shower are unsteady and the ones that come out once she is dressed, hair still wet and mangled, are not much better. Her head spins as she tosses the dirty clothes into a pile by the luggage rack with the others. When was the last time she ate?

Begrudgingly, Dani orders a take-out meal from another restaurant she can't recall ever having heard of. The knock comes sooner than expected, but when Dani opens the door, it is not a Pad Thai that greets her.

It's her brother.

"Hey, Dani," Matt says, as if seeing his formerly dead sister is nothing out of the ordinary at all. "How are you holding up?"

"Matt?" The word barely makes it out, the familiar visage inciting none of the relief Dani might have expected.

Dani can feel his arms wrap around her briefly before they both make their way back inside the motel room. Matt takes a seat on the mattress and Dani joins him, hardly aware she crossed the distance at all.

"I, wow, I can't believe you're actually here," he says. "Are you okay?"

"How are you – did Nickie *tell you* about this?"

"Nah. Nickie and I are kind of on the outs. You know how it is with us. It was an angel that told me."

"Hanael?"

"No, Michael."

Dani's ears are ringing. "Michael? As in, the archangel Michael?"

"I guess?" Matt says. "He stayed long enough to tell me

35

about your, well, situation. Which you still haven't said much about yourself."

Dani's head is spinning. The entire conversation feels wrong.

"I'm managing, Matt."

Matt looks unconvincingly around the motel room. "Yeah, I can tell."

Dani shifts from her place on the mattress. The banter is familiar and yet not. Not like how it was with Nickie, but –

"Listen, I appreciate you coming here, I do. But –"

"You need your space. Totally get that." He's already standing up to leave and Dani doesn't try and stop him. "I'll be in town as long as you need, alright? Already put in my leave for work. This is kind of a big deal, you know? So, I'll be here."

Then he's gone. The slamming of the motel door echoes far louder than Dani thinks it has any right to.

What the hell just happened?

Question of the year.

She begins pacing then, only now realizing how cramped and stuffy the motel room was. When was the last time she went outside?

Feeling more deprived of fresh air by the second, Dani's pacing takes her into her sneakers and out the door. One foot in front of the other. One block after another. Her surroundings once again blurring into an abstract portraiture that Dani can't be bothered to dissect.

When Dani feels her feet abruptly stopping, the whiplash is dizzying. She blinks, vision clearing just enough to make out the outline of a tall, white, and steepled building.

Figures.

Still, her feet continue onward. Onward through the

stained-glass doors, where rows of empty velvet seats stare back at her. Onward down the center aisle as she runs her hand along the smooth surface of the pews. Until finally she reaches the front and, not knowing what else to do, settles into a seat.

Dani had always secretly envied those who could find such comfort inside churches. *It must be nice,* she used think, *to have an entire building dedicated to feeling safe and welcome and loved.* Now all she feels is pity.

Pity and loathing.

She glances up and is met with the goading sight of an angel statue situated at the center podium. It's made of an aged grey marble, hands clasped neatly together, and gaze turned upward.

Dani is tempted to push it down and watch it shatter.

"Dani?"

Dani's head jerks behind her to see Hanael walking down the center aisle. She's wearing a lace white sundress that curves around her breasts in a way that makes Dani think, were there a service in session, would have more than a few people dropping their bibles.

Her mood upturns at the thought, though only slightly.

Hanael settles into the seat next to her. Neither of them say anything for a while, although Dani feels tempted to say a lot. *Can you see it?* She wants to ask. *Can you see me? Any part of me that Hell hasn't ruined?*

What she actually ends up saying is, "I like your dress."

Hanael beams. "Oh, thank you. I really like this one as well."

"What are you doing here, anyway?"

"I sensed your distress," Hanael says. "And I wanted to see if you were alright. *Are you* alright?"

"I just talked to Matt," Dani says, the memory already

beginning to take on a surreal quality. "Said Michael told him about my situation. Do you know anything about that?"

"Michael?" Hanael asks. "Michael talked to Matthew? Are you sure?" The look on her face does not inspire confidence.

"I'm sure," Dani says.

Hanael's eyebrows scrunch up further.

"That's a bad thing, I'm guessing?" Because what's one more to add to the list, right?

Hanael turns to look at her, expression softening. "No, not at all. A bit surprising, seeing as it's not Michael's domain, but nothing to worry about."

"Why didn't they tell you?" Dani asks.

"They don't tell me much."

Dani is about to ask why when she feels her head swim, Hanael's face blurring into a nauseating stream of colors.

"Dani?" There's a hand on her cheek. A jolt of energy rushes through her, vision clearing to give way to Hanael's concerned pale-blue eyes. "When was the last time you ate?"

Oh. Right. "I was getting to it."

Hanael stands, offering out a hand to her. Dani stares at it.

"Come on, then," Hanael persists. "We'll get lunch. My treat."

"You eat?" Dani asks, wearily accepting the appendage.

"I can eat, so I see no reason not to," Hanael says. "What kind of food do you like?"

"I don't have a preference, really. Italian is good. Thai –"

Dani has barely made it to a standing position before she feels a *'whoosh'* of air that forces her eyes closed. When she opens them, Dani finds they are no longer in the church. No longer in America, by the looks of it.

"Florence, Italy," Hanael announces proudly. "They have some wonderful restaurants here."

Dani has a biting accusation on the tip of her tongue, but the look on Hanael's face keeps it there. The angel was trying stupidly hard to make things right. And well, if Dani was going to have an existential breakdown anyway, why *not* have it in Italy? Sure beats the musty interior of her motel room, if nothing else.

Hanael is practically giddy as they trek onward onto a bustling palazzo, her Italian impeccable as she names off this and that shop, restaurant, or cathedral. It's all so very human that Dani forgets for a moment that she isn't.

Dani seems to be forgetting a lot of things lately. Though perhaps this one she'll allow herself to lean into.

Just for a while.

Dani arrives back at her motel room some five hours later. Lunch was...nice. Nicer than Dani had been expecting. As was the impromptu retail therapy.

Maybe that's all she needs, yeah? To keep busy. Hana seemed willing enough to provide a distraction, elaborate as it may be.

Though Dani has the distinct feeling that perhaps the angel needed one as badly as her.

Juggling her two shopping bags, Dani fumbles the keycard into the slot and enters back into her darkened motel room.

"And here I thought my place was depressing."

Both bags drop to the ground and Dani curses. The door

slams shut as Dani spins around to find Nickie sprawled out on the recliner, feet dangling carelessly off the arm. Dani isn't even going to ask how she got in.

"Damnit, Nickie," Dani hisses at her, grabbing her bags and tossing them onto the bed. "Do not sneak up on me like that! Not right now."

A brief look of guilt flashes across Nickie's expression as she makes her way to her feet, though it is gone as quickly as it came.

"Well, if you bothered to keep me updated, I wouldn't have to," Nickie says, eyes traveling to the shopping bags in growing interest. "Oh, fancy. Where'd you go?"

"Italy."

"Funny."

"Not joking," Dani says, as she makes her way over to said bags in an effort to add some kind of organization to the room. "Hana took me there for lunch."

Nickie's eyebrows rise comically high on her forehead.

"Don't start, Nickie," Dani warns. "It was just something to distract myself. And Hana seems nice enough, all things considered."

Her eyebrows rise further. "A nice distraction, you say?"

Dani slams the current pair of jeans in her hand back onto the bed. "Matt stopped by, did you know that?"

"What? No. What?" Amusement fades into a scowl. "When the hell was this?"

"This morning," Dani says. "He said another angel told him about me. Didn't stay long, though I guess he'll be in town for a while."

"Why am I just now hearing about this?"

"Make up your mind, Nickie!" Dani snaps at her. "Either you want to help me or you don't. But I can't play these games with you right now."

They look at each other and Nickie's face crumbles. Wordlessly, she approaches the bed and takes a seat next to Dani.

"I don't know how to deal with this shit, Dani," Nickie chokes out. "How are you dealing with this? How do you always deal with shit and not go completely insane?"

Dani laughs. "And what gave you the impression I wasn't insane?"

"I'm serious."

"So am I."

Nickie looks at her, unconvinced, and Dani finally admits to her what she hadn't been able to admit to herself for the past week.

"Nothing feels real anymore," Dani says. "I can't pinpoint the moment things stopped feeling real, or if they ever felt real to begin with. I can't sleep because I'm terrified that when I wake up, it's going to be in Hell. I don't feel like myself and I'm not *dealing* with it, Nickie. I'm just trying to survive it."

Nickie is silent. Eventually, she slides her hand into Dani's and says, "I know it's not the same thing, but I feel that way sometimes too. Ever since I OD'd. Like, hell, maybe that was it, you know? Or that I'm brain dead in a hospital somewhere."

"Nickie..."

"No, no, let me finish. I'm trying to be insightful here," Nickie says, gripping her hand tighter. "You are brave as all hell, Dani. And if it turns out you're actually still there, then hey, I guess I am too. So, we'll just have to *Dante's Inferno* this shit together."

Dani laughs, genuinely, for the first time in what feels like forever. "*That* was supposed to be insightful?"

"It was clever."

"It was morbid."

They both laugh and finally, *finally*, Dani can feel the barest silhouette of her former self return to her.

"Hey, come back to stay at my place again, yeah?" Nickie says. Her eyes trail down to the bed sheet under them. "Pretty sure I can count the semen stains on here."

"What, and yours is any better?"

"Hardy, har, har. Come on, get packing." Nickie stands from her place on the bed to give Dani a knowing look. "Before I get bored and pick a fist fight with your brother."

Dani stands up with a sigh. Yes, definitely getting back to normal.

...Was that a good thing?

CHAPTER 5
HANAEL

Hanael stares blankly at her melting bowl of gelato. Dusk was beginning to roll in over the quieting city, tourists and residents retreating to the safety of their hotel rooms and homes. Hanael envies them.

She had flown Dani back hours ago, only to return and find herself sifting through the markets and shops along the Arno River, desperate to calm the agitation in her mind. It didn't help, and neither does the gelato that has now found itself on the receiving end of her glare.

It wasn't that she had a bad time with Dani – quite the opposite. They had a lovely lunch. An even lovelier shopping trip. *Dani* was lovely and Hanael enjoys spending time with her.

Which is why Hanael is so very angry that she couldn't fully engage herself without the looming cloud of 'Michael' hanging over her.

It is, perhaps, just as she told Dani; surprising but nothing to worry about. It's not as if Michael's presence in human affairs was unprecedented. Perhaps the archangel wanted to see her squirm, if nothing else.

It is perfectly reasonable. A perfectly reasonable lie that Hanael would do well to keep telling herself.

"Mi scusi signora?" Hanael's head jerks up at the sound of the waiter's voice. "Stiamo chiudendo."

Hanael forces a smile, places her money on the table, and stands to leave the same way she came.

Once outside on the now dark cobble way, Hanael cranes her head skyward, glare fading into a well-timed grimace.

But this wasn't about her, was it? Dani deserved a real answer. It is the very least Hanael can do, to momentarily push her hang-ups regarding the Heavenly Host aside to find it for her.

Hanael was due soon for a status update, anyway. She could surely find some way to work it into the conversation. Worst case scenario, they offer her an unpleasant smile and tell her it is "above her pay grade". So, business as usual.

It is with that thought that Hanael approaches a nearby church, snaps her fingers, and the previously locked double-doors open, bathing her in light. With a springless step, Hanael enters.

Hanael enjoyed speaking with her superiors about as much as one might enjoy an anesthesia-less root canal. Though in Hanael's case, the latter might be less painful.

Heaven is as bright, bare, and dispassionate as always. Hanael treks along the main corridor, shifting through the Sixth, Fifth, and Fourth Spheres before finding herself in front of the conference room door of the Third.

With a deep breath and Dani's face in the back of her mind, Hanael opens the door and walks inside. Her eyes instantly meet Michael's. They are alone, and Hanael tries and fails not to startle when the door slams shut behind her.

"Hanael, nice to see you. Take a seat." Michael motions to the large, oval table and Hanael has to fight every urge to take her feet in the opposite direction. When was the last time they had spoken directly?

"I am taking over for Remiel in regard to your status update," The archangel continues as he takes a seat himself. "Nothing to concern yourself with. Please." He motions to the seat directly across the table and Hanael can do little else but take it.

Michael looks relatively unchanged from the few times Hanael had seen him. Same stony, dark eyes and immaculate appearance. Collected, professional, laser focused. An undoubtedly surreal contrast to his actual energetic signature.

"Would you like me to come back Hanael, or can we get started?" And with the kind of arrogance only Heaven's leader could manage.

"Of course. Apologies," Hanael says. "Things with Dani – Danielle – are going about as well as can be expected." Not that you didn't already know that. "I've been doing all I can to help her, but the adjustment has been difficult, to say the least."

"Well, as you said, that's to be expected." Michael pauses as he jots a few notes down on his celestial clipboard. "And who else knows about Danielle's situation? Just her brother and one Nicole Allbright, I presume?"

He's goading her, he must be. A test of some sort. Though of what variety, Hanael isn't going to speculate. "Yes, but I presume you already knew that."

Hanael waits with bated breath as Michael raises his

eyes from his clipboard, rakes them over her once, and returns back to his notes.

"Ah, yes. I do recall speaking to Matthew. I had assumed you were informed of that."

"I was not."

The sound of pen against paper echoes maddeningly into Hanael's skull. After what feels like an eternity, Michael sets it down and says, "Anything else we should be informed of regarding this mission? Any closing concerns or questions?"

Don't push your luck. Don't push your luck. Don't –

"I think it would be beneficial for Danielle to have more information regarding why she was sent to Hell. It's all rather...unprecedented, wouldn't you say? This 'clerical error'."

"Humanity is becoming increasingly complex," Michael says without missing a beat. "It should come as no surprise, certainly not to someone as versed on the subject as yourself, that errors in the sorting system are bound to occur."

"Of course," Hanael says, biting down any further remarks. At least she could say she tried.

The clipboard blinks away. Michael's eyes never leave hers.

"While we are on the subject," he says. "I would like to discuss a reassignment, if you are so inclined to accept it."

Hanael swallows. "A reassignment? You mean with Dani's case?"

"No, no. You said it yourself, didn't you? The adjustment has been quite difficult for her. I am suggesting a permanent reassignment to Earth. I do believe you put in the request for that some time ago?"

A millennia ago. "I did," Hanael says, choosing her words carefully. Surely it couldn't be that easy. Surely. "But

I thought Cassiel was the angel currently assigned to Earth?"

"Cassiel has requested a reassignment herself," Michael says. "So, the position is yours, if you'll have it."

"I – yes, of course. I would love the position."

Hanael is waiting for the moment Michael breaks out into hysterical laughter at her gullibility, but instead the archangel pulls out another clipboard.

"Sign here, please. You can expect to report back to Heaven every century. Aside from that, you are free to perform miracles in the interest of humanity as you see fit."

Hanael eyes the fine print wearily. All of it ends up being standard Heavenly jargon. Once the realization hits, she can't sign quickly enough.

The clipboard blinks away and Michael stands, ushering a hand towards the door. "Thank you for your time, Hanael. I'm sure you will do fine work on Earth."

Hanael exits the conference room in a daze. Even when she is back on Earth in her rental home, she can't seem to make her thoughts align.

What just happened?

She's pacing then, the ends of her floral sundress whipping against her ankle boots. Everything she's ever wanted handed to her on a silver platter by the leader of Heaven himself? They must take her for a fool.

Still, the reassignment contract was legitimate, as legitimate as they come. Even now, Hanael can begin to feel her energy align seamlessly with the earthly dimension. She stops pacing, eyes landing on her bookcase. They stay there only a moment before a buzzing in the pocket of her dress startles her back to reality.

Hanael unlocks the device and sees it's a text from Dani. Her stomach flips.

Where would Dani fit into all of this?

'Hey. At Nickie's shop, if you have a minute. - Dani'

She did have a minute. Hanael had more minutes than she would ever know what to do with now. That was, if –

No.

Hanael would enjoy this while she could. Because if she's right and there is something more sinister at play, then there is nothing more to do than wait for the other celestial shoe to drop.

Smoothing out her dress, Hanael takes flight to A New Dawn.

Hanael finds Dani sitting at one of the small tables near the café section of the store, a pile of books to her right and a coffee to her left. She looks about as unimpressed at the current bible in her hands as the angel had been herself when she first got her hands on it.

"How much of this stuff is actually accurate?" Dani asks.

"Not much."

Dani slams the book shut and tosses it into the pile with the others. Hanael approaches the table and, noticing a second coffee in the seat across from her, asks, "Is Nickie sitting here? Or...Matthew?"

Dani looks up at Hanael, following her gaze to the empty seat. "Oh. No. Nickie ran out for a meeting with the shop owner. And Matt, well, I haven't seen him since that once at the motel. Coffee's for you." Dani frowns. "Though by the look on your face, I can't help but think you'd appreciate something stronger."

Was it really so obvious? "Thank you, for the coffee,"

Hanael says. Dani continues to stare long after she's taken her seat.

"Seriously. Are you okay?"

The mental gymnastics Hanael's mind goes through to formulate a believable lie are laughable. It eventually gives up, focusing her attention back on her coffee.

"Hana?"

"I lied to you," Hanael blurts out. "About Michael. It's not nothing, but I'm struggling to figure out the significance of it. I asked him about it, just now. Tried to get more information regarding this...joke of a clerical error." Finally, Hanael raises her eyes from her coffee to meet Dani's. "I'm sorry, Dani. I wish I could have gotten you the answers you deserve."

"I had kind of figured there was something more to the Michael thing," Dani says, surprisingly unbothered. "Are you okay, though? You're not like, in trouble or anything, right?"

"Quite the opposite," Hanael says. "I've been promoted to Earth indefinitely. A position that I've been vying for a millennia."

"And you, what? Don't think it's a genuine offer?"

"I think I would be mighty foolish to assume it was."

"And here I thought I had some bad bosses when I worked retail," Dani says, gaze hardening. "Don't do that again, alright? I don't want you sticking your neck out for me. It's not worth it."

"I beg to differ."

Dani stares at her before a small smile begins to tickle at her expression. Hanael quite likes the look of it on her.

"So, I think I mentioned alcohol a few minutes ago," Dani says as she begins to type out a text message. "And since I'm guessing I won't find any more answers in all that," she waves a vague hand over to the pile of books, "than I will from your bosses, why don't you let me buy you a drink? And you can tell me all the secrets of the universe that you *do* know."

Hanael mirrors her smile. "That might take a few drinks."

"Then I guess we better get a head start on it, huh?" Dani says, grabbing her jacket from the chair's back as she stands from the table. Hanael rises to meet her and watches as she makes quick work of putting away the books and closing up the shop on Nickie's behalf.

They both exit A New Dawn, Hanael pushing any remaining morose thoughts aside. Which, in Dani's presence, ends up being far easier than the angel anticipated. A growing trend, it seemed.

Hanael should probably keep an eye on that.

Then again, Hanael should probably do a lot of things that she can't be bothered to.

CHAPTER 6
DANI

I t wasn't very often that Dani didn't regret emotionally driven trips to the bar. The last one did, after all, land her six feet underground.

Though as Dani was coming to find, Hana seemed to be the exception to a lot of things.

The bar is loud but not too loud. There's a dim purple light that casts a glow over the environment. Hana's hair almost seems to reflect it, the light cascading down over eyes that were currently absorbed in a drink menu.

"You girls ready to order?" The bartender asks. Dani's attention snaps back before she answers, "An old-fashioned. With Bourbon, please. Whatever's good."

"Sure thing." He turns to Hana and she smiles politely before saying, "One Sex on the Beach. Thank you."

Dani smirks. "You know, for an angel, you're not all that angelic."

"And for a human, you are *extremely* angelic. Sure you don't want to trade places with me?"

"Nice try. But by the sounds of your bosses, I wouldn't last a day." Dani pauses, glancing over at the bartender preparing her drink. "What's the story behind all that, anyway?"

Hana stiffens. It's only for a split second, but it's enough to make Dani feel bad for asking.

"I'm not well liked," Hana says. "Resented, is probably a better word. Many of the other angels feel it's blasphemy that I'm still in Heaven at all."

"What?" Dani balks. The more she hears about Heaven, the less she thinks their bureaucracy was any better than Hell's. "That's horrible. Why would anyone think that?"

Hana falters before admitting, "I Fell. Or was supposed to Fall. With Lucifer."

Dani's heart jerks down to her stomach. A single emotion settles somewhere in the back of her mind, unreachable. Even so, it takes a lot of work to push down before she asks, "What happened?"

Hana shrugs, shoulders stiff, as she takes a long swig of her drink. "I'm still not sure of the semantics. I was marked to Fall and then the mark...disappeared. As if it was never there."

"So, it was a mistake then, you being marked to Fall," Dani guesses. It made sense, didn't it? That Dani wouldn't be the only 'clerical error' out of the bunch. She grimaces at the thought.

"I suppose," Hana says.

"Sounds to me like they need a reason to justify their treatment of you," Dani says, feeling a little surer. "You're a good person, Hana. You don't deserve to be anywhere near Hell." Smiling grimly, Dani finishes, "Despite my previous remarks on the subject."

Hana relaxes, giving her a smile much brighter than Dani's own. Dani begins to relax, too.

It's a new kind of feeling for her – relaxing, trusting,

speaking freely. Normally, this would be the point in the evening where Dani would inevitably pull away. Put up her usual barriers and call it a night.

But normal had become a contradictory concept as of late. It mocked and screamed and told her she was damned if she did and damned if she didn't.

So, Dani relaxes. She relaxes and she tells normal to go fuck itself.

Dani and Hana are laughing. They're both comfortably drunk, though the effects fade far quicker on Hana. Dani pities the fool who challenges the angel to a drinking contest.

What were they laughing about, again? Another tale of celestial mishaps, Dani's sure. Hana seemed to have a lot of them: Mary was actually quite perturbed about the whole thing; you can blame Cambiel for the meteor that took out the dinosaurs; and that's where the demonic possession myth came from.

It's a surreal kind of balm for Dani's soul. Not comforting per say, but it somehow made Dani feel less alone. Which was more than enough for right now.

Dani chances a glance at her watch and blinks, only partly surprised to see that three hours have passed. It was almost too easy to talk to Hana.

Their laughter dies down and another song begins to play in the speakers above the bar. "Eyes on Fire", if Dani is recalling correctly. What was that from? *Twilight*?

Dani laughs. She wonders if Hana keeps up with any kind of popular culture.

"Do you want to dance?" Hana asks suddenly. Dani

stares at her, the only response she's able to come up with being, "I'm a terrible dancer."

"So am I." Dani very much doubts that, but she is just drunk enough to call Hana's bluff.

And so, Hana leads her to the far end of the bar, into a small section of black tile that passed for the dance floor. It's quieter now, most of the happy hour customers having already cleared out. The intimacy of the moment sobers Dani significantly.

Though apparently not enough to stop it.

Hana lifts her left hand as she begins to lead. Flawlessly, of course.

"Liar, liar, pants on fire," Dani says. "I doubt there's a single dance you don't know."

"Oh, there's plenty I don't know," Hana says as she goes to spin her. "Plenty I'm terrible at too, as I said." She's smiling again, animated and radiant and all too human. "But I was on Earth during the twenties, when ballroom dancing had gotten an overhaul. Couldn't help myself, really."

"Oh, I'm sure," Dani says with a laugh. Her drunken brain not-so-helpfully decides to conjure images of Hana in a red flapper dress. It's distracting, but preferable to what her vision does end up catching over the angel's shoulder.

There's a sort of lapse in time before Dani's brain processes the image. A buzzing assaults her ears, sinister and angry and familiar in a way that Dani doesn't understand.

After what feels like hours, her eyes meet the familiar brown of her brother's.

He meets her gaze once, winks, and finishes the drink in his hand before proceeding to make his exit.

"Dani?" They've stopped dancing, though Dani still feels like she's spinning.

She's out of Hana's grasp before she knows what she's doing, stumbling across the bar and out the door. A few passersby are on the sidewalk, but none of them are her brother.

Dani only has a chance to yell his name twice before Hana is beside her again.

"Dani, what's going on?! Are you alright?"

What *was* going on? Was Matt screwing with her? Where could he have possibly gone that fast?

Dani meets a pair of concerned blue eyes and swallows.

Was Matt even here?

"I —" Dani tries, throat constricted. "Give me a minute, okay?" She pulls her phone out of her back pocket, hands shaking, and dials Matt's number.

"Hey, Dani. How are you feel —"

"Were you at the bar just now?" Dani demands.

"What? What are you talking about?"

"The bar!" Dani yells. "On Demont Street! The Purple Cat! Were you here?" Several pedestrians have stopped to stare, and Hana ushers them onward with an awkward smile.

"What? No," Matt says. "I've been at my hotel all afternoon binge-watching." Dani can faintly hear a TV in the background. "Do you need me to pick you up? You sound plastered."

Dani hangs up, takes a deep breath, and tries not to scream.

"Dani?"

"I'm just drunk. Can we go now, please?" Before she starts hallucinating something worse.

"Of course we can. Come on." Hana wraps one arm

around her shoulder as she begins to lead her down the sidewalk. "Do you want me to sober you up?"

"You can do that?"

"Sure. Alcohol is a toxin, like any other. A little healing and it will be completely removed from your system."

Dani stops walking, stares at Hana a moment, before finally nodding her head.

One expertly placed hand on her temple later and Dani is completely sober. And at least two percent less insane.

"Thank you," Dani says.

"Of course," Hana says. "Would you like me to fly you back to Nickie's? If not, I can call a cab."

Flying. Right. Because Hana was an angel. A literal angel that Dani, for the life of her, could not stop fantasizing about.

She should have stayed drunk.

"Dani?"

"Yes, yes. Flying is fine." Everything was fine.

Hana doesn't look convinced, but takes Dani's hand regardless. There's that familiar *'whoosh'* of air against Dani's face and when she opens her eyes, they are in front of Nickie's apartment.

"Thanks," Dani says. Hana only smiles and nods while Dani shifts from foot to foot.

"Listen, Hana, I —" What? What was she supposed to say? "Whatever this is between us, I mean, if there's anything at all because let's face it," Dani laughs raggedly. "My brain isn't exactly 'all there' right now. I just — I don't think I can do it right now, okay? I'm sorry."

"I hadn't expected you to," Hana says. "I'm sorry, Dani. I...shouldn't have put you in that position. I hadn't realized —" She shakes her head. "I've been extremely selfish. I apologize."

"What? No!" Dani rushes out. "You've been the *opposite* of selfish, Hana. You have no idea how much I appreciate what you've already done for me. I just –"

Dani's remaining words are drowned out by the sound of Nickie's front door swinging open.

"So! Not to brag or anything, but –" Dani's head jerks toward the voice of her best friend, whose mouth had now settled into an impressive 'O'. "Ugh. Bad time?"

"I should let you go," Hana says, already turning to leave. "I'll text you?"

"Yeah, of course. Anytime."

Hana smiles, a little pained, before making her exit. Dani follows suit, proceeding to brush past Nickie into the apartment. She throws her jacket over the back of the couch before collapsing on it, eyes screwed shut.

After a few minutes, Dani hears Nickie say, "So, can I assume we *won't* be calling the U-Haul?"

Dani wants to scream at her, maybe go hide in her now designated bedroom for the next week. She's too tired to do either.

"You said you had something to brag about?" Dani says instead, eyes still closed.

There's a long beat of silence before Nickie says, "Maybe now's not such a good time."

Dani's eyes fly open and she pushes herself to a sitting position, eyeing Nickie wearily.

"Nickie, what did you do?"

"I didn't do anything. Christ." Nickie glares at her. "You wanted answers about this crap and so that's what I've been trying to find."

"And did you? Find anything, I mean." Though if Hana couldn't get a straight answer, Dani doubts anyone could.

"Sort of."

"Meaning?"

"Well, you know that lady who owns the shop I work for? Lily?"

"Yeah?"

"Well, we were talking shop earlier today and I sort of, maybe, *accidentally* told her about your situation."

"You're joking," Dani says. She can already feel the migraine coming on. "You're not joking. Nickie, are you insane? We can't be dragging other people into this."

"Lily would've figured it out anyway," Nickie says with a wave of her hand. "Hell, she was already halfway there. I may have prematurely brushed off her whole 'psychic' thing." Nickie raises her eyebrows conspiratorially. "Makes you wonder what *else* is out there we don't know about."

Dani begins to massage her throbbing temples. That's all she needed right now – a nosy psychic on top of her unhinged best friend.

"Anywho! Lily's more than willing to help. She's got a ton of ancient occult texts that we can look through. Offered to do an energy reading on you, if you're up for it. I mean, what do we have to lose, right?"

Just more of her sanity. "What makes you think some psychic is going to have any more answers than Hana?"

"I don't. I just thought it was worth a shot."

Maybe it was. After all, it's not as if the whole 'back to normal' plan was getting her anywhere.

"Fine. Fine! But I reserve the right to change my mind at any time."

Nickie perks up at her answer and they settle into comfortable conversation before ordering delivery and retiring to their respective rooms.

It would be a good distraction if nothing else, Dani

thinks, as she readies for bed. A distraction that was decidedly not Hana-shaped.

Dani lets out a groan as she collapses backwards onto the bed.

∽

Dani and Nickie leave early that next morning. Too early, really, but it's not as if Dani had been sleeping.

The house they pull up to is somehow both charming and decrepit. If it weren't for the adorned gardens out front, Dani would think the place abandoned entirely.

The questionable aesthetic does nothing, of course, to stop Nickie from eagerly ascending the pathway to the porch. Dani reluctantly follows behind. When they arrive at the front door, it swings open before Nickie has a chance to knock.

"Right on time. Come in, girls."

Lily looked like the psychic type. Pin-straight black hair that flowed down over a bohemian, off-patterned dress. The stereotype only manages to unfold further as they follow Lily into the house, and Dani feels as if she's stepped into a wonderland of occult paraphernalia.

She was committed, Dani would give her that. She takes the offered scone and tea gratefully as they all take a seat at the dinner table.

"Nickie tells me you've had quite the stroke of bad luck," Lily says. "Or good luck, I suppose, depending on who's asking."

"I wouldn't call it luck of any form, quite frankly," Dani says.

"Perhaps not," Lily says. "Nickie also tells me you've been speaking to angels?"

59

"Angel. Singular," Dani says. "Though Hana didn't have any answers either. Not that she didn't try but, well –" Dani picks at her scone. "Upper management apparently doesn't have a 'suggestions' box."

"Unsurprising, really," Lily says. "Abrahamic deities have quite the bureaucracy going on." As if to emphasize, Lily drops a large, leather-bound book in front of Dani's plate, rattling the table.

Dani eyes the book with interest before moving to pick it up. It's massive, dusty, and as Dani flips through the pages, sees is handwritten in a language that Dani isn't sure is a language at all.

But looks achingly familiar.

"Now, I can't promise that will have the answers you're looking for, but it's the best I have on Abrahamic deities. That angel of yours should be able to translate it."

"You keep saying Abrahamic deities," Nickie cuts in before Dani has a chance to ask about the text. "What do you mean by that?"

"Sweet girl," Lily says with a suggestive smile. "You didn't think Yahweh was the only god, did you?"

Lily and Nickie delve into conversation, but their voices drown out quickly. Dani stares at the symbols on the page in front of her. Where had she seen them before?

Dani grimaces. *Hell, probably.*

"Dani?"

Dani's head jolts up to find Nickie and Lily staring at her.

"Lily asked if you wanted her to do that energy reading now," Nickie continues, a frown forming. "You good, dude?"

"I – I'd rather dive right into this, if it's all the same," Dani says, already standing. "Raincheck?"

"Sure," Lily says. "But you take good care of that book. It wasn't an easy find."

"Of course," Dani says, eyeing her barely touched scone guiltily. "I'm sorry I can't stay longer."

Lily smiles at her, sharp and knowing. "Don't apologize, my dear. It's a woman's Achilles heel. You just take care of my book and yourself. You know where to find me."

Dani returns her smile. She can see why Nickie liked the woman so much.

The book is heavy under Dani's arm as she and Nickie make their way back down the pathway to Nickie's red sedan, which now housed a particularly impressive raven on the hood.

It stares at her, even as Nickie shoos it away. Dani swears it's still staring mid-flight.

Her grip tightens around the book as she shuffles into the passenger side.

CHAPTER 7

HANAEL

anael hasn't been able to read. Pity, seeing as she could have used the distraction.

What a mess she's made of things.

Of course, messes were nothing out of the ordinary for Hanael, as the Host so loved to remind her. But this? Hanael isn't even sure what *this* is.

It was strange, in any capacity. To feel the connection she does to Dani. It's never happened before – certainly not with a human – and Hanael doubts it will happen again.

Perhaps for the best. After all, Hanael still may or may not have a Heavenly bullseye on her back. It wouldn't do to be dragging Dani into the crossfire. She had suffered enough already.

Hanael looks down at the current burnt cupcakes on her stove, scowls, and tosses the entire pan into the trash-can. It's about the fourth time she's done so. No distractions to be found anywhere, it would seem.

A *'ding'* from across the countertop brings Hanael's attention to her phone. She pats her floury hands off on her apron before crossing the distance and picking the device up. A new text from Dani.

At least, Hanael reasons, she hadn't turned the woman off her completely.

'Can you translate this? It's in Enochian.'

Hanael opens the attached file and frowns. It was a table of contents from a metaphysical book that Hanael doesn't recognize. Ancient but accurate. Hanael wonders, more than a little concerned, where Dani could have gotten it.

She is in the midst of voicing those concerns via text when a sudden prick to her neck causes both her hands to go lax. The phone slips through her fingers and falls to the ground with a *'thud'*. Hanael's body joins it.

Through her spotting vision, Hanael can see a male figure standing over her. Dark eyes and dark hair and – oh.

Oh, no.

CHAPTER 8

DANI

D ani slams her smartphone against the table. They were back at A New Dawn, though the shop had very little in terms of translating the Enochian of the book. The internet even less so.

Nickie makes a sound from her place across the shop. Something between a scoff and snicker. Something that said, 'And you haven't called Hana yet, why?'

Dani isn't quite sure herself.

The entire conflict with Hana seemed to have poked at an extra-sensitive part of herself. A part of herself she didn't know existed until, you guessed it, Hana had entered the picture.

Or maybe all parts of her were sensitive right now. That is, the parts of her that were still *her*.

Another hour passes of internal agonizing before Dani gives in and texts Hana the table of contents. Or at least, what she thinks is the table of contents.

Hana answers quickly, listing out the translated chapters. They go back and forth like this for a while, before Dani discovers a *'Divination'* section of the book, followed by a mantra that was supposed to reveal all things hidden.

It sounded promising enough.

Hana seems to think so too, and gets to work making any needed edits. Hana also seems confident that it's safe enough for Dani to try on her own. That, and she probably just didn't want to see her.

God, she had really screwed up, hadn't she?

Dani doesn't waste any time with the mantra. She lights her single black candle, burns her Kava Kava Root, and sits down on her ceremonial mat, all while wondering idly if any 'revealed secrets' would be able to make it past the screaming in her own head.

Nickie watches her, eyebrows pinched. "And you're sure this is safe?"

"Hana said it was." And despite everything else, Dani knows that's not something the angel would lie about.

If Nickie looks unconvinced, she doesn't voice her concerns aloud.

Dani closes her eyes, concentrating hard. Answers. Answers. That's what she wanted, right? Okay.

"URAN! URAN! CIRP CRIP BALIT. LAP A CANSE MALPHAS I OL OOANOAN. LRASD CNILAM, LRASD TRIAN, OL FIFIS OL ULS."

The Enochian rolls off her tongue easily. Strangely so.

Dani shakes off the unease and repeats the mantra. Black begins to spot at her vision, which Dani takes to mean it's working. She repeats it again and her vision blackens completely.

Something is wrong.

She realizes it a second too late. A second before a deafening ringing has her hands flying to her ears in a failed attempt to block out the sound.

No, no, no, no, no! What –

She tries to scream out, but there's a vise against her throat. Electrical. It moves quickly. Up, up, up. Until it hits her brain with one single shock.

And finally, Dani's thoughts quiet.

There is nothing.

No sense of direction or time or color. Dani can't even call her current surroundings black. It's just...nothing.

So much of nothing that Dani begins to question her existence in relation to it. The thoughts don't last, however. They too, fade – fleetingly – into the nothingness.

Then, there is something. It starts out as a small something. A speck of light in the distance. Until that speck of light becomes a huge ball of light that is hurtling straight towards her.

It hits her and color returns. Blinding. Vivid. Inhumanly vivid.

They scatter and morph until finally taking shape, forming...something. Images. Memories? Dani likens it to a cosmic movie theater, minus the exit.

Where she's playing the starring role.

She's in a cave somewhere, underground. There is a river. Next to the river is a woman, long flowing red hair and a forced smile. She holds out a chalice for Dani's movie counterpart to take.

Dani watches as she takes it, drinks it all down in hazy indifference, and then the screen goes black.

It starts again.

Same cave. Same woman. Same chalice. Again, and

again, and *again*. Until the hazy indifference begins to sharpen.

"*Who are you? I've been here before, haven't I?*" Her counterpart asks, visibly afraid. The woman only smiles sadly, snaps her fingers, and Dani's shaking hand is forced back around the chalice.

Again, and again, and *again*.

Dani feels ill. This was worse than Hell. What was this?

Dani feels a *'snap'* against her body. Then a burning – in her chest, her lungs, her throat. She is suddenly very aware of the need to breathe. Aware that she now has a body to breathe into.

Except she can't. All Dani can manage is a painful, choked gasp.

Lights and colors blur around her. Frantic voices and the tell-tale *'beeping'* of medical equipment. She is now fully aware of being wheeled through a hospital.

She is now fully aware.

Dani wishes she wasn't.

The images start back up again, but this time in a very different way. They begin to blend with the reality around her, darkness flooding through the hospital hall, decimating everything in its path.

The lights go next, flickering in quick succession before exploding, sharp glass piercing Dani's skin. She tries to scream, but the blood in her mouth chokes her.

And then the darkness silences her completely.

It covers her, suffocates her, until it begins pulling her down, down, down –

Dani knows what comes next.

She knows before she opens her eyes again what she will see. Knows that there is no escape, and that maybe, there never was.

It's less of a surprise than she imagines.

CHAPTER 9
HANAEL

Hanael awakens slowly, head heavy with confusion.
Actually, everything was heavy.

The weight presses down on her as Hanael attempts to help herself to a standing position. It's difficult, and alarm bells immediately blare in her mind.

What happened?

Her still adjusting eyes make contact with her phone, lying only a few feet from where her body had been moments ago. Hanael picks it up, gritting down on the pain that shoots up her spine at the action.

It only takes a moment of scrolling through her most recent texts for the memories to hit her. Panic follows.

The texts aren't from her. Dani's brother must have sent them. *Was it* Dani's brother? The presence was obviously demonic. Hanael doesn't know how she missed it from her first encounter in that coffee shop.

Hanael's eyes find his most recent text and her heart shoots into her throat.

'URAN! URAN! CIRP CRIP BALIT. LAP A CANSE

MALPHAS I OL OOANOAN. LRASD CNILAM, LRASD TRIAN, OL FIFIS OL ULS.'

Malphas. Malphas! By God, what would Lucifer's second in command want with Dani? Hanael can't make heads or tails of the incantation. Some sort of binding?

Hanael tries to unfurl her wings but is hit with a tearing pain in her shoulders. She tries again and cries out, hunching over.

Whatever Matthew (Malphas?) had knocked her out with was subduing her powers. It would wear off, but not as quickly as Hanael needed it to.

How horrifyingly human she feels.

Perhaps that was the point.

Hanael stumbles across her living room and over to the garage door. She had bought a car shortly after the confrontation with Michael, among making several other 'human' contingency plans.

Looks like she'd be needing them.

Even before Hanael arrives at the hospital, she knows she is too late.

There is a loss that grips her as she races, wild-eyed, into the hospital emergency room. Hanael's never felt anything like it before and she hasn't the slightest idea how to process it.

So, she doesn't. Her celestial compartmentalizing was still working fine, and so that is what Hanael does. Which isn't a great hindsight, seeing as *something* had to take the grief's place.

It is this jaded rage that finds Azrael standing outside of Dani's now empty hospital room. And Azrael, with her designer black cloak and sanctimonious aire, has the gall to look surprised.

"You look like something the cat dragged in," Azrael says.

"I was attacked," Hanael spits out. "And so was Dani. Her death was foul play on Hell's part. You need to bring her back."

"I *need* to bring her back?" Azrael laughs. "I don't think so. If you want the girl back so badly, resurrect her yourself."

Hanael wants to scream at her that she can't right now but swallows the urge. Level head. She needed to keep a level head.

"Fine," Hanael says. "Just tell me what Sphere and room number Dani was assigned to in Heaven."

"Danielle isn't in Heaven. So, if you want to know what room she was assigned to, you'll have to take it up with Lucifer."

Time slows to a crawl. The words don't connect for a long while, and by the time they do, Azrael is no longer there for Hanael to take her anger out on.

Instead, she finds herself on the receiving end of Nickie's.

"You piece of shit!" Is all Hanael hears before hands are on her, and her already throbbing spine collides with a nearby wall. Hanael doesn't try and stop her.

Nickie is able to get a few good punches in before hospital security pulls her off.

"It wasn't *me*," Hanael spits out, blood coating her teeth. "Dani's brother knocked me out before taking my phone and sending her those translations."

Nickie's face pales, though not in any way that was surprised.

71

Interesting.

Hanael tries to convince the security guards to let Nickie go, but only manages to get herself kicked out of the hospital alongside her.

"You're lying," Nickie says, eyes blazing again once they're on the sidewalk outside. "Matt couldn't possibly know those translations –"

"Yes, like he couldn't possibly know how to depower me," Hanael bites back. Her hand travels absently to her broken nose to align it. "His presence is demonic. That's all I know."

"So, what? Matt's possessed now?"

"No. No, demons can't possess humans. That's an old wives' tale."

"Well, if he's not possessed, then what the fuck is he? What the fuck happened!"

"I don't know!" Hanael shouts, gaining the attention of several exiting hospital patients. "I don't know, Nickie. But I'm – I'll figure something out." What? What was she supposed to figure out?

Hanael can feel her stomach curl the moment her mind supplies the answer.

"We need to get Dani's body. I can preserve it. It will buy us time until I can resurrect her." Until she is forced to storm the one place whose occupants might hate her more than Heaven's.

Nickie stares at her. Finally, she begins, voice low, "Thin. Fucking. Ice. That's what you're on, Hanael." A good five inches shorter, Nickie still seems to tower over her. "Dani trusted you. Hell, more than that. So, if you ever give me a reason to believe that was in vain –"

"It wasn't," Hanael says, though somehow the words taste like a lie. Hanael should have seen an attack like this coming from a mile away. She should have been there. And perhaps if she hadn't stupidly let her feelings cloud her judgment, she would have been.

Nickie stares at her again, seemingly searching Hanael's expression for any signs of deceit. When she finds none, she says, "We'll see. Let's just get to the damn morgue before I change my mind."

Hanael follows limply behind Nickie as they maneuver their way back inside the hospital and down to a sterile grey room that reeked of death. Both Hanael and Nickie bite down a gag.

Something changes in Hanael when she sees the body. Her previous mental defenses lower, and every attempt to put them back up are miserable failures.

She can see it then, as visibly as the lifeless look on Dani's face, the point where it snaps.

That precarious branch Hanael had been clinging to for as long as she could remember. Too much of a coward to take the leap herself. Too afraid of the fall.

Hanael can feel it now, like air whipping through her hair as she plummets down, down, down, the impact inevitable. Because it was always inevitable, wasn't it?

As Hanael gently picks up Dani's body and she and Nickie make their hasty exit, Hanael wonders what she had ever been afraid of.

Hanael doesn't remember much of the car ride back to Nickie's apartment. Wheels are turning in her mind too quickly for Hanael to properly dissect. Spinning, motivating, like electricity coiling to strike.

"You said something about preserving her body?"

Nickie's voice jerks Hanael's attention back to the present moment. She's in Nickie's living room and there's a dead body on the sofa.

The wheels turn faster.

Hanael drags her feet over to the sofa. It's hard to look at Dani's face, but Hanael forces herself.

This is what they do, an inciting voice in her mind says. *Playing with humanity. Playing God. But God left a long time ago, didn't He?*

"Hanael?"

Mechanically, Hanael waves a hand over the length of Dani's body, emitting a soft, blue glow as she does. The angel can feel the telltale *'fizzle'* and *'pop'* under her skin once she finishes, indicating that her powers were all but depleted.

Still, Dani didn't have the kind of time needed for Hanael to wait for them to replenish.

"Dani's in Hell again, isn't she?" Nickie's right beside Hanael now.

"Yes."

"Bastards," Nickie says with a grimace as she lays a blanket over Dani's body. "So, what's the plan?"

"I'm going to Hell to get her back."

"You mean *we're* going to Hell to get her back."

Hanael gapes at her. Nickie's being completely serious. Which, if the girl's recent actions were anything to go by, meant she would be a huge liability.

Dani couldn't afford that either.

The wheels turn again; spinning, spinning, into Hanael's back pocket to retrieve the syringe she had forgotten she swiped from the hospital. Nickie almost knocks it out of her hand. Almost.

Nickie's body goes limp into Hanael's waiting arms. She

makes quick work of maneuvering her body over to a nearby armchair, lying a blanket over her shoulders as an afterthought.

All for the best, she convinces herself as a final wave of her hand materializes her sword from the ether. It is, Hanael knows, the last miracle she will be performing for a while.

CHAPTER 10

DANI

D ani is determined to keep her eyes shut for as long as she can. A thought that immediately strikes her as odd, seeing that she had the option at all.

The hospital gurney has long since been replaced by a hard stone slab that cuts painfully into her back. Her surroundings are silent aside from the sound of her own breathing. Not that she needed to breathe, but old habits die hard, Dani supposes.

Was it ever this silent before? No. No, it wasn't. Something was off. Why wasn't she back in her Hell loop?

"Did you ever stop to think that you never left?"

Dani shoots to a sitting position, eyes flying open in search of the raspy voice – only to land on herself.

Or at least, a demonic-looking zombie version of herself. It looks like what Dani might have looked like if she had crawled out of her grave without being embalmed.

Pitch black sclera's center on her as the creature limps and contorts towards her in a way that suggested half its bones were broken. Dani carefully makes her way off the slab, standing her ground.

After all, what could it possibly do to her that hadn't already been tried?

"What? No more Hell loops?" Dani says, a bitter grin forming. "Let me guess – budget cuts?"

The creature certainly seems surprised at her response. Until it isn't.

A deafening screech echoes against the stone walls before it dissolves into a puddle of steaming black goo on the floor in front of her. Dani stares at it a moment before muttering, "Right. Why not?"

Her surroundings aren't any more impressive. Stone slab. Stone walls. Arched stone doorway. All blurring together in a disorientating shade of grey. Though Dani knows it could be worse.

Keeping this thought in mind, Dani slowly begins putting one foot in front of the other, half expecting the ground to collapse under her. When it doesn't, she continues toward the doorway.

The ice-cold cobble burns her bare feet as Dani makes her way into a hallway that stretches endlessly in both directions. She looks down to find she's now wearing a thin, white slip. A gaze back to the doorway informs her that the room she came out of no longer exists.

Dani proceeds left, overriding her first thought to go right.

The floor is smoother here, but no less painful to walk on. And the more Dani focuses on the pain, the worse it gets. She grits down, continuing onward, before being assaulted by a gag-inducing odor.

Sulphur, Dani's mind helpfully supplies. Too helpfully, considering the circumstances.

Dani's attention is drawn to a nearby mirror, hanging precariously against the grey stone wall. Dani sees a flash of movement in the reflection, and finally, dread grips her.

She tries to retreat, but only manages to move herself closer to the mirror. Though it's not her reflection she ends up seeing.

Dani almost wishes it was.

The sickening, black eyes of Hana stare back at her. Mocking. A feral and utterly wrong smile twisted on her lips. They begin to move, inhumanly, before saying, "You didn't actually think you could trust me, did you?"

A knot rises in Dani's throat. She isn't sure if she needs to scream or throw up.

She ends up doing neither, instead throwing her fist forward into the mirror, shattering it on contact. On her next blink, it vanishes completely.

Was it ever here?

"Get it together, Dani." Nothing here was ever *here*. And even if she wasn't in her Hell loop, the fundamentals were all the same.

She needs to remember that.

"My name is Danielle Olivia Argent," Dani tries as she shakily continues forward. "My brother's name is Matthew Owen Argent. Nicole Allbright is my best friend. And Hanael –"

Dani's knees give out. There is a skull-splitting pressure in her head, that, combined with the sulphur in the air, has her dry heaving.

Dani throws another punch, this time to the stone floor. She is only vaguely aware of the bone-crunching sound and hot pain that flares up her arm at the action.

Focus on the pain, Dani reminds herself. Use it. Ground yourself with it.

But what was there to be grounded to? What does she seriously expect the best-case scenario is here?

The pressure increases and Dani curls in on herself. There's a silent scream in the back of her mind that Dani realizes had been there for a very, very long time. Seemingly on the verge of becoming not-so-silent anymore.

Remember, it seems wanting to scream. *Remember!*

For fucks sake, remember what?

Very abruptly, things quiet. The pain vanishes and Dani is left gasping, knuckles bloody and shaking.

"Hello, Danael."

Dani tries to look up at the approaching footsteps, but the movement only manages to blur her vision further. Blackening spots follow, and the last thing Dani is cognizant of is that she does remember.

She remembers a garden.

When Dani wakes up again, she isn't sure that she wakes up at all.

Everything is fractured – reality, memories, emotions. As if being viewed through a sinister kaleidoscope. Each panel of the refracted reality gives her a different image, some familiar and some not. Though even the unfamiliar panels evoke some sort of emotion.

Dani tries to blink, shake it off, but it does little. She wonders if she's dreaming.

But no, that wasn't right, was it? She was – she had died. She was back in Hell, right?

Right?

"Welcome back."

Male. Unemotional. Vaguely familiar. Where had she heard that voice before?

Only with a great amount of effort can Dani focus on the single refracted panel of the man in front of her. Dark hair, dark eyes, and seemingly dressed to impress.

Dani wasn't impressed.

"My name is Michael. You don't remember me, but not to worry. Your current state is only temporary."

Michael. Dani does remember Hana mentioning how she had talked to him. Hana! Hana would hear her prayers from down here, wouldn't she?

Dani tries and feels like her brain is hit with a cinder block of electricity. She bites down a scream.

"I suppose you still believe Hanael will come to your aid," Michael says. "I am afraid your trust is vastly misplaced."

"It's not."

The archangel stops pacing and stares at her before saying, "Is that so? Then why, pray tell, is she not here already?" He smiles. "Perhaps because she is the reason you are back down here to begin with?"

Dani goes cold. The spell. Hana. Hana had translated the spell that —

No. Hana wouldn't do that. She wouldn't. It was another trick. Another lie. It had to be.

"Yeah, and why are you here?" Dani says, voice hoarse. "Obviously not to help me."

"Help you? Oh, but I did. I gave you exactly what you asked for. How you choose to interpret the situation is entirely up to you."

Before Dani can ask what the hell that's supposed to mean, a loud *'clanging'* brings her attention to a sword dropped at her feet.

"And here I am, helping again," Michael says, eyes drifting to the weapon. "I would keep that close. You'll be needing it."

He vanishes then, and if not for the sword still resting on the stone floor, Dani might doubt the interaction took place at all.

She still doubts.

The blade is silver, almost glowing in the otherwise grey crypt-like surroundings, and there are a variety of symbols carved into the black gemstone handle. Dani tries to decipher them, but a sick feeling rises in her stomach at every attempt.

So, Dani stops trying. What good would any answers do her now? But a weapon – yes, that might be good for something.

Dani picks it up. The handle fits seamlessly in her grip.

Knowing there was no other way but forward, Dani forces herself to a standing position and exits through a stone archway. A chill of Déjà vu prickles at the back of her neck that she pointedly ignores.

Dani wishes she hadn't.

Though in hindsight, Dani wishes she hadn't done a lot of things.

Something is wrong. Or maybe something is right. Dani stopped being able to tell the difference about two days ago.

It's about how long she's been roaming the lower divisions of the Seventh and Eighth Levels of Hell, for a running total of four days. Which equated to roughly four hours Earth time and four days Heaven time.

How does she know this?

No clue. But the celestial info dump has at least provided enough information to navigate Hell semi-effectively. Unfortunately, not enough to escape, but Dani had put that idea to bed after her failed attempt at a prayer.

It's those thoughts, of Hana and clerical errors and unanswered prayers, that cause that silent scream to finally vocalize. It tears through her mind, loud and angry, and Dani – Dani is all too willing to let it.

The handle of the sword digs into Dani's palm as she hops over another crevice of questionable origin. There seems to be a lot of them in the Eighth Level; a disorientating pitch black that tries very hard to draw you in. If Dani listens closely, she can hear screaming.

Dani listens, breathes, and can feel her hand further tighten around her sword as they begin to synchronize with the screams in her head.

She continues on, weaving and ducking this way and that. It was a rather precarious Level, Dani knows. The lower divisions, especially. But she can't afford to run into any demonic foot traffic, and so the hellish subterranean route was the best she could hope for. At least until she made it to the Ninth Level.

The Ninth Level, her celestial laden mind reminds her, had magick. It's what made all the other manifestations in Hell possible. And if Dani had magick, well, she was still figuring that part out.

You could get revenge, the scream offers. Though not so much a scream now as a prodding hum under her skin. *Think of how much you have suffered. How you have been wronged. When will you start fighting back?*

The voice sounds like hers and not hers. Dani considers it.

Michael. Lucifer. The entirety of the Heavenly Host. The entirety of Hell. All puppeteering you this way and that. How long will you allow it to continue for?

Dani can feel the power of the Ninth Level approaching. Just a few more miles.

Hanael. Matthew. Nicole. What have they done to deserve your love?

Dani stops, heart hammering in her chest.

"I love Nickie," Dani says, probably too loudly. "I love my brother. I love —" Dani shakes her head. "They don't have to do anything to earn it."

"Well, I'm flattered."

Dani spins around, almost falling backward at the whiplash. Though she knows, even before her vision settles, who she will see.

"Matt?" Every logical instinct tells her it isn't. Matt isn't here; Matt can't be here. But the newly discovered celestial instinct tells her the opposite. And it hadn't been wrong yet.

"Yes and no. Name's Malphas. Well." He smiles and it's a punch to Dani's gut. "My real name, at least."

Malphas. Major demon. Second in command to Lucifer. One part of her brain continues to relay the information while the other vehemently denies it. Nausea builds.

"It almost doesn't seem like a fair fight," Malphas says, closing the distance between them. Dani can feel his breath on her face as he finishes, "But then again, what would you know about fair fights?"

"What are you talking about?" Dani hisses into his face. Rage curls under her skin as the denial slowly but surely makes its exit. "I did everything for you! I sacrificed EVERY-THING for you! Ever since the day you were born!"

"In this life, maybe," he says. "But that's twenty-two

years. A blink. Worthless, to both of us." He takes a step back, eyes falling bitterly to her sword. "Not after what you and Hanael did."

It's that name, that does it.

Dani lunges for him, sword brandishing and teeth barred. He ducks, but Dani is able to land a slice to his arm. He grips the bleeding appendage and looks up at her, partly amused and partly like he wants to rip her entire head from her body.

It's not a look she hasn't seen before.

It's that single thought that has Dani faltering. It's only a second, but it's enough for Malphas to capitalize on.

Dani feels a searing pain rattle her skull. Rattle everything. Shadows and skeletons let loose to wreak havoc on her mind.

She's on the ground now, watching as Malphas lands a kick, this time to her ribs. That's all she's doing now – watching. Merely an observer of her own actions and his. Had she always been an observer?

Dani doesn't know.

She doesn't know as Malphas blinks off in retreat. Doesn't know as she watches her own eyes stare unblinking into her sword, blood dripping from her mouth.

Even when Dani begins to regain control of her body, she finds herself wondering if it was ever hers to begin with.

Dani doesn't know, and that, she thinks, is her worst revelation yet.

CHAPTER II

NICKIE

W hen Nickie wakes up, she's pissed.

Scratch that; Nickie was already pissed. She's goddamned livid now.

She's up in an instant, despite the spinning of the room. Her hand grips at the side of her neck in a grimace. What the hell had Hanael given her?

Nickie's eyes land on Dani's body and the grimace tightens.

Stupid, *stupid*. This is what she gets for entertaining this supernatural bullshit for a second. Hah! Maybe that had been her problem with Matt. And here she thought him your run-of-the-mill sociopath.

Hanael wasn't lying about that, at least. Loathe as she is to admit it, Nickie doesn't think there's much Hanael *is* lying about. Still, it was a dick move to knock her out and Nickie regrets not punching the angel harder.

At a lack of anything better to do, Nickie screams. Once to get it out of her system and a second time for good luck. With a burning in her throat, Nickie looks skyward, puts her hands together in mock prayer, and says, "God grant me the serenity to accept nothing because this is bullshit, the courage to kick your fucking ass when I see you, and the wisdom to know the difference. Amen."

With a fresh spring in her still slightly inebriated step, Nickie saunters over to the breakfast bar, grabs her keys off the counter, and proceeds out to her car.

Alright, first stop – Lily's. Nickie is sure she'll be able to point her in the right direction. Hell, Nickie would take any direction at this point.

Thoughts of Hell and Dani and celestial bullshit threaten to overwhelm her again and *again*, Nickie has to work overtime to stomp out the emotional fire as she makes her way up the pathway to Lily's house. Though one of these days, she knows, she's going to stomp it right into a puddle of gasoline.

Nickie just hadn't figured that day would be today.

The smell of blood is unmistakable, even before Nickie enters the foyer. And when Nickie does enter the foyer, well.

Once her brain fully processes the image, her hand flies to her mouth in some vain attempt to stop the violent half-sob, half-gag that comes out.

Lily's throat is slit clean. A familiar kind of clean. While her body lay crumpled against one of the bookcases. Her light blue eyes are blown wide open, and even dead, Nickie can see the terror etched into them.

"Shame you missed all the good bits."

Very slowly, Nickie raises her head to meet a pair of familiar brown eyes. They're almost glistening now, unapologetic in their sadism. It's a look Nickie has seen often, and one she only wishes Dani had acknowledged. Maybe then her best friend wouldn't be in this mess.

The idea of Matt killing someone is woefully unsurprising. Not the first time and Nickie doubts it will be the last. Really, she's surprised the asshole hasn't already lit the place up. He loved his arson.

"I see those cogs turning in your head, princess," Matt says. His voice *is* different. Less restrained, maybe. "Turning, turning, turning." He smiles wide, making a counterclockwise motion with the still bloody knife in his hand. "But never making any connections."

Nickie schools her expression, takes in a stuttering breath, and pulls the knife from her boot. She's about to start swinging until she sees the entirety of his eyes blacken. The knife clatters to the floor and Nickie doesn't have time to curse before Matt is backing her into a corner.

Matt. Was that even his real name? God – she probably has some kind of demonic STD now.

"Funny, isn't it?" He says as her back hits the wall. His eyes are unchanged, though Nickie is beginning to find them unimpressive. "How everyone close to you ends up dead."

"Oh, not everyone, unfortunately."

Matt laughs and takes a few steps back. Nickie instinctually begins scanning her surroundings, looking for anything that might be of some use. What was supposed to hurt demons? Holy water? Fuck. She knew she should have memorized that exorcism.

"Self-preservation for the win, baby," Matt says, walking languidly around Lily's living room, almost daring Nickie to try something. "Not that you would know anything about that."

Nickie just as casually begins making her way over to a nearby bookcase. "Yeah, silly me and my empathy for other living things."

Something in Matt's expression darkens. He approaches

her and Nickie backs up, spine hitting one of the bookcase ledges.

"It *is* silly," he hisses. Nickie can feel his hot breath against her ear as she maneuvers her hand to the ledge behind her. "It's downright detestable. And you know, I tried with you, Nickie. I really did. You could have been something glorious. *We* could have been something glorious. Instead, you were a fucking junkie that –"

'*Crack!'* goes the vile of holy water against his head. Nickie rubs the remaining bits of glass off on her jeans as she hears him cry out like the little bitch he is. A plaster of chemical burns begins to cover his cheek as he stumbles backward. Nickie grins.

"Would you look at that. Looks like the horror movies got something right after all."

Nickie can feel the full weight of Matt's body slam into hers as he topples them both over. Nickie's back hits the floor and the thought barely crosses her mind of the luck of it being carpet when she feels pressure on her throat, choking her.

"You think I won't kill you?"

Oh, she is absolutely sure of it. If he hadn't already, after all their vicious fights and proverbial daggers, he wouldn't now. Still, Nickie doesn't call his bluff (not that she could right now) and instead chooses an unapologetic knee to the groin.

The hands release and Nickie lets out a string of choked gasps. Her throat burns and already Nickie can tell it will leave a mark. She glowers before crawling over to him and landing a blow to his jaw. *You killed my best friend.* Then another. *You killed the woman who was the only mother figure I'll probably ever have.* And another. *You killed your own fucking parents*. She has no plans to stop, but an unfamiliar male voice forces her hand.

"Huh. You need a lot less help than I figured you would."

Nickie's fist freezes above Matt's face as she turns around to see a shortish, brown-haired, moderately attractive dude. Or at least, what Nickie assumes is a dude. Because if Matt was any indication, god only knows how many supernatural nasties could be crawling around.

Nickie can feel Matt's hand jerk around her wrist and twist it behind her back. Followed by a firmly placed knee that sends her flying about four feet forward. Weakly, Nickie forces herself to a standing position, though is almost knocked back down by a sudden blinding light that erupts from where Matt was previously standing.

Nickie stumbles, rubs her eyes, and they clear to once again reveal the mysterious brunette.

"And who the hell are you supposed to be?" Nickie spits out, only vaguely aware of the blood coating her lips.

"Name's Amy," he says with a smirk before his attention catches Lily's body. Nickie stiffens as she sees him approach it before leaning down and touching the back of his hand to her neck.

"I'm sorry," Amy says. "She's been dead too long now. I can't revive her."

"So, what? You another one of those dick angels?"

Amy laughs. "I used to be. Though lately I've made my home more south of the border, if you catch my drift."

"Hell," Nickie grits out, working overtime to keep her cool. She couldn't afford to drive off the one person who might be able to help Dani. "Demon, I'm guessing? Like Matt?"

"Demon, yes. Like Malphas? Hell, no. I can't stand that prick."

At least they had something in common. Wait –

"Malphas?" Nickie confirms. "*That's* Matt's real name?" Stupid name. "Has he always been a demon?"

"Yep and yep," Amy says, popping the 'p's'. "I assume you have questions."

"No shit. But I'm guessing you're not going to be giving them out of the goodness of your heart."

Amy places his hand over said organ in mock hurt. "You wound me, darling. But you're not wrong. I do have quite a bit riding on this situation. Though to be fair, so does, well, everyone."

"What do you mean?" Nickie asks, not sure she wants to hear the answer.

"The apocalypse is nigh. And you and me," he makes a motion between the two of them, "Are gonna have to be the first line of defense to stop it."

Then again, when was the last time Nickie ever got what she wanted?

Nickie asks Amy to repeat himself about four times. She still ends up understanding only about half of it.

Matt was the demon Malphas reincarnated (?) into the body of Dani's brother. Except, according to Amy, was just not a thing demons did. Hence his investigation into the matter. Hence the apocalypse being nigh.

What part Dani had to play in all of this was still unknown to Amy. *Convenient*, Nickie thinks, despite having followed the demon to the outskirts of town in search of a crossroad. Scratchy thorns and brush continue to attack her knee-high socks as Nickie grimaces at the surrounding deserted field. Nothing for miles. No one would ever hear her scream.

But what was the alternative? Every minute that Nickie spent on her ass was another hour that Dani spent in Hell. Not to mention that Nickie *really* doesn't want to come to find she somehow inadvertently jumpstarted Armageddon.

It couldn't have been zombies, could it? This would have been so much easier if it had been zombies.

"Penny for your thoughts?"

"Just trying to figure out what use you think I'm going to be to you in Hell," Nickie says. Because that was the golden question, wasn't it?

"Despite the fact you're kind of a badass for a human –"

"You know adding 'for a human' to the end of a compliment," Nickie says, almost tripping as she tries to pull out another thorn from her sock. "Takes away from the compliment. And makes you a dick."

Amy laughs. "Fair enough. To answer your question, there are two main reasons. First, you have a personal connection to Dani. That connection will help us find her. Hell is still a wonderland of horrors, even for demons, so you being there will cut our navigation time down threefold. Second, you are a human soul who is the farthest thing from damnation as one could get. Which will, in fact, be *very* useful to me. A sort of energetic camouflage, if you will."

Nickie freezes. There is a lot to unpack from that – namely the idea of being a literal human shield – though, naturally, what Nickie's brain ends up fixating on is, "'The farthest thing from damnation?' Is that supposed to be a joke?"

Amy stops as he turns to frown at her. "No? Your soul

is...unnaturally bright, Nickie. Pretty, even. Reminds me of Heaven when I look at it."

Nickie gapes and Amy clears his throat.

"Anyway," he says, pointing to their far-right, where the field began to give way to a dirt road. "Crossroad's over there, which is where we'll open the portal to –"

"Why do you even want to stop the apocalypse?" Nickie says, mind still reeling from Amy's previous statement. It's a lie. It has to be. "You're a demon. Aren't you supposed to, I don't know, *want* the world to end?"

"What gave you that impression?"

"Answer the question!" Nickie shouts, storming up to him. "Why is this so important to you? Why are you willing to risk your neck to help me?"

The demon obviously hadn't expected her outburst. Nickie stands her ground, and slowly but surely, she can see cracks of vulnerability begin to appear on his expression. Now it was Nickie's turn to be surprised.

"I hope that if I help stop the apocalypse, I might gain Heaven's attention. In a good way, I mean," Amy says. "In a 'your trespasses are forgiven' kind of way."

That...wasn't a lie. "You want to go back to Heaven? Why?" Nickie asks. "From what I've heard, neither side seems particularly stand-up."

"It's home," Amy says with a shrug.

Home. Nickie could never relate to the idea, at least not as a physical place. Before being placed in foster care and meeting Dani, the only 'home' to Nickie had been one she couldn't wait to be taken from. Even now, at twenty-two years old, Nickie still sleeps with a knife under her pillow.

Though if they are talking in terms of a person, well, that one went without saying. Maybe her and Amy's goals aren't so misaligned after all. Maybe.

She really was going to do this, wasn't she?

"Fine!" Nickie blurts out. "But if I come to find you're screwing with me, trust me when I say you're going to wish you never met me." Hanael had already fooled her once and she'd be damned if she was going to have the celestial wool pulled over her eyes a second time.

"I think I'd be pretty hard-pressed to wish I never met you," Amy says, grinning. He turns around and starts toward the crossroad. And against every better judgment, Nickie follows him.

The actual opening a portal to Hell part is amusingly anticlimactic.

Amy draws some kind of sigil in the center of the cross-road with a stick before slicing his hand and letting the blood drip into the crevice of dirt. The blood begins moving until there is a bright crimson sigil that begins to glow in their current surrounding dusk.

"You ready?" Amy asks.

"Not even a little," Nickie says. "Just get on with it."

An ancient string of words begins to roll off Amy's tongue, causing vibrations to rise in the air around them. Nickie can feel them progressively prickle against her skin until there is a sudden *'crack!'* in the atmosphere, giving way to a crack on the ground at the edge of the sigil.

Out of that crack rises a door. And out of that door rises Nickie's heart into her throat.

Amy gives her a look and Nickie nods. He turns the handle.

Darkness. It's all Nickie can see as she looks into the

doorway. All she can feel as she sees Amy step through and disappear into nothing.

"Abandon all hope, ye who enter here," Nickie mutters under her breath before stepping through the threshold, swallowed whole.

CHAPTER 12
HANAEL

Something was wrong. Or perhaps something was going according to whatever asinine plan was being concocted. Hanael is betting on the latter.

Dani wasn't in a hell loop. In fact, Hanael is beginning to wonder if Dani was in Hell at all. There is certainly no trace of her energetic signature anywhere to be found.

Add that to the fact that Hanael has not been approached by a single demon, and Hanael's mind begins to go to some very colorful places.

Or perhaps that was an effect of being in Hell.

It's harder to navigate than Hanael was expecting. Disorientating. Like walking through a labyrinth at nighttime. Along its walls an infinite number of doors, the barest echo of screams behind them.

Hanael can taste the torment in the air. She swallows it, walks faster.

Her angelic sense of direction was still working well enough to tell her she had entered the portal from Earth into the Fourth Level; one of the three which housed human souls. That's about all it tells her.

Well, that and Lucifer's main living quarters being three Levels below her.

Once upon a time, she and Lucifer had been quite close. Or as close as one could be to Lucifer if you weren't Michael. She had always considered him as a brother. Still does, despite everything.

This isn't to say that Hanael supported his cause. Not at all. But she had respected it enough to create the apple tree at his behest.

It's still her proudest accomplishment.

Yahweh hadn't said much about it at first, instead turning it into a kind of test for Adam and Eve. Until they failed, Yahweh left, and Michael more or less took His place.

Which, Hanael suspects, might have been Lucifer's goal all along. Though his other half certainly doesn't end up seeing it that way.

Hanael often wonders about her own twin flame. Most of the angels don't remember the whole separating debacle. At least the ones that separated correctly –

Hanael stops walking. Why was she thinking about this? How long had she been walking?

Dani. She needed to find Dani.

There's a sudden rumble from somewhere deep underground; vibrations that physically shake her. Hanael coughs as a film of sulphuric dust clouds the air. When it clears, there is a black, steel elevator standing in front of her.

It opens and Hanael knows, instinctively, where it leads.

Still, she steps in, back ramrod straight as the doors close and it takes her down. The haze that had previously been occupying her mind clears just enough for Hanael's heart to jump into her throat.

Was she *insane*? She can't seriously think Lucifer will help her. What if Dani wasn't even in Hell?

Hanael swallows down the lump as there is a *'ding'* and the elevator doors open to reveal a misty abyss of a hallway. She steps out and can feel the magick laced in the air. The mist swirls around her, prodding at her energy, and, once realizing she is not a threat, disperses to reveal what appears to be an elaborate and ordained mansion.

The transfer is jarring.

As Hanael's senses focus, she finds that she is now seated on a vintage violet settee. Her fingers run along its cushion, velvet soft and smooth under her fingertips.

"It's been a long time, Hanael."

Hanael's head jerks up to find Lucifer lazily preparing them both a drink. She watches, dazed, as the archangel approaches her, handing off a caramel-colored liquid in a glass tumbler. It takes a few moments for Hanael to stop the shaking in her hands enough to take it.

Though Lucifer is as always, in no rush.

She watches as he takes a seat on the recliner opposite her, taking a sip of his own drink before crossing one designer pantsuit leg over the other. Like Michael, he looks quite unchanged from the last time Hanael saw him, though perhaps a bit more mentally stable.

A closer look at his energetic signature says otherwise.

Hanael realizes that Lucifer is waiting for her to speak. There's a knowing smile on his face, cocky, as if to say *'Yes, the one that got away. I always knew you'd return to me.'*

Hanael is surprised her grip on the tumbler doesn't cause it to shatter. She takes in a steadying breath before saying, "I am here about a soul. Danielle Olivia Argent. Recently deceased. I would like her current location, seeing as she isn't in a hell loop."

"Ah, yes. The clerical error." Hanael's jaw ticks. "Strange she isn't in Heaven. I rather thought that was the whole point of resurrecting her."

"Strange, indeed," Hanael says with a bite.

Lucifer looks at her in contemplation before saying, "Must be something special, for you to venture all the way down here."

"She is."

With a slight roll of his shoulders, the archangel is back on his feet and making his way over to a bookshelf. He pulls some sort of turquoise crystal off before tossing it to her, the sigil-covered gemstone resting heavy in her hands.

"Hell's very own compass. One of my own inventions, of course. You just need to focus on this human of yours and the stone will help you hone in on her energetic signature. It's quite impossible to do so otherwise down here."

"...Right," Hanael murmurs. "And what exactly is it going to cost me?"

"How cynical you've grown in our time apart, sister. No, no. First one is on the house."

"You mean first deal?" Hanael asks. "And what makes you think there would ever be a second?"

Lucifer's hand stops cold as it is trailing along the spines of his books. He turns to her and says, "Why would an already ostracized angel who has gone against the *direct* orders of the Host need to make a deal?" He smiles. "I do wonder."

Hanael's face grows hot. Like with her recent confrontation with Michael, Hanael's brain begs her not to push her luck. This time she actually manages to listen.

Wordlessly, Hanael stands, placing her untouched tumbler on a nearby table. She gives Lucifer a curt nod and turns around to find the steel elevator has returned. She wastes no time in shuffling into it.

The doors close and Hanael looks down at the now glowing crystal. The Ninth Level. Dani was on the Ninth Level.

Hanael presses the '9' button on the elevator and as she begins to ascend, can only hope she will find Dani in one piece.

CHAPTER 13
NICKIE

Nickie realizes it too late.

That familiar euphoria. The dangerous kind of calm. Like being under water, drowning. Your only fear in the world being dragged back to the surface.

There is no come up. When Nickie crosses through the threshold into Hell, there is nothing to indicate anything is wrong at all. That should have been her first clue.

Her second should have been the look on Amy's face when he asked her how she was faring and she answered, "I'm fucking fantastic," genuinely.

There is some sort of way that Nickie thinks she should be feeling – will feel later, if she survives – but it slips out of her grasp as easily as any other fear, apprehension, or horror that Hell tries to throw at her.

And so, Nickie keeps her mouth shut and decides to take it for the respite it is.

It's dark, on the Level they enter onto, which Amy tells her is the Eighth. Their goal is apparently the Ninth, but that one doesn't have an entrance from Earth.

Her surroundings aren't much to speak of – dark, damp,

musty. There's a smell in the air that Nickie recognizes from somewhere. She breathes it in deeply.

Nickie starts walking forward through the current hallway, somehow knowing exactly where to go. Amy struggles to catch up with her.

"How can you see down here?" Amy puffs out. "*I* can barely see down here."

"Good internal compass, I guess."

"I guess."

They walk for what feels like days, but Amy assures her has only been a few hours. They talk, and Nickie begins to find his presence less annoying with each passing conversation.

He's quite handsome, Nickie realizes suddenly. Just not in the way that Malphas was. They smelled different, too. Which is weird, seeing as they were both demons.

"So, is Malphas high on the food chain down here or something?" Nickie asks.

Amy shoots her a strange look as they pass under another stone stairwell. "Yeah, actually. He's Lucifer's second in command. Why do you ask?"

Why did she ask? What's wrong with her? And why the *hell* is she thinking about what they smell like?

"No reason," Nickie says a little too quickly. "How much farther?"

"About an hour."

They fall into an only semi-awkward silence and Nickie resigns herself to not ask any more questions. Not from lack of temptation but more because Nickie cares less and less about the answers with each passing moment.

Why does she feel high? Because she was in literal Hell. Next question.

101

Was her mother somewhere down here? Who cares? If she is, the bitch deserves it.

Where is Hanael? Again, who cares? The only way it's relevant is if the angel ends up finding Dani before her.

Dani's safety truly was the only relevant thing remaining.

"Why do you have a chick's name?" Nickie does end up asking out of sheer boredom.

"Gender is boring," Amy says breezily as they pass over a stone bridge. "And not a thing for celestials. We all have some pretty weird names anyhow." He smirks. "Why? You want to see what I look like with boobs?"

"Maybe another time."

"Alright! It's a date."

Nickie has a scathing reply ready, but it is swallowed at the sight in front of her. It's the first time she genuinely startles since arriving in Hell.

"What the fuck is that?!" Nickie curses. It's – god, some kind of leech-infested *moat*. The pitch-black creatures swaying back and forth like a tidal wave of nightmares.

Nickie can feel her stomach churn. The previous high joins it, curling inward, inward – all the way up to her throat.

"Fatum sanuisugae," Amy says gravely. "Leeches of death. One of the few creatures that came into existence in Hell by themselves. No doubt from all that magic seeping out of the Ninth Level."

"I repeat, what the fuck?"

"We just...have to be careful, that's all. See that bridge over there?" Amy points to the far left, and like most things in her direct line of vision, seemed to just materialize. "We cross that, enter through the foyer, and we'll be in the Ninth Level."

"Yeah, and what happens if we're not careful?"

Amy grimaces. "Nothing good. Lucifer has full control over the leeches and let's just say it wouldn't bode well for us if one were to take a bite." At Nickie's look of incredulity, he puts his hand up in placation. "Hey, we made it this far, right? And what? You seriously find this the scariest part of our journey so far?"

"I don't like bugs!"

"Then we can face our mutual entomophobia together. Come on." Amy is already on his way towards the bridge and Nickie can do little else but twist her face in contempt before following him.

The good news is they make it into the Ninth Level in one piece. Which ends up being the only good news.

Easy, Amy had said. Concentrate on Dani and the magic of the Ninth Level would take care of the rest, Amy had said.

Yeah, right.

"Maybe...focus more?" Amy suggests.

She opens a single eye to glare at him. "What the hell do you think I've been doing?" The consequence of her failure certainly isn't lost on Nickie.

She feels close, too. So close. The power is *right there*. Nickie can feel it humming under her fingertips, accentuated by the dim red glow of their surroundings.

"Alright, alright," Amy says. "I can try something else. A grounding spell might help you –" Amy's words trail off as his eyes focus on something behind Nickie. Nickie doesn't have a chance to turn around to look before Amy pushes her behind him.

"I suppose I should be thanking you." Nickie shoves

past Amy at the sound of the voice, despite his physical attempts to keep her back. Standing only a few yards from them is Malphas, joined by what Nickie can only assume is two demon lackeys. The holy water burns are healing but still visible, and Nickie sends him a knowing smirk.

He returns it.

It's strange, seeing her ex and knowing what she knows now. They were always playing games with each other, sure. Mental chess. Though only now is Nickie starting to see the whole board.

Malphas' grin turns from her to Amy. "You really have saved me so much time, Amy. Bringing this one to me almost gift-wrapped."

"You and I both know you can't lay a finger on her down here. Her soul is spotless," Amy says, the confidence in his voice betraying his coiled body posture. The demon lackeys take notice.

"Are you sure about that?" Malphas says as he spares another grin in her direction. He still knows something Amy doesn't and Nickie intends to find out what.

"You want me?" Nickie says, taking several generous steps forward before throwing out her hands. "Come on, then. Let's walk and talk. Seems we're long overdue, *Malphas*."

Malphas is positively beaming, while Amy looks ready to rip the smile off his face. Nickie isn't entirely sure he won't.

"No way," Amy says, attempting to grab Nickie's wrist, but she shoves him off. His eyes are begging. "Nickie, please. Think about this. You don't want to go with him."

"Nickie is a grown woman," Malphas chimes in. "She can think for herself. Isn't that right, princess?"

Nickie can feel her fingers twitch toward the knife in her

back pocket, but this time she manages to control herself. Another game, that's all this was.

"If I go with you, you *will* take me to Dani," Nickie says. "And you'll tell me why she's here to begin with."

"I will."

Nickie searches his expression and, after finding what she's looking for, begins to move forward. Though Amy, the idiot, tries to beat her to it. He doesn't get far; dropped to his knees via a dart to the neck courtesy of a demon lackey.

Nickie glares at Malphas.

"Your boy toy will be just fine," he assures, extending a hand for her to take. Nickie slaps it down and brushes past him into the tunnel he came from. There is a slightly darker tinge of red here and Nickie can hear the echo of Malphas' footsteps as he catches up to her.

"You did a number on my face, you know." Is the first thing he says. Nickie can hear the grin in his voice. "It'll probably leave a scar."

"Good. Might give you a little character."

"You always say such sweet things to me."

"Cut the shit," Nickie snarls, stopping in her tracks to face him. "And tell me why Dani is here. Why did you target her? This was all planned, yeah?" Her chest is only inches from his. "From the moment you killed her parents."

"I'm not the only reason Dani is here," Malphas says. "I'm barely a reason at all. I simply chose not to look a gift horse in the mouth when Lucifer gave me the orders."

"The orders for *what*? And what the hell do you have against Dani, anyway?"

"You're still asking the wrong questions," he says. "Instead of asking what Hell wants with Dani, ask yourself what Dani could have done to get Hell's attention in the first place."

Nickie is about to spit out vehement denials, but something stops her. It's the same something that had been nagging at her since Dani had returned. The same something that had, on several occasions, made Nickie hesitant to be around her.

Because Dani *was* different. Up until now, Nickie had written it off as some kind of Hell-induced PTSD, feeling like the shittiest best friend on the planet for even entertaining the idea it could be anything more. But well, if Malphas had the power to reincarnate into a human body –

A connection is made then, cutting razor sharp into Nickie's skull. It brings her to her knees and Nickie cries out, clawing at her ears. Vaguely, Nickie recognizes that the previous spell she had tried to locate Dani with was finally taking effect.

Except it's not Dani's voice that Nickie ends up hearing.

"*And you're certain everything is in place, Lucifer?*"

"*Ye of so little faith, Michael.*"

A beat.

"*Oh, don't give me that look. Yes, yes. Fine. Hanael is on her way as we speak to meet up with her other half. The rest is, as they say, history.*"

Nickie gasps back to the present moment to find Malphas' fingers digging into her shoulders, his eyes wild. "What was that? What did you see?"

Nickie elbows him in the eye. He's quick to make his way back to his feet, but Nickie's blade is quicker. She presses it firmly against his crotch, right at the edge of his ball sack.

"Start talking."

Malphas inhales and Nickie can visibly see his pants tighten. She gives him a disgusted look.

"Oh, no. That's all on you, sweetheart," he says, still somehow managing a smirk.

Nickie is about to transfer the blade to his throat when a scream in the distance causes her to remove the weapon entirely.

That was Dani's scream. It's unlike anything Nickie's heard before. Unlike anything she thought capable of coming out of her best friend's mouth. Or anyone's, for that matter.

Nickie doesn't offer Malphas a second glance before she runs in the direction of the sound. He doesn't try and stop her.

CHAPTER 14

HANAEL

T he Ninth Level is infinitely easier to navigate than the Lower Levels, Hanael finds. For one, she could actually see – thanks to a faint red glow that lights up the surrounding stone pathways. Her pace is also less strained, and Hanael no longer feels like she is walking through molasses.

Time does feel...different, somehow. Changed. As if the time in Hell has aligned with the time on Earth.

Hanael shakes off the feeling and looks down again at the turquoise stone as she continues toward where its magnetic field was pulling her. Dani shouldn't be far off now.

Hanael is about to call out Dani's name when she sees the reflection of a sword on the steel stone to her left. She ducks and can hear the *'whiz'* of the blade as it goes over her head. Her own sword is unsheathed from her waist the next instant, as Hanael readies herself for anything except what she ends up seeing.

Aside from the Rebellion, the sight of true avenging angels was few and far between. They are all warriors certainly, but rarely did angels care enough about an issue to enact their full wrath.

Dani had always cared quite a bit though, hadn't she?

Hanael's mind short-circuits. Unfortunate timing, as Dani lunges forward again, with all the grace and nuance that only a fighter trained by the Heavenly Host could exhibit. Hanael's brain comes back online just in time to angle her own sword above her head.

The *'clank'* of Dani's sword into hers leaves Hanael's ears ringing.

"Dani. Dani it's *me*. It's Hanael." But could the same be said for Dani? Her energetic signature has morphed to one of entirely angelic origin. Hanael can see the energy rage and twist before taking a generous step back.

"And that's supposed to mean something to me?" Dani hisses, taking another swipe with her blade that Hanael narrowly avoids.

The words cut into Hanael worse than any blade ever could. Doubt follows, reeling her brain until all that remained was the possibility that Dani had been an angel all along. Nothing more than a Heavenly trojan horse used to manipulate her. What other explanation was there?

Pain explodes against her right arm. Hanael grips it and can feel the blood slick against her fingers. She raises her head to meet Dani's expression and finds it's one she doesn't recognize at all.

Hanael feels sick.

She tries to get angry then. Enraged enough to hurt Dani; to kill her.

It's a miserable failure.

"You were in on it the whole time, weren't you?" Dani truly looks deranged.

"In on what?" Hanael bites back, gripping her injured arm pathetically.

"Malphas!" Dani screams. Her fist goes flying towards Hanael's face, and Hanael blocks it with her good arm. Dani glowers over the obstructed appendage. "My own brother was a *demon*. And you sent me back to Hell with that translated text. I'm in Hell again because of you!"

Doubt reels back to confusion. Why would Dani be so angry if she was the one working against Hanael? Was it possible she was as clueless as Hanael?

Any such hope dies, however, when a sharp pain explodes in Hanael's abdomen. Hanael's hands are shaking as they travel downward to feel the gushing blood escape.

She was going to die.

The thought barely makes itself known before Hanael collapses. It almost feels as if she collapses into a set of waiting arms, though Hanael is sure she can blame such frivolous ideas on the blood loss.

Her vision has long since spotted and Hanael can feel the physical sensation of her energy begin to turn in on itself. Where did angels go when they died? Did they go anywhere?

It's not peaceful, in any case. If Hanael had the energy, she'd be screaming. Perhaps she is. She hears someone screaming.

It's Dani. Dani is screaming.

Not out of anger anymore, but grief. It's a horrible sound and it echoes wildly around Hanael's skull. Echoes, echoes, until violently slamming into another echo. One similar but not. Then another and another until –

"I do not like it," Hanael mutters despairingly to Dani – no, Danael. They are in the Seventh Sphere; in the Garden, centuries before Adam and Eve will be created. Danael looks much the same, though her 21st-century casual wear has been replaced by golden armor.

"It feels wrong being separated," she continues, before roughly plunging her hands into the moist soil. Danael leans down to join her before saying, "I know. But it is our Creator's will, and His will shouldn't be questioned. We should embrace His new concept. Duality."

Hanael doesn't look at her. She can feel the roots of a future cherry blossom begin to form under her fingertips. A fore-warning doubt joins it.

～

"Is there something wrong with us?" Hanael asks Danael one day. They both have long since adjusted into their new roles – Hanael the Virtue of the Seventh Sphere and Danael the Power of the Ninth Sphere – though Hanael still feels empty.

"It is not just us," Danael reminds. "Michael and Lucifer seem to be suffering a similar affliction. As do Malphas and Asbeel, among others."

"Perhaps our Creator has made a mistake, then." Hanael can see Danael visibly flinch at her words. Still, she placates her, "Perhaps."

They could lie to each other now. It is such a new concept, lying. Hanael isn't sure if she likes it.

～

"You are spending a lot of time with Lucifer," Danael says offhandedly one day. Danael has been joining her in the garden

more these days, fascinated with Adam and Eve. Hanael still wonders what happened to Lilith.

"You spend a lot of time with Michael," Hanael replies.

"Michael is my superior," Danael says. "We are not...friendly, as you and Lucifer are."

Hanael smirks at her. "Envy is a sin, Danael. You know I would never care for anyone as I care for you."

"I am not envious. I am worried."

The Rebellion hits Danael like a whiplash. Hanael, less so. Though the branded sigil that appears behind her neck comes as an unpleasant surprise.

"Hanael, what did you do?" Danael cries out when she sees the unmistakable Mark of the Fallen on Hanael.

"I suppose it was the Tree of Knowledge," Hanael says, more unbothered by the entire thing than she has any right to be.

"I thought our Creator asked you to make that?"

"No. Lucifer did."

Danael glares at her, all manners of livid and hurt and resentful. It is the only aspect of the situation Hanael regrets.

Despite the obvious dissonance it causes her, Danael tries to hide Hanael from the ongoing witch hunt for as long as possible. Though Hanael knows they are only buying themselves time.

"No!" Danael screams, fighting back against Asbeel as the newly fallen angel attempts to drag Hanael away.

"I am doing you both a favor!" Asbeel spits back at her. "Hanael will stand far better a chance at Lucifer's side than not. Look at how many of us have already been slaughtered like

animals!" She pushes Danael backwards. "And where is our Creator? Gone! We are all abandoned! Forsaken! Fallen or not!"

Asbeel turns back towards Hanael and Hanael is quite content to go with her before she sees the glint of Danael's sword from her peripheral. Danael would keep trying to protect her, Hanael realizes with a growing horror, up until the moment of her own death.

Unless Hanael gave her a reason not to.

Hanael plunges her sword into Asbeel's abdomen. She watches with forced emotionlessness as the other angel's body falls limp at her feet, bloodied abdomen on full display.

Her head rises to meet Danael's, hoping to see disgust, rage, hate – anything other than the pronounced determination she actually ends up seeing.

"I am going to fix this," Danael says gravely, and before Hanael can stop her, she is gone.

Danael is only gone a short time, but it is long enough for the Mark of the Fallen to be inexplicably removed from Hanael's person.

The panic is thick in Hanael's throat. She cannot imagine what lengths Danael must have gone through to ensure such a fate. The angel doesn't have to imagine for long, however, as Danael and Michael materialize in front of her and the archangel announces, "It is your lucky day, Hanael. It seems your other half is quite motivated to ensure your safety." His voice is thick with bitterness. "I only wish I could have said the same of mine."

"Danael, what did you do?"

Danael only smiles at her sadly. An apology. It's the last

expression Hanael remembers seeing on her. Well, if she had remembered Danael at all –

So too, do Hanael's last memories of Danael in this moment consist of an apology. Though not with a smile this time, but a scream. Piercing and vibrating and the kind of emotionally charged energy that could very well break an apocalyptic seal.

The sound carries Hanael all the way into approaching darkness.

CHAPTER 15
DANI

Dani comes to with blood on her now shaking hands. It isn't hers, but Dani wishes it were.

A blink later and Dani is desperately working to slow the bleeding from the gaping wound in Hanael's abdomen. Her eyes are stinging as they catch sight of her sword, menacing and bloody, only a few feet to her right.

"No. No!" Dani cries out. How could she do this? How could she *ever* do this? And Hana – Hana hadn't known anything! Dani remembers that part clearly enough. And she had just kept *going*.

This was worse than a Hell loop. Was this a Hell loop?

Hanael's eyes are glazed; focused on something nonexistent behind Dani. She coughs and a mouthful of blood follows. Dani screams.

It knocks something loose that Dani hadn't known existed.

"Please help us," Dani gasps out through her ragged sobs. She only realizes it's a prayer when her head is craned upward toward the current red, misty abyss. "Please help her. Please save her."

There is no answer. Dani doesn't know why she expected there to be. Though there is that voice again, telling her she knows exactly why. It's starting to sound more and more like her own voice with each passing second.

"Fuck You!" Dani screams skyward. "I've never asked for anything from You! I've always been loyal! And the one time I ask for Your help, You can't even –"

Dani sobs again, followed by a scream. It releases something old and powerful that burns like acid coming out of Dani's throat. When she stops, her vision blurs, almost causing her body to topple over beside Hana's.

When it clears, Dani can see Hana's breathing slowing down. She can see something else, too – an energy surrounding the angel. A beautiful swirl of green and purple hues that was, too, fading quickly.

The realization that she's seen this energy before, is intimately familiar with it, gives Dani a disorientating pause. Like what one might feel if they were seeing their own bloody and displaced limb in front of them.

Her hand reaches out, mesmerized, to touch it. A jolt of electricity follows, not more than a pinprick, but enough to blast open the locked doors in her mind that she hadn't realized were locked.

Dani still can't see the memories inside those doors, but it's enough to know to place her hands over Hanael's chest and push her own energy forward into the angel's. It's draining and celestial alarm bells are going off in her head, but Dani persists.

Only when Dani is physically unable to give Hanael any more of her energy does she collapse next to the angel. Her heart throbs in protest and it is the only noise against the otherwise silent hallway.

It didn't work. Why did Dani think it would? Oh, God, Hanael's really –

Dani's eyes are screwed shut and she has no plans to open them until she hears a gasp from beside her.

Her body shoots up and there, eye-level, is a very not-dead angel.

"Hanael?" Dani chokes out. She doesn't want to get her hopes up. Not when it could be another trick of Hell.

But then Hanael looks at her and Dani knows it's real. Because *nothing* could replicate that look.

Dani's not sure who bridges the gap between them first. Her hands dig into Hanael's back and it doesn't take the angel's adjoining shoulder long to grow damp. Dani isn't sure if she's thankful that the angel hasn't pushed her away or not.

"I'm so sorry. I'm so sorry." It sounds worthless. It *is* worthless. How could she ever apologize for something like this?

"It's not your fault," Hanael breathes into the crook of Dani's neck. "You were coerced; manipulated. You didn't have a choice."

Didn't she? "I almost killed you."

"But you didn't," Hanael says, separating them. Dani feels a hand cup her cheek and she sucks in a breath, closing her eyes. "You healed me. You overcame whatever hold was on you and you *healed me*. And even if you hadn't, I still wouldn't have blamed you."

Dani opens her eyes and the familiarity she sees in Hanael's, the absolute agony of it, has Dani gasping, "What's happening to me?"

Hanael opens her mouth to reply, but the words are drowned out by a male voice from behind her, "Oh, I'll tell you what's happening."

Both of their heads shoot in the direction of the voice, which, after a moment of brain-wracking, Dani identifies as Michael.

"You both," Michael says as he stalks towards them. "Have tested my patience for the absolute last time."

Dani tenses. She recognizes that look, that fury. It has her springing to her feet, dragging an equally incapacitated Hanael up with her. Dani tries not to think about their odds as she positions herself in front of the angel.

"Do you have any idea how much work you've undone?" Michael is practically foaming at the mouth. "How much planning and foresight and sacrifice? How dare you –"

"How dare we? How dare we, what?" Dani seethes. "Survive? Not be a pawn in whatever sick game it is you're playing? How dare *you* act so despicably while hiding behind some false sense of righteousness!"

The doors inside her mind open a little more.

"Extremely rich coming from you," Michael says. "Though projection seems to be an ongoing theme with you, doesn't it?" His eyes trail to Hanael. "With you both."

Dani bites down her reply in favor of supporting Hanael when she sees the angel is having trouble standing. Her gaze trails down to the onyx stone floor to discover her bloodied sword several feet out of reach.

That sword wouldn't work on an archangel, anyway, the voice reminds her and Dani frowns.

"Now, now, Michael. No need to cause such a scene, is there?" A new and unfamiliar male voice joins the fray. At least unfamiliar to Dani. Hanael's body grows rigid at the sound and Dani tightens the grip on her arm.

"And you!" Michael spins around to face the newcomer. "I assume you knew about this?"

The light-haired, overly dressed man quirks an eyebrow at Michael before saying, "I know about it now, certainly. What are you insinuating?"

The two stare at each other and Dani can feel the hairs on the back of her neck rise. She does recognize the charged energy between them, and that's when her mind helpfully supplies a name.

"Nevertheless," Lucifer continues, turning his attention back towards Dani and Hanael. "There is more than one way to start an apocalypse, and as luck would have it, I am nothing if not an avid planner."

The apocalypse, her celestial voice rounds off. *To be jump-started by either an act of God, cataclysmic event, or unprecedented release of energy.*

Dani's attention settles on the last of the three as she begins to feel sick. Hanael is shaking beside her. Dani isn't sure if it's out of fear or anger.

"Sadly for you, Danael, your presence will no longer be required."

Something *twists* inside Dani and she screams. The white-hot pain has her wishing for death.

"Lucifer, STOP!" Hanael yells, and much to Dani's relief, he does. Though it is short-lived. "You want me, yes? So, go on. Name your price. Name your deal."

Dani's eyes travel to Hanael's as if moving in slow motion. They beg her to stop. Hanael's gaze remains pointedly fixed on Lucifer.

"You will thank me eventually, Hanael," Lucifer says. "The terms are simple. I will provide you protection from the Heavenly Host, allow you to join me on the winning side, and your precious Danael is free to leave here in one piece. All I ask in return is your abiding loyalty."

Hanael does meet her gaze then and Dani wishes she

hadn't. It's resigned; a silent apology. Why does it seem so familiar?

"Lucifer, this is not what we agreed on."

"Plans change, Michael."

"Dani will be safe," Hanael interrupts. "You will let her return to her body and she will be left alone."

"As I've already said, Danael is of no use to me anymore. However, should she try and enter my domain again," Lucifer looks to Dani as he finishes, "I will kill you both."

Any contemplations of escaping with Hanael die in their synapses. Had they ever stood a chance?

Hanael gives Dani one final glance before saying, "Deal."

It's that final word that does it. The whiplash of déjà vu brings Dani to her knees.

"*Hanael will be left alone. She will not Fall and Lucifer will not have her. Can you guarantee me that, Michael?*" She's in a colorless void of a room that might look like something akin to an office if such things had existed at the time.

"*I can,*" Michael says, and Danael doesn't once question the honesty of the statement. What a fool she had been. "*You do realize you will never see her again? I haven't seen such a punishment bestowed since Cain's.*"

"*It is not a punishment,*" Danael says. "*It is a willing sacrifice.*"

"*It's a shame is what it is,*" Michael replies bitterly as he begins putting together the celestial paperwork. "*That such martyring couldn't be utilized where it is truly needed – here, with the current War.*"

Danael holds her tongue.

"*Though I suppose it will serve to be useful,*" he continues. "*Having this sort of Heavenly informant on Earth. Ignorant as you may be to it all." Michael hands over an inscribed stone tablet and the weight of it feels monumental in her hands.*

"Do you, Danael the Power of the Ninth Heavenly Sphere, agree to the terms that have been set forth?"

"I do."

Dani gasps back to the present moment and it is like waking from one long and convoluted nightmare. Only to have a worse one waiting to fall into.

The picture she had been so desperate to see is useless to her. Everything had been useless. They still ended up in the same place.

Dani's head swims as she forces herself back to a standing position. Hanael is crossing the distance to meet Lucifer while Dani desperately searches her own energy for some remaining angelic power. There had to be some, Dani reasons, or she wouldn't have been able to heal Hanael.

All she finds is a sharp pain in her abdomen that doubles her over. So that's what she had felt twist inside her earlier. Lucifer *would* have multiple contingency plans.

"What the fuck –"

All four angels' attention draw to the left side hallway and Dani feels her stomach sink further. Of course, Nickie would have to be here, too. Losing Hanael couldn't be enough, could it?

Only a moment later is her best friend joined by a very out-of-breath male demon. Dani panics further until she sees him take a protective stance in front of her.

"Ah, yes. Amy," Lucifer says. "How nice you've returned. Saves me the trouble of sending my Hounds after you."

Amy transfers his gaze from Lucifer to Nickie and then back to Lucifer before paling. Dani doesn't have a chance to guess what that might be about before the demon in question is blinked beside the archangel.

Things become a blur of movement after that.

Nickie tries to run toward Dani and Dani tries to run toward Hanael. They are both knocked back down by an earthquake-like rumble that shakes the surrounding walls. By the time Nickie drags them both back up, a chasm has already opened in front of them, blocking any path Danael might have had to her other half.

Dani stares down inside the five-foot gap – a bottomless void that could very well stretch until the ends of Hell. Fitting. Her head rises in hopes of seeing Hanael one last time, but she, along with Amy and Michael, are already long gone.

It's that feeling in her chest, unmeasurable in its severity, that Dani knows will be worse than anything that was to come. Was worse than any reincarnation cycle she had ever faced.

"It's been a pleasure, girls," Lucifer waves. His gaze lands on Nickie and the look causes a bile to rise in Dani's throat. "Especially you, my dear girl. I'm sure we'll be seeing each other soon enough."

Nickie looks ready to spit back a reply, but Lucifer, too, disappears into a mist of nothing.

Dani thinks she feels herself disappear as well.

CHAPTER 16
NICKIE

And here Nickie thought things had been going bad before. Ha!

She supposes she should be glad she found Dani in one piece. Then again, her best friend's current state doesn't leave much to the imagination.

Dani's eyes are glued to the spot where Hanael had disappeared from. There's a rumbling sound that echoes from somewhere above them and dust filters down, clouding the air. Dani doesn't seem to notice.

"We need to go," Nickie says, grabbing her hand. Dani doesn't acknowledge her. "We can figure this shit out later, Dani. But we need to be alive to do that!"

Nothing. Somewhere in the distance Nickie can hear an inhuman growl and she resigns to dragging Dani's unresponsive body back the way they came. It's not ideal, but Dani at least isn't fighting her.

Time is...different. They're running and Nickie actually feels like they're running. Was that something to do with the apocalypse? Jesus. The world really was ending, wasn't it?

It's a good thing she's high right now.

Dani still hasn't said a word. Nickie wouldn't know what to say to her if she had. She still doesn't know all the details but it's enough to paint a pretty fucked up picture.

Nickie grimaces at the shriek she hears from somewhere far behind them and picks up the pace. They were almost back in the Eighth Level, and with the time change, should be able to make it to the portal in less than an hour. What was it Amy had said about the time differences in –

Amy. Shit. What was going to happen to him? Obviously nothing too peachy keen if Lucifer's comment was anything to go by. Not even mentioning what he said to *her*.

No. Shut up! Focus. She needed to focus or they were both dead.

Nickie's grip tightens on Dani's arm as she tries very hard to ignore the growing chaos around them. Which does work, for all of twenty seconds, before Nickie catches sight of a moat whose leech occupants look even hungrier than before.

"Right," Nickie breathes into Dani's shoulder. "So, hell leeches." She extends one foot to test that the bridge was intact before maneuvering a still unresponsive Dani under her arm. "Just...don't fall, okay?" God – *please* don't fall.

Nickie likes to think it's going well enough, at least until she can feel Dani begin to tense under her.

"Dani?"

Dani cries out before doubling over. Nickie curses. She narrowly avoids losing balance and tipping them both over the edge, where she can see a wave of leeches eagerly swarm to.

"We're almost across," Nickie tries to reassure a current whimpering Dani. "Try and –"

Nickie's words die off in a disarray of Dani's flailing

limbs and body spasms. Fuck. She's delirious. Nickie works desperately to clamp down on her best friend's seizing form while trying to drag her the remaining few feet across the bridge. Was it getting narrower?

They're only a couple of steps to solid ground when another spasm rocks Dani's body. She starts fighting against Nickie's hold then, eyes wide and terrified. Nickie is not able to correct their balance this time around.

Nickie drives her own body into Dani's and over the remaining distance onto solid ground. A stinging sensation cuts across Nickie's abdomen on the impact, but aside from that, she seems okay. Dani is less so, but Dani also isn't in the state of mind to care.

Nickie envies her in that respect. The remaining mile to the portal is no cakewalk. They're about halfway there when Dani starts speaking in tongues. Enochian, if Nickie is recalling correctly. It's garbled for a while until it turns into a monotone mantra.

"ZIRDO IL SAMVELA NAZPS. ZIRDO IL SAMVELA NAZPS."

At least Dani's stopped struggling against her. Which is much appreciated considering how much the pain in Nickie's stomach was spreading. There's no visible blood, but Nickie is too afraid right now to survey the damage.

Another twenty minutes and Nickie knows the portal is only a few minutes away. It's dark in the hallway. Darker than Nickie remembers it being on the way in. Shadows creep into her peripheral and Nickie further tightens her grip on Dani as they round the final corner.

A sudden jolt of dread stops her. Her eyes are fixed on her boots and Dani's bare feet, but Nickie can feel the presence of something directly in front of them. She really doesn't want to look up.

Nickie looks up.

It's her. Well, it's her if she was the main attraction at a horror theme park.

Its skin is pale and gray, rotting, and Nickie can see some area where the bone is exposed. Maggots crawl in and out of these areas, all while the double smiles inhumanly at them. Nickie takes a generous step back and Dani continues to mutter incoherently to herself.

Despite all of this, it's still not the worst thing Nickie's seen today. She tells the thing as much.

It laughs. Nickie can hear the *'crack'* of bone as it twists its head at an unnatural angle to look at her before saying, "The worst thing you've seen today, sure. But what about tomorrow? Next week? Month?" Lips twist upward to reveal a row of equally decaying teeth. "Take a good look at my face, Nicole. I promise it'll be yours soon enough."

Nickie doesn't get the chance to dignify it with a reply before the doppelgänger lets out a banshee-like wail and disappears in a cloud of black smoke.

"Right," Nickie breathes out. "We'll unpack that later." Or not. Preferably not.

The portal is within sight now. Nickie's hands are shaking as she yanks forward the doorknob to reveal that familiar void, wasting no time as they both stumble through.

Nickie's body lands with a *'thud'* in the same field she and Amy had originally entered from. A crack of thunder follows. The soil is moist as Nickie digs her fingertips into the ground beneath her. The ground that Nickie was more than a bit tempted to kiss because holy shit – they made it!

Her grin is painful as Nickie turns to where she expects to see Dani only to be met with an empty field. It promptly drops off her face as she staggers to a standing position.

"Dani! Dani? Shit!"

There's another crack of thunder before the trickle turns to a downpour. Dani is nowhere to be seen. Neither is the door they entered from. The only indication Nickie hadn't hallucinated the entire ordeal is a sword that she only vaguely recalls being cemented in Dani's grip as she dragged them both out of Hell.

A scream is at the back of Nickie's throat, ready to be released into the night air, when a thought occurs to her.

Dani wasn't in her body. Not like Nickie was, at least. And if her sword was here, that meant she had to be on Earth somewhere, right?

Maybe it's a stretch. Maybe Nickie is prolonging the inevitable. But Nickie was also too exhausted to entertain any what-ifs her garbage brain was providing her with.

Said exhaustion becomes worryingly apparent when Nickie tries to take a step forward to have her legs give out from under her. A sharp pain explodes in her abdomen and Nickie is forced to finally survey the damage. Which proves to be less damage and more Hell leech stuck to her fucking stomach.

Nickie screams and her hand shoots down to rip it off. It's body is slimy and burns to the touch; a horrible combination for actually getting a grip on the thing. Though Nickie is nothing if not persistent, particularly where bugs were concerned.

Finally, Nickie can feel the sting of its teeth unlatch from her skin and chucks it to the side. It wiggles and screeches on the damp soil before stilling, body melting into the ground below it.

"That's right," Nickie chokes out, trying very hard not to think of Amy's previous warning about the little bastards. "Tell your friends."

It doesn't hear her, of course. No one does. Nickie is alone in bumfuck nowhere, soaking wet with a hellish leech bite to boot.

She doesn't want to stand up. Doesn't even want to attempt to face whatever it was that waited for her outside this field. It all feels too big, and more than Nickie will ever be able to handle.

Nickie isn't sure how long she stays like that, feet pulled up to her chest, raindrops pounding against her skin, when eventually, it stops.

It's surreally abrupt. When Nickie looks up, the night sky is as clear as Nickie can ever remember seeing it. The only indication of it having rained is a shallow puddle at Nickie's feet, a bright reflection of the moon on its surface.

Nickie does force herself to a standing position then. She searches her pockets and is pleasantly surprised to find that her phone is still charged and functional. Which Nickie ends up being very thankful for when she limps back to her car to find that it won't start.

The gratitude is short-lived, however, as Nickie sees the headlights of the cab some twenty minutes later. Her stomach sinks.

Dani was right. Post-Hell cab rides suck.

"Are you alright?!" The driver's eyes are wide, and the suggestion of a hospital seems to be on the tip of his tongue.

"Fantastic," Nickie says as she shuffles into the backseat. "Best day of my life. Just drive." Dani's sword is stationed tightly in her arms and one look at the sizeable weapon is all it takes for the driver to heed her instruction.

That's one problem solved. That just left, oh, about a hundred in its place.

It's hard to sit still. Nickie still feels like she needs to run, and the weight of Dani's sword in her hands doesn't help. Then again, what would?

Nickie wants to be glad to be alive, but she can't help but think that maybe she would have been safer in Hell. Would feel safer, at the very least, even if it was because of the high.

Fuck. This comedown was going to be nasty.

The car stops suddenly, and Nickie is jolted forward in her seat, an eerie silence filling the vehicle. She looks up to see that her entire apartment complex has been burnt down, fresh smoke filling the night air.

Nickie wonders if God is laughing at her.

"Figures," Nickie says, throwing her money at the driver and slamming the car door behind her.

The parking lot of her complex is a mess. Paramedics, police, and firefighters are all racing around like chickens with their heads cut off. There are no tears amongst the witnesses but there is fighting. Pointed fingers and violent verbal sparring.

Nickie shudders before weaving herself around the chaos and towards the first cop she can find.

"What the hell happened?" She asks. The officer looks down at her sword a minute, seemingly bypassing her disheveled appearance before saying, "No idea. At least not yet. Are you a resident?"

"Yeah."

"You're lucky, then. No one that was home made it out alive."

Nickie feels sick. She quickly makes herself sparse and the officer doesn't follow. The shouting and conflict in the parking lot only seems to be growing and out of her peripheral, Nickie catches two bodies being carried out on a stretcher. Both are unrecognizable from the burns except for the charred pearl bracelet on the second body.

Yep. That would be her landlord.

Nickie averts her gaze and forces her feet forward until she finds an alleyway at the end of the street to collapse in. The disarray of the scene is now a dull echo against the pounding in her own ears.

Nickie's head falls back. The stars are out and Venus is directly overhead. She stares and stares and stares before squeezing her eyes shut and clasping her hands together in front of her chest.

"I don't know if you're alive enough to hear this." Nickie swallows. "But you're an angel, right? So, I figured it was worth a shot. Shit's fucked, Dani. And I can't – I can't do this without you. I need you not to be dead. Don't be fucking dead, alright?" Somewhere in the distance, Nickie can hear a scream. "I'm just – I'm going back to the shop. Meet me there. Amen."

The praying feels as hollow as it did when her mother forced her to do it as a kid. At least this time, Nickie thinks bitterly, she wouldn't have her head held under bathtub water for getting a verse wrong.

Using a nearby pipe for support, Nickie forces herself back to a standing position. She briefly considers calling another cab before scratching the idea. The air around her tenses in a way that makes Nickie weary of putting her safety in the hands of anyone operating heavy machinery.

Grabbing Dani's sword off the ground, Nickie makes her way back towards the crowd and to option number two.

No one seems to notice the presence of Nickie or her sketchy-looking sword. Which makes hot-wiring her land-lord's car that much easier. After all, it's not as if the woman would be using it.

Nickie hightails it, cranking up the radio. Highway to Hell by AC/DC comes on and Nickie wishes she could laugh.

ACT 2

CHAPTER 17

DANAEL

I n the beginning, there was already quite a lot. That's because it wasn't *the* beginning, it was just Yahweh's beginning.

Dani, admittedly, must give credit where it was due. Yahweh created the Earth; humanity. Then again, after thousands of lives lived as a human, Dani questions how much that credit was worth.

Because humans *were* created in his image. Wrathful. Petty. Selfish. Not that the angels were much better.

None of them had names or identities back then – just formless shards of energy formed from the Void. Up until the day they separated into their own unique halves. Duality was, as Yahweh explained, a way to establish balance in the material world.

It failed spectacularly.

Still, the separation isn't an issue for most angels because most angels separate entirely and go on their merry way to begin Yahweh's humanity project. Those that don't, however, well, they start a Rebellion.

Or make a deal to try and save their other half from said Rebellion.

A deal that turned out to be meaningless. A deal that Dani is beginning to doubt was a deal at all. Was any choice she had ever made her own? For how long had she and Hanael been the Host's puppets? Dani almost wishes she could crawl back into her existential hole of ignorance.

Dani remembers very little after her confrontation with Michael and Lucifer. She remembers Nickie finding her, remembers the tell-tale signs of the approaching apocalypse ala a quaking Hell, and remembers the devastation of knowing she would have to leave Hanael behind in it. That's about the time she blacks out.

It's not like how it was with Dani's revelation with Malphas. This hits harder, too close to home, and the acclimation is overwhelming. Not so much her angelic heritage, but what came after – the deal, the reincarnations, *Hanael*.

The dark and oblivious space that previously occupied her mind is now filled with mirrors. All her previous lives surround her, taunt her, and the weight of them feels like more than Dani will ever be able to bear.

She tries to force the images into a single mirror, but when she turns around to look at it, her reflection is of Hanael. Hanael – bright and magnificent and what might be the best thing that ever happened to Dani.

Or the worst, depending on who was asking.

Love was funny like that.

Dani takes a deep breath and steps through the glass.

There's fire.

At first, it's a small flame. As if someone's lit a match in the very far distance. She's not aware of any surroundings beside that single, barely visible flame. Not sure, really, if any other surroundings exist. Nothing exists except Dani and the flame.

And then someone drops the match.

It's Dani. Dani drops the match.

She's not six years old anymore but feels just as powerless. Emptiness replaces the previous panic, and Dani lets it fill her, watching as the flames consume the structure around her.

She still screams, though. She screams until there is nothing but smoke and ash. Until her throat is raw and the charred base-boards burn beneath her bare feet.

Only then does Dani walk away from the wreckage.

When Dani comes to for the final time, she is back at the graveyard. Her bare feet sink into the moist soil of the Earth as her eyes trail idly over her gravestone. A hospital gown hangs loosely over her body, charred, from a fire that she can't seem to care about the semantics of.

There is a sudden burst of lightning in the distance, but Dani doesn't startle. Dani doesn't startle because Dani is dead. And this time – Danael actually allows her to rest.

Danael has never received a prayer before. When she was in Heaven and humanity was still new and well aware of the existence of the divine, there had been no reason for them. Though Danael supposes that much hasn't changed.

It is strange, having Nickie's voice echo around in her head, though not unwelcome. The relief of knowing Nickie was alive and out of Hell is unsurmountable. At least until Danael lays eyes on her at A New Dawn.

The stench of Hell is so strong on Nickie that Danael does a double take of their surroundings. Which makes little sense, seeing how bright Nickie's actual energetic signature is. Far brighter than Danael would have expected it to be.

Still, Nickie startles at the sight of her. Even more so when Danael asks her if she is alright.

"Nickie?"

Nickie stands from her place at the café table, slowly, before approaching Danael and saying, "You're going to have to speak English if you want me to understand you."

"What?" Oh. That was German, wasn't it?

Danael tries again and is met with a growing look of irritation.

"Now I *know* that's Japanese. Try again."

Danael does. It takes a few good minutes, but eventually she can begin, "Are you okay, Nickie?" Though it still feels like she's using the wrong dialect.

"I'm managing," Nickie says, posture stiff and tightly gripping Danael's sword. "Are you?"

No. "I'm managing."

Nickie's eyes trail down her, unconvinced, before she hands Danael her sword. The weight of it in her hands feels both too heavy and not heavy enough.

"What happened?" Danael asks, dialect beginning to smooth over. "Why were you in Hell? *How* were you in Hell?"

Nickie limps back to the café table before collapsing on its chair with a flinch. Danael wishes she could heal her, though she wonders if Nickie would even let her.

"You died," Nickie says. "Hanael went crazy. Malphas

137

killed Lily, strangled me, and then another demon named Amy showed up declaring the end of times. Knew you had something to do with it and offered to take me to Hell to get you back —"

"And you, what? Followed some random demon into Hell? Are you insane?"

Nickie's jaw ticks. She looks at Danael and the angel flinches back at the expression she sees. "Well, excuse me for saving your fucking life. Believe you me, I will not be pulling the hero card again anytime soon. Trying to save the world. Hah. What a joke, amirite?"

Danael frowns. She opens her mouth to reply when the distant sound of glass shattering brings both their attention out the window and to the apartment complex across the street. A husband and wife descend from the first floor in a heated argument. Danael barely has time to blink before the wife pulls out a gun, points, and pulls the trigger.

Not that she could have done anything anyway, right? War was here and Danael was powerless to stop it. Perhaps Nickie was onto something after all with her anti-heroism sentiments.

"We should leave," Nickie says, sitting up and heading for the exit.

Danael follows her out to an unfamiliar blue sedan. She makes no comment as they slide into their respective seats and Nickie hot-wires the engine.

"So, where are we going? Cause' my place isn't exactly an option anymore."

"Why?"

"It burnt down."

Oh. *Oh.*

Danael's tongue is heavy as she says, "Valerian Drive. It's a few miles north of the Sunset Park Hiking Trails."

After all, it's not as if Hanael would have any use for her rental home now.

The heaviness sinks into Danael's chest as Nickie begins driving.

~

It takes Nickie about thirty minutes to pull up to the large and secluded off-green bungalow. The property is nestled so closely among the trees and nearby lake that unless one was looking for it, they'd risk missing the turn completely.

It's beautiful, Danael thinks, as she can feel the almost silent crunch of leaves under her feet. An echo of wildlife joins it, and as Danael breathes in the fresh scent of pine, she is reminded of Heaven.

Danael is reminded of a lot of things once they enter the house.

Stopping at the entrance into the foyer, Danael runs her fingers along the spines of Hanael's books. She closes her eyes and takes another deep breath. Even for the short time Hanael had been here, the house sings with her energy.

"So, what exactly is the game plan here?" Danael's eyes shoot open and she turns the corner to find Nickie sprawled out on a couch, nursing a bottle of Hanael's gin. The TV is on, and Danael can hear the thinly veiled panic of the newsman as he announces the possibility of World War III.

Danael grimaces before saying, "We try and survive."

Nickie takes another generous swig from the bottle. "Try being the key word there, I assume."

Danael says nothing. Nickie stands, raises her bottle with a tight "cheers", and makes her ascent up the staircase. Danael stares long after she's left.

Eventually, Danael hears the upstairs guest shower

begin to run and allows her own feet to lead her across the living room and into a side hallway. It doesn't take her long to find Hanael's bedroom.

Only after the door is closed and locked behind her does Danael allow her body to slide down against the frame.

Her hands are shaking and as Danael only now notices, so is her sword. She tosses the weapon to the opposite wall and it lands with a loud *'clang'* next to Hanael's bed.

"I'm so sorry." Danael isn't sure who the apology is directed at. Perhaps Hanael; perhaps everyone; perhaps only herself. It's harder to deal with emotions now. Were angels ever wired for them? Danael wonders.

It is with that wondering that Danael wills her hand to stop shaking.

Their options were woefully limited. Without her power, Danael wouldn't make it three feet into Hell before Lucifer made good on his promise. For now, Hell was the safest place for Hanael.

Anyway, Hanael was, for once, the least of her problems.

Or at least, that's what Danael tries desperately to convince herself of as she angelically compartmentalizes every Hanael-related emotion as far down as it will go.

"I'm so sorry," Danael says again, and it is a prayer that she almost hopes Hanael doesn't hear. "You made your choice and now I have to make mine. Please stay safe."

With a shuddering breath, Danael picks herself up off the floor, retrieves her sword, and exits the room.

Danael doesn't sleep that night (not that she needed to

anymore) and instead uses the remaining six hours before dawn to gather supplies, food, and weapons.

The stores are packed. Danael makes little progress and finally decides to call it a night when she is nearly shot grabbing the last two first aid kits at the local drugstore. War wasn't wasting any time.

It does strike Danael as odd, how fast things were progressing. It makes her wonder if Michael and Lucifer weren't speeding things along to get to their grand finale of earthquakes, blood seas, and the annihilation of mankind.

Once Danael returns to Hanael's rental, and what little supplies she could gather are unpacked, she begins putting up warding.

Enochian protection sigils carved into the doors and window frames. Holy water lining all the doorknobs and entryways. It wasn't much, but it was the best Danael could do for right now.

She's finishing up the last blood-made banishment sigil when the sound of footsteps brings her attention to the stairwell. When had the sun come up?

"Oh, great. More freaky blood circles," Nickie grumbles before making a beeline for the coffee pot.

"They're for protection," Danael says, wiping the blood off her palm and following her. At least she had some of her angelic healing back.

"Yeah, well, they're freaky."

Danael frowns as she watches Nickie pour herself a cup with shaking hands. Her best friend barely makes it to the breakfast bar without incident.

When did Nickie have the time to use?

"I gathered what supplies I could while you were asleep," Danael says instead, motioning to the dining room table. "Which wasn't much, unfortunately."

"Mhm."

"And I'll try to do more research today. Maybe Hanael will have something here that will prove useful."

"Cool."

The rest of their makeshift breakfast is spent in silence. Nickie breaks it when she rises unsteadily from the breakfast bar and towards the front door.

"Wait, where are you going?" Danael says. "Nickie, you know it's not safe out there –"

"I've been to Hell and back. I think I'll manage."

"Will you at least tell me where you're going?"

Nickie turns around to face her, and for once, Danael can't begin to pinpoint the expression on it.

"I'm going back to my apartment to see if there's anything salvageable. Also, as fun as grand theft auto is, I'd really like my own car back."

Danael frowns but knows better than to try and stop her. She should get started on that research anyway. Maybe get a list going of any information she already –

"FUCK! WHAT THE FUCK?!"

Danael startles and looks up to find Nickie grabbing her hand in pain, all while glaring daggers at Danael. "What the hell did you put on the doorknob?"

"It's...holy water. Nickie, what happened?"

Nickie's expression pales and she is out the door before Danael can stop her. A worry settles as she touches the handle of the door, noticing nothing amiss.

Letting out a sigh, Danael slams closed the front door before making her way down the hall to Hanael's study. Hopefully it was the withdrawals. And if it wasn't, well, it was still the least of their problems.

It is with that thought that Danael opens Hanael's laptop and gets to work.

CHAPTER 18
HANAEL

Lucifer, so far, had been surprisingly hospitable.

He conjures up a large guest bedroom for Hanael in his quarters, prepares a grand meal for them each evening, and has given Hanael unrestricted travel to any Level of Hell she desires.

It's almost the kind of behavior one would see towards their second in command, which Hanael quickly gains Malphas' contempt for. Though Hanael supposes if she had to be here, she might as well allow herself the small win of the demon's psychological unrest.

Then again, there seemed to be a lot of that to go around.

Between Lucifer and Malphas. Michael and Lucifer. Malphas and whatever perceived wrong of Nickie's.

Nickie. Now that was one Hanael didn't see coming (neither had Michael, if his and Lucifer's continuous arguing was anything to go by). Should have, but her foresight had been sorely lacking as of late, hadn't it?

She needed to get back to Danael.

But how? Already she's been here a week and found no

possible means of escape from her deal. Or Hell, for that matter. Certainly not with Lucifer's demons all on apocalypse duty.

Letting out a frustrated sigh, Hanael retreats down the steps from her guest bedroom to find Malphas and Lucifer arguing. Or more, Malphas arguing *at* Lucifer.

"–demoting me to guard? Are you fucking kidding me?"

He doesn't get far, as Hanael takes her final step off the staircase to find Lucifer's hand around the demon's throat, choking him mid-air. Hanael breezes past them into the kitchen and over to the espresso machine.

"I refuse to humor this insubordination any longer, Malphas," Lucifer sneers, squeezing his hand so hard the demon chokes up blood. "You should be honored to serve me in any capacity. Question my orders again and you will have far more to worry about than a demotion." Malphas is dropped to the ground with a *'thud'*, letting out a string of choked gasps.

Hanael takes her coffee over to a nearby armchair, only gaining interest when her name is called.

"Hanael? See to it that Malphas begins work at his new post immediately. He will be replacing Valefor as the guard to Amy's cell."

Her jaw ticks as Hanael is forced to set down her coffee cup in favor of approaching Malphas. The demon looks about as eager to begin their journey to the Fourth Level as Hanael.

"I wonder how Dani is faring," Malphas says as soon as the elevator doors close. "I wonder if she is beginning to realize yet what a mistake her original sacrifice was."

Hanael doesn't dignify him with an answer. He gives up his goading after a few minutes and the two step out of the elevator to begin their trek along the dark labyrinth of doors.

Malphas, however, seems intent to direct his anger somewhere. Once they reach the prison cells on the far end of the Level, Amy is awoken to a canteen of holy water in his face.

Hanael says nothing as the other demon chokes and flails about, instead focusing her attention on the current clipboard in her hands. She records the information to indicate Malphas' arrival before the clipboard disappears in a puff of black smoke, back to Lucifer's archives.

"You always were intimated by strong women," Amy says, despite his current burns. "Boy, oh, boy. Can I not *wait* to see Nickie cut your lying tongue right out of your mouth."

Malphas' smile doesn't falter. "You may be waiting a while. I think Nickie's grown quite fond of my 'lying tongue'. Particularly when it's between her legs."

Amy rages silently. Malphas laughs, "You're too easy."

Hanael clears her throat before saying, "I wonder what Lucifer would think of these opinions", and watches in satisfaction as the demon's confidence finally begins to wane.

"You forget your place, Malphas. Now leave us a moment; I would like to talk to the prisoner in private."

"I don't take orders from *you* –"

"No? Was it not *me* Lucifer tasked with seeing to your new post?" Malphas' lip curls upward. "Unless you were inclined to challenge his orders again?"

A few moments pass before Malphas falls into a forced laugh, "You want to scheme? Then by all means." His arms open wide towards Amy's cell. "Though I would encourage you not to forget your place either. Because trust me, sweetheart, it's not any better position than mine."

The steel entrance door to the room slams behind him.

"You're awfully interested in Nickie's wellbeing," Hanael moves forward until only the steel bars separate them. "Why is that?"

"You wound me, darling," Amy says, putting his hand to his heart in mock distress. "I *am* capable of caring about others beside myself. Or else I wouldn't do this –"

A hand locks around her wrist and Hanael is about to yank it back before she hears another voice broadcast in her mind.

'Okay! We'll have to make this quick. There's a sort of loophole with deals – Lucifer tricked you, right? Gave you an ultimatum?'

'Of course he did,' Hanael shoots back. *'That's what he does.'*

'Which most people think is a moot point concerning him, but here's the thing – deals are legally binding contracts. Contracts that are created on the basis of free will. Take that away and the whole thing is null and void.'

'So, what?' Hanael asks, unconvinced. *'You think I can just walk out of here and he can't do anything?'*

'Of course not,' Amy says. *'Free will is a pretty grey area with celestials, anyway. You'll need help. You know how humans have lawyers for this type of stuff? Same wheelhouse. You'll need to summon some type of entity or god relating to justice and law. I'm sure you'll be able to find what you need in Lucifer's library.'*

Hanael is still not inclined to trust Amy, but she supposes there's not much she can do to make things worse. Though it does raise the question, *'Why are you helping me?'*

'What else do I have to do while locked in this Hell hole. Hah! Get it? Hell hole.' Hanael glares at him. *'But if you are feeling particularly grateful, I wouldn't be opposed to a jailbreak – '*

Both celestials are startled from their telepathic conversation by the sound of the prison ward's door clangoring back open. Hanael quickly puts some space between herself and Amy before Malphas comes sauntering back into the room.

"We done here?" Malphas asks.

Hanael gives him a stiff nod before turning on her heel and returning to Lucifer's quarters.

It certainly isn't hard to find a relevant summoning spell among Lucifer's extensive library.

Hanael settles on Varuna, as Hindu deities tended to be generally agreeable. And the last thing the angel needs is to get stiffed by another ill-planned deal.

Though performing the ritual might prove to be a challenge.

"I think it's about time I familiarize myself with the Levels," Hanael says to Lucifer three days after her meeting with Amy. The archangel pauses from the current vegetables he is chopping, knife unmoving as he replies, "Rude, wouldn't you say, to leave as your host is preparing dinner?"

"Not any ruder than having to eat dinner to the backdrop of you and Michael's domestics."

Lucifer stares at her a few moments before returning to his chopping. "Fair enough, I suppose. Though do be mindful of your time; we have a busy day tomorrow."

"Fair enough," Hanael says. "I don't suppose I could use another one of your compasses to help with that?"

Lucifer laughs. "Had you not figured it out, sister? That was not a compass leading you to Danael; it was a compass leading Danael to *you*. It's only purpose was to further her deterioration."

Hanael turns on her heel toward the elevator before she can rip the knife out of Lucifer's hands and shove it through his neck.

It takes quite a bit of trial and error to make it back to the Ninth Level. At least, Hanael reasons, her wing was now healed enough that she can cover the distance in flight.

When Hanael does arrive at the location where she had made her deal, she has to work hard to push down the growing nausea. *How much had Danael sacrificed for Hanael to make it all in vain?*

Hanael still doesn't know the extent of it; isn't sure she wants to. Where had Danael been all this time? How did Michael erase her memories of her? Had all the angels memories been altered?

All questions for another time, Hanael supposes. If she went down that particular rabbit hole right now, the angel isn't confident she'd make it out. She had dug enough holes for herself as it was.

The Ninth Level is quiet; suspiciously so. The only present noise being that of the faint buzzing of energy coming from the hazy red of her surroundings.

Any icy wind brushes against the nape of Hanael's neck. She drops her satchel and quickly begins setting out the supplies.

The ritual itself is easy. Hemlock and Buckthorn sprinkled into one of Lucifer's favorite wine glasses. Joined by her own blood and a vial of consecrated water. All set out on the uneven stone floor in front of her.

Here goes nothing.

"He mahaan dev varun, mere vnatee suniye –"

The remaining words turn to a painful choke as Hanael can feel an energetic vise coil around her throat. She struggles, tries to rip it off with her own power, but it's already weakened her to the point of near unconsciousness.

Hanael's vision is beginning to darken as she hears, "It's a shame." *Lucifer.* "I had such high hopes for you, Hanael."

Oblivion drags her down, and somewhere in its expanse, Hanael thinks she can hear Danael praying.

CHAPTER 19

NICKIE

The shitty thing was, Nickie had been clean.

Sure, she still kept some morphine in her medicine cabinet, but she didn't touch it. She just...needed to know it was there. That she had a way out, you know?

...What way out was there for her now?

The comedown is worse than she was expecting. Pair that with whatever the hell happened with Hanael's doorknob and hello, downward spiral!

Nickie's hands are shaking as she searches frantically through her charred medicine cabinet. It's a lost cause, Nickie already knows. Though somehow the burnt and unsalvageable pill bottle manages to break her a little more.

"FUCK!" Nickie screams, before falling into a fit of chokes. The stench of imbedded smoke does nothing for her building nausea.

Okay, so she had two options. Each sucked, but at least one of them might give her the chance of retaining a shred of her sanity.

Maybe.

How much longer would she be alive, anyway? It was

the god-damned apocalypse. And Dani's optimism will only get them so far.

Dragging her feet across the length of her destroyed apartment, Nickie takes out her phone. She scrolls through her contacts and is about to hit the 'call' button on her old supplier Jake, when she's reminded that she's broke.

Nickie curses.

An incoming call notification pops up and she curses again before answering with a terse, "What?"

"Oh. Uhm, yes. Is this Nicole Allbright?"

"Unfortunately. Who's this?"

"Nina Valdez. I'm with the Jefferson and Sons Law Firm. I was just calling to inform you that a Miss Lillian Devere has passed away and you have been named the sole beneficiary on her will."

Shit. Lily. What would Lily say if she saw her using again?

"Miss Allbright?"

"Uh, yeah. Hi. Still here. So, a will. What's on the will, then?"

"A large monetary amount that will be disclosed at our office. As well as a business in the name of A New Dawn."

She – fuck. She left all that for Nickie? Seriously?

"Right. Okay. That's –" Convenient. Or inconvenient, depending on who's asking. How do all the people she cares about manage to guilt trip her even from the grave?

"I can understand how overwhelming this process can be, Miss Allbright. Though rest assured that all we need from you is a few signatures. If you have time today, we have a couple of slots that opened for this morning?"

"Sure, whatever." A detour – that's all this was. And then she'd call Jake.

Or at least, that's what she tells herself as the law firm lady finishes setting up her appointment.

The call ends and Nickie is brought back to the current wasteland that used to be her bedroom. Guess it's a good thing she never got too attached to it, eh?

"Fuck me," Nickie says, stomping out of the ashy hellscape and back to her stolen vehicle.

It's a miracle Nickie makes it to the law office without incident. She doesn't remember the drive over and already her shirt is soaked with sweat. An appearance that ends up being a particularly amusing backdrop to the obviously upper-scale office.

Or would be if Nickie was in any state of mind to be amused.

Nickie checks in for her appointment and the receptionist, while giving her a side-eye over the computer screen, wisely makes no comment.

Turning her attention to the waiting room, Nickie's spirits are at least slightly lifted by the sight of a self-serve coffee machine.

"Thank god," Nickie mutters under her breath as she helps herself to a cup. She is about to take a seat before an echoed shouting causes her to spill its contents all over the designer couch.

"Fucking figures." And burning the same damn hand that had already been assaulted by the doorknob!

As Nickie tries and fails to mop up the mess with a few napkins, the shouting continues. Two men. Nickie can see the shadow of their outline through one of the shaded office windows.

"I know you slept with my wife, you son of a bitch!"

"Oh, you're flattering yourself now, Dave. I wouldn't touch that cow with a ten-foot pole!"

Why did she come here, again?

"I am so sorry, Miss Allbright!" A female voice from behind her says and it's a good thing Nickie hadn't gone for a second cup or she would have dropped that, too. "Don't worry about the mess. I don't know what's gotten into those two."

Nickie holds back any innuendos in favor of following the woman into her office. Said woman, one miss Attorney Valerie Jefferson, apologies several more times before they both take a seat to go over paperwork.

"This is all pretty standard. House. Business. Assets..." Valerie begins and already Nickie is spacing out. Blah. Blah. Blah. Just tell her where to sign so she can –

Valerie's voice suddenly trails off. The hairs on the back of Nickie's neck rise.

"ALL HAIL THE MORNINGSTARS! BEHOLD THE GLORY OF YOUR LIGHT! WE ARE NOT WORTHY! WE ARE NOT WORTHY!"

Nickie flies out of the seat and across the room like her ass is on fire. Her head swivels to meet Valerie's and, half expecting to see another creepy Hell creature, Nickie is no more relieved to find the attorney's expression as startled as hers.

"Good lord! Are you alright? Do you need me to call someone?"

Nickie shakes her head before taking a few hesitant steps back toward the desk.

"Easily startled," Nickie mumbles, picking up the pen and beginning to sign. "I've been through a trauma recently, you see."

"Oh, dear," Valerie says. "And I'm sure Dave and Ricardo's arguing didn't help, did it?" Her expression hardens and Nickie signs faster. "Rest assured, those two will have me to answer to after this. Are you sure you don't want me to call someone?"

"Nope. Nope. All good. All done." Nickie shoves the stack of paperwork her way. Valerie briefly checks it over before nodding. "The funds should be transferred within twenty-four hours to your specified bank account. The other assets may take up to a week to be put into your name. We'll be in contact if we need any additional information."

Nickie hardly hears her. She's already at the door. "Sounds great. All great. Bye now!"

Dave and Ricardo are still arguing when she hightails it out the exit.

The good news is, Nickie is now wide awake. It's the only good news.

Fuck it. She doesn't have the energy to deal with whatever the hell that was. Twenty-four hours, Valerie said. She just needed to last twenty-four hours and then –

And then, what? Get high? While freaky shit was apparently lurking around every corner? What if something happened to Dani?

Fuck.

Alright. Okay. One step at a time. Her car. She still needed to get her car. She could figure the rest out later, right? Right. Okay.

The drive back to the crossroads is as normal as can be expected. Well, at least until she enters the turn off into the wooded area that would lead her to it.

It's broad daylight but it doesn't feel like it. It's too still; too quiet. A flurry of brown and green bypasses the car windows and somewhere in the distance she can hear a raven caw.

Nickie swallows. She should turn around. Probably would, on any other day. But Nickie needed a distraction right now more than she needed any faux sense of safety.

Cause that's all it would be, right? It's not like there's anywhere on this god-forsaken planet that was safe now.

"Get it together, Nickie," she curses under her breath. The echo of the car door slamming behind her rings in the not-night air. She pulls her jacket tighter before unloading the jump starter from the trunk and connecting the two cars.

The sound of her own car's engine starting is like music to her ears.

"Thank fuck." Nickie doesn't waste any time disconnecting the cars, slamming both hoods closed, and getting back into her own.

Still considering how to dispose of her dead landlord's car, Nickie begins adjusting the radio.

No signal. Unsurprising. She *was* in the middle of bumfuck nowhere.

Just as Nickie is beginning to speculate if the nearby lake would be deep enough to drive the other car into, the static on the radio goes silent.

It's like the feeling that had come over her in the law office but worse.

Alarm bells blare as she tries desperately to open the

driver's side door. Jammed. Nickie raises her elbow to break the window when the grip of a hand stops her.

"Cool it." Malphas. Why is she not surprised?

Nickie elbows him in the jaw before sending a hard glare into the rearview window.

"Touchy, touchy," Malphas says, rubbing the side of his face. "Then again, you always were a bitch when you didn't have your go-go juice."

"And you're just a bitch," Nickie says. "Don't you have some kind of apocalypse duties to attend to? You know, skinning children, animal sacrifice, the genocide of all mankind?"

Malphas smiles wide, resting his chin on the back of the passenger side head rest. "Well see, now that's why I'm here, princess."

Before Nickie can try and land another elbow, Malphas pulls out a vial of red, glowing liquid and any malignant thoughts are silenced.

Everything is silenced.

It's like being in front of the portal to Hell again, except this time Nickie knows what's on the other side. She craves it, salivates for it. Realizing, horrifyingly, that opioids would never have been enough.

"Essence of Hell," Malphas attempts to hand over the vial and Nickie barely manages to stop her hand from jerking forward to take it.

The demon smiles again. "If you don't want the vial, we could always, you know," he whistles, making a suggestive motion with his hands. "I'm sure it'd have the same effect."

Nickie wishes she could strangle him, fight, curse, yell, do *anything* besides just stare, wide-eyed, and horrified.

"But you gotta get some aspect of Hell back into you," he drawls on. "The transition has to be completed, one way or another." They meet eyes and Nickie notices he almost looks serious. Almost. "Or you'll be dead."

Malphas drops the vial into the cup holder next to her. "And we both know that you're not the type to go down easy."

On Nickie's next blink, Malphas vanishes. The blink after that, she screams.

CHAPTER 20
HANAEL

Everything was going according to plan.

The Horseman are being executed remarkably well despite the time constraint. Malphas was on his way to finalize the connection Nicole had to Hell. A bit of celestial conquest later and Earth would be theirs for the taking.

Everything was going according to plan. So why does Hanael have the nagging feeling that it isn't?

She's felt quite unwell lately – fatigue, headaches, dizziness – the sort of things humans are afflicted with. The thought causes an internal blanche.

It takes a week of this before Hanael confronts Lucifer.

She finds her brother in the kitchen, immediately hit with the smell of fresh oranges. She smiles. A mimosa would hit the spot right about now, wouldn't it?

The smile falls, however, when her brother hands her the drink. Her fingers tighten around the glass as she stares at the colorful liquid.

"Something on your mind?"

Hanael shakes her head in an effort to clear it. "No... well, yes, actually. I suppose there is. I –" Something gives

Hanael pause, though she isn't sure what. "I've been feeling rather unwell lately."

"Unwell?"

"Tiredness. Headaches. Human illness."

"Ah," Lucifer hums, pouring himself a generous serving of scotch into his favorite wine glass. Wine glass. *Wasn't there something she needed to do involving a wine glass?*

"I do apologize, sister," Lucifer continues as he motions them over to the loveseat and armchair near his bookshelf. "The apocalypse is taking much of Hell's power, as you well know. Particularly with the modifications we made. The demons are suffering from similar afflictions."

"I see," Hanael says, wondering why the assurance doesn't offer any relief. "Thank you for telling me."

"Of course." Lucifer smiles through his drink, both now seated opposite the other. When Hanael takes a sip of her own, it tastes unusually bitter.

The next few days continue as usual, though Hanael's symptoms only worsen. Unease follows; a dark, sickly thing that screams at Hanael to listen. Somewhere in it, she can hear a woman praying.

The voice is familiar, but fleeting. And every attempt to focus on it results in another migraine that Hanael doesn't need. Particularly when she still had so many apocalypse-related duties to attend.

Hanael considers, briefly, bringing these issues to Lucifer's attention. Only to reconsider when she is at the door of his office and the unease is like a noose tightening around her neck.

She barely makes it back to her own quarters before vomiting into the wastebasket by her bed.

Inconsistency. Inconsistency. Her days are filled with inconsistency.

It's easy enough to ignore, at first. Memories that don't entirely line up. The look a demon gives her that says it knows something she doesn't. All minor details that Hanael can attribute to the stress of apocalypse planning.

The time loss is a bit harder to ignore.

Still, Hanael tries. Desperate in her need to make the puzzle pieces form a believable picture. It is only when Hanael begins cramming in pieces that don't fit – could never fit – that she realizes she has a very big problem, indeed.

Hanael cannot ever recall having a nightmare.

Then again, Hanael is having problems recalling much of anything.

There is blood on her hands – sticky, warm – as her fingertips brush against the cold stone wall of the Second Level.

Even through the misty obscurity of her environment, Hanael can see the letters she spells.

D – A – N – A – E – L

Hanael's heart is in her throat. Danael. Danael? Dan –

She's screaming. The sound echoes through the dark and still bedroom as she jolts up in a cold sweat. Which there is some comfort in – feeling the safety of her silk sheets grasped under her fingertips – until Hanael looks down at them.

Dried blood.

Barely dried blood.

And Hanael realizes, perhaps too late, what a subjective experience safety is.

Perception comes in as a close second in subjectivity. Even easier to distort. The only question remained was who (or what) was doing the distorting.

Though Hanael can surmise a guess.

Certainly not one that involves the 'draining' effects of the apocalypse. Of which, Hanael wonders how much longer she could realistically remain competent (see: sane) to oversee the planning of.

Her next orders from Lucifer test the limits of this.

"Malphas has momentarily left his current post to retrieve Nicole. In his absence, I would like you to eliminate Amy."

"Of course," Hanael says, as she always does. Refusal was not an option. Had she ever had options?

Lucifer gives a single curt nod before busying himself in the library. Hanael watches him, hand twitching, before making her exit towards his elevator and the Fourth Level.

Hanael's trip to the Fourth Level is as brief as always. The lightless, soundless abyss of her journey is a much-needed balm for the current fiery of her mind.

The reprieve doesn't last. As before Hanael can grasp

onto the handle to open the entrance to Amy's designated cell area, she begins to overhear voices.

Her hand hovers over the doorknob. Didn't Lucifer say Malphas had already left his post to retrieve Nicole?

Hanael lowers her hand in favor of maneuvering herself to a position that would allow for better hearing.

Two male voices. One obviously belonging to Amy and the other – Hanael startles at the realization of.

"I would like to offer you a proposal," Michael says, his words echoing off the steel door that was now a mere inch from Hanael's face.

"So, what? You making deals now, too? Hard pass." Hanael chills at Amy's word. Deal. Deal. There was something involving a deal, wasn't there?

Her hand slips from the cold metal and Hanael barely steadies it before it can make an impact against the door.

"A mutually beneficial agreement," Michael corrects. "I will release you. Right this moment. I will even see you reinstated back to your former angelic glory." Could he do that? "All I ask is that you kill Lucifer's abomination."

There is a very long pause before Amy answers, "Why do you want Nickie dead? And why the hell come to me about it?" He is struggling to keep his voice level, Hanael notices. She wonders if Michael does as well.

"You are the only demon that is not loyal to Lucifer in his entirety and regrettably, my only option. Ordinarily, I would order one of my own subordinates to do it, but I am not confident suspicions wouldn't arise." Another pause. "As for your other question – Nicole has served her purpose in ushering in the first Horseman. An existence that is dragging on far too long for my liking."

"And you think Lucifer is going to, what? Take that crap lying down?" Amy laughs humorlessly. "I can see it now!

162

The Rebellion Part Two: Electric Boogaloo. Well, either that or you end up like Hanael –"

Hanael's ears are ringing. She stumbles backward from the door, staring wide-eyed at the metal silhouette as if it might swallow her whole.

A part of her wishes it would.

Hanael's feet are propelling her forward before she makes the conscious decision to run. The angel wishes she could take flight to the portal to Earth on the Fourth Level, but her current surroundings would make it far too disorientating. And she couldn't risk attracting any attention to herself.

Just get to the Third Level, Hanael keeps repeating to herself like a mantra. It was the only thing she had left. *Just survive. You just need to survive.*

Hanael takes a sharp turn down another oblivion-filled hallway. Her legs feel close to giving out and every breath stings painfully into her chest. A very bad time to be sleep-deprived, indeed.

She can see the entrance to the Third Level now – a tiny flicker of blue light in the distance – and pushes forward even harder. She pushes and pushes and pushes and –

She's falling.

Her leg catches on some unseen piece of rubble and Hanael's body follows it down against the hard gravel. Pain explodes in her left ankle and when she looks down, can blurrily make out the protruding bone.

Just survive, Hanael repeats to herself again before traveling her hands down her bloody leg, aligning one hand over the bone and the other to the opposite side of her ankle. *You just need to survive.* Hanael makes a hard press inward and nearly bites her tongue off. There is an audible *'crunch'* and Hanael gags.

You just need to –

"Quite the fall you've had."

The hope drains from Hanael's body as quickly as any remaining body heat. She is hunched over her bloody ankle as Lucifer stalks forward. Hanael doesn't look up.

"Fool me once, shame on you," Lucifer says before leaning down. His hand grips her chin to jerk it upward, forcing Hanael to meet his gaze. "Fool me twice, well –"

His expression reads no more than mildly disappointed. Hanael thinks she should change that.

Hanael laughs, manic in her need to land the last blow. "You want to talk about people fooling you? Why don't you talk to Michael?"

It gets the desired response. Hanael can feel Lucifer's energy twist and snarl, confirmation of what the archangel had probably been suspecting ever since he and Michael began arguing.

Darkness comes for her before his wrath. Though it does not take her under. Instead, the surreal obscurity lifts her up and finally –

Hanael is awake.

CHAPTER 21

DANAEL

P oetry. It's the only thing Danael ends up finding of note on Hanael's computer.

Danael supposes she shouldn't be surprised. Hanael had always loved the arts, and it was obvious from her bookshelf that she was still an avid reader.

Danael wonders what Hanael would think of her reading it. If it was something the angel would have shared with her, had they not been apart. Danael wonders what it matters anymore.

A rose by any other name would smell as sweet

Or would it?

For what are we without our absurd labels and expectations?

A rose smells sweet for those who enjoy roses

A rose smells sweet until it doesn't

Until decay ravages the garden and thorns cut deep into the flesh

Until we realize that the rose was nothing more than the idea of what we thought it was

What we wanted it to be

What should a rose be?
I do wonder
Danael swallows.

CHAPTER 22
NICKIE

Nickie's still in the car. Still in the woods by the lake with a vial of what she has now deemed Satan's Heroin in the cup holder.

She doesn't know how long she's been here. It must have been a few hours, at least, if the sun's position is anything to go by.

Nickie releases her death grip from the steering wheel, exits her car, and heads over to that of her dead landlord's.

The lake would definitely be deep enough, Nickie decides as she hot-wires the engine again. Just drive it to the edge, push it in and then –

Then, what? Wait painfully to die? Or get high off hell juice? Which, if Malphas' demeanor was anything to go by, would only make her wish she *was* dead.

Nickie presses her foot slowly to the pedal.

And if somehow, by the grace of someone, she manages to make it out of the other side unscathed, it wouldn't last. The apocalypse would do her in one way or another.

The lake is approaching, and Nickie doesn't lift her foot from the pedal.

Dani, though. Dani might make it out alright. She had all this time, hadn't she? A little worse for wear, sure, but still. Dani would be okay.

And if she wasn't, well – Nickie isn't afraid to admit she's too much of a coward to want to be there for it.

She would die a coward, but she wouldn't die a high coward. Which is probably the best Nickie could hope for at this point.

The car rattles, heavy, as it dips forward into the lake. Water seeps in and Nickie looks at it disinterestedly.

It's a pathetic death, but at least it would be on her terms. And hey, maybe Amy will have turned out not to have been bullshitting her. Maybe she'd actually make it into Heaven.

Maybe.

Chills grip her as the water begins to pool around her midsection. Growing inpatient, Nickie floors the gas pedal.

And yep – that does it.

...

..

.

It's not peaceful. Fuck. Wasn't drowning supposed to be peaceful?

Her lungs burn, screaming at her to listen to her survival instincts. In defiance, Nickie takes several deep breaths of the surrounding water. Only on the sixth breath does her mind start to slow.

Slow and quiet.

Quite. Quite. Dark. Cold.

Cold. Why is it so cold?

She's floating. She's –

Something wasn't right.

She's floating down. It's too dark and something even

darker latches onto her ankle, tugging her down faster. Nickie tries to scream but her chest is heavy and unresponsive. Shadows in the water blur past her until they're all that remains.

Shadows. Darkness. Fear. Regret. A...park? A tree.

An apple tree.

Nickie walks toward it, suddenly oblivious to anything that had previously led to this moment in time. The grass feels alive under Nickie's feet as she pads barefoot towards a discarded apple. It's even more vibrant and inviting than her surroundings and, mesmerized, Nickie takes a bite.

She spits it out.

The apple drops from her hand as she sees the decay and rot inside. As soon as it hits the ground, the vibrant green grass turns rough and dead, cutting against Nickie's feet. When she looks up, she sees herself. Or more specifically, she sees herself the night of Dani's death.

A shadow appears over Nickie's shoulder right before she drunkenly mumbles out about 'appletinis.' Nickie is yelling, crying, begging Dani not to listen to her, but it's like trying to talk underwater.

Dani falls and the crack of her spine is like a gunshot in the otherwise silent night air. The shadow disappears and Nickie sees herself collapse at Dani's side.

And Nickie realizes, sickeningly, it's not the first time she's seen that shadow.

She sees it the night of her mother's death, when all she can feel is a smug kind of relief. She sees it when she takes her first hit of heroin, knowing it's not enough but it will do for now. She sees it when Malphas kills someone and she knows she should feel something, anything, other than the darkness that creeps in at the sight.

But it's always there. The darkness is always there.

Lucifer is always there.

Nickie never stood a chance.

The scene warps – memories being sucked back into the shadows. Somewhere in them, Nickie sees herself. Sees Lucifer too, though he thrives in them.

"Give it time, my darling daughter. One day very soon, you will as well."

Nickie screams. A violent tearing in her throat that finally manages to escape. The pain spreads downward and settles in her chest, where all the weight of her shadows seems to rest.

Hah. That rhymed.

Then she's coughing. Choking. Water rushing out of her lungs like a fire hose –

"What the actual fuck do you think you're doing?!"

Nickie startles back at the voice of Amy, fingernails digging into the damp shore of the lake. Eventually, the coughing begins to subside and Nickie spits the last of the water onto the demon's face.

"What the fuck am I doing?" Nickie growls, forcing herself to a standing position. Amy tries to reach for her and she pushes him backwards. "What the fuck are you doing, you lying piece of shit? I trusted you! I actually gave a shit about you!"

"I didn't know!" Amy shouts. "I didn't, Nickie. I swear. I only found out when I saw you and Lucifer standing near each other. How similar your energy was." His expression crumples and Nickie collapses back down to the ground, not having the energy to fight him.

"I'm so sorry, Nickie. I would have never taken you to Hell if I had –"

"Save it," Nickie bites back. "Why are you here?"

Amy collapses next to her, something unreadable in his

expression. The only sounds between them are the soft, crashing waves of the lake. Finally, Amy says, "Michael sent me here to kill you."

Nickie laughs, bitterly. "And what? You wanted the honors of doing it yourself, is that it?"

His expression hardens, lip curling and eyes blazing. It's the first time Amy actually looks demonic.

"Do you know what I just gave up to save your life? Do you have any idea?"

What *he* just gave up? Is that a joke?

"I'm not your consolation prize for doing the right thing, dickbag," Nickie snarls, the fire in her eyes matching his. "'Right' being a pretty grey area at this point. I'm dying anyway, so why bother?"

Amy pales, eyes frantically beginning to search her energy, and paling further at what he finds. He really didn't know, did he? About any of it.

Nickie thinks it might have been easier if he had.

"Okay. *Okay.*" Amy scrambles to a standing position, hoisting an uncooperative Nickie up with him. "Something...something from Hell would –"

"Yeah, Malphas already gave me the hell juice spiel," Nickie says, yanking her hand out of his. "It's not gonna happen."

Amy's expression darkens. "When was Malphas here?"

"The fuck does it matter?"

Amy throws his hands up before settling them into a prayer. "Dear Danael of whatever Sphere you used to be in. Your best friend is trying to kill herself –"

Nickie tackles him back down to the ground. Her fingernails dig into his wrists as she pins them above his head, teeth barred inches from his face.

"I'm not letting you kill yourself," Amy says calmly.

Cool as a cucumber, the fucker. "We'll figure something out, but it's not gonna be *that*."

Amy stares at Nickie. Nickie glowers at Amy. It's only until Nickie realizes that she's quite literally straddling him that she rolls off and retreats over to a nearby tree to collapse against. Vaguely, she can hear Amy finish his prayer with directions to their current location.

How did things manage to get even worse?

It's the punchline to her already cosmic joke of an existence. Because oh, yes. She was very much meant to exist, wasn't she? Couldn't have an apocalypse without good ol' Nickie Morningstar to brandish the starting flags.

Fuck her fucking fucked up life.

Nickie wonders, somewhere in the dark recess of mind space she's now found herself in, how she didn't know.

There was always something wrong with her; something dirty, unclean. Her mother saw it. Her teachers saw it. Dani saw it, no matter how much she might deny it. And Malphas – well.

I see those cogs turning in your head, princess. Turning, turning, turning – but never making any connections.

Nickie shudders. Why couldn't the stupid bastard let her die? Why couldn't *either* of the stupid bastards let her die?

Nickie wallows in her own self-pity a bit more before forcing herself back to a standing position and over to Amy, who was now eyeing the Satan's Heroin in his hand with crinkled brows.

Dani enters the scene only moments later.

She's pissed.

"You tried to *kill yourself*?"

"I'm the Antichrist. I think I'm entitled."

Dani reels back, blazing eyes shooting from Nickie to

Amy. The demon holds his hands up in placation before saying, "Minor missed detail, I'll admit. But, yeah. She's... Lucifer's daughter."

Dani's eyes trail back to her, slowly. They're full of pity and guilt and everything Nickie hates. Dani closes them, takes a deep breath and says, "And I'm an angel whose obsession with my other half *started the apocalypse*. Do you think I should kill myself?"

Low blow. "You know I don't."

Dani's nostrils flare in the way they used to when Nickie was using. Angry, upset, but resigned to the deafening silence of reality. She does now what she did then – wraps Nickie in a crushing embrace and says, "We'll figure it out."

And like back then, Nickie replies, "Will we?"

Except there are no additional placations this time around. Just a tight smile from Dani as Nickie is all but forced to follow her and Amy back over to Nickie's car. She's about to grab for the passenger handle when Dani freezes in place, eyes locked on Amy.

"I remember you," Dani says. "Amy. We used to work in the same Sphere. You...Fell? How? Did you even side with Lucifer?"

Amy blinks owlishly at her before saying, "No, I didn't. So, your guess is as good as mine. You were in the Ninth Sphere, then?" Amy frowns. "I don't remember you."

"I figured as much. Suppose I have Michael to thank for that," Dani says. "But yes, we were, well, I guess you could say friends." A sad look crosses her face. "You were such a good angel, Amy. I envied you sometimes."

Nickie stiffens as she can feel Amy's eyes on her. She meets his gaze and it softens, never leaving hers, as he replies, "Yeah, I guess we have Michael to thank for a lot of things."

Not another word is said between the three as they enter Nickie's car and Dani begins the drive back to Hanael's. Only in the silence does Nickie begin to wonder what Michael could have offered Amy in exchange for her death.

Though the silence answers, as it has started to as of late, that she already knows.

CHAPTER 23

DANAEL

There has been a menacing little voice in the back of Danael's head ever since she regained her memories. A quiet but constant throb that told her how much the current apocalyptic events were her fault.

That voice is screaming now.

There weren't many people that had taken such a center stage in Danael's life besides Hanael. She cared about the people in her past lives, of course, though none could hold a candle to Nickie.

Perhaps that should have been Danael's first hint her best friend wasn't human.

Lucifer's daughter. A Nephilim. The Antichrist.

Dying.

The latter is the only label Danael seems to care about.

So much for keeping her priorities in check.

"I told you to get that shit out of my face!"

Danael's head jerks up from its place over her current research. They've been back at Hanael's only a few hours, but already Nickie's withdrawals (could she even call them that?) were reaching a peak.

Amy remains unfazed as the two continue a stare off, white knuckling the vial of Hell essence in his hand. "You're *dying* –"

"Oh, no! The Antichrist is dying," Nickie deadpans. "What ever will the world do?" A maddening grin appears. "Probably fucking recover from this bullshit apocalypse."

Amy's eye twitches and Danael sighs. Poor bastard. Loving Nickie always was a losing game.

"Amy, can I talk to you a minute?" Danael asks.

Reluctantly, Amy removes himself from Nickie and follows Danael into a study adjacent to the living room. She shuts the door behind them before saying, "We're running out of time."

"I know," Amy says, running a hand through his tattered hair. "Have you found anything?"

"Maybe," Danael says as she approaches Hanael's desk and a stack of various occult printouts. "An unlinking ritual. If we can severe Nickie's link to Lucifer and Hell, her condition might improve."

"Might?"

"It's the best we have for right now," Danael says. "Keep an eye on her, okay? I'll need a good four or five hours to gather the supplies."

"Sure, okay," Amy gripes. "And what if our best isn't good enough?"

Danael's grip tightens around the paper in her hand. "We'll cross that bridge when we come to it."

"I'm not letting her die."

"Neither am I."

~

The supplies take longer to procure than Danael had been expecting. It would be a hassle on a good day to find the needed candles, rope, and herbs, but with War still on full display – well. Let's just say it's a good thing Danael wasn't too attached to the scarf she had been wearing.

By the time Danael makes it back to Hanael's, it is well past dark. She enters through the foyer and is greeted by the sound of shouting. Which she initially takes no mind to until the sound of shattering glass joins it.

Danael's heart jumps to her throat as she races into the living room to find a bruised Amy, wild-eyed Nickie, and very much destroyed vial of Hell essence.

Danael approaches Nickie slowly, holding out her hands in front of her. Nickie doesn't seem to register either of them.

Suddenly, her best friend's gaze darts to a far-right corner before she screams, "Get out of my fucking head!", and drops to the ground, shaking.

"Nickie!" Danael yells, before attempting to run to her side. A grip on her shoulder stops her.

"She can't hear you," Amy says. "Don't try and touch her." His expression tightens. "Trust me."

"Oh, Nickie," Danael whispers. You're going to hate me for this.

"We can't perform the unlinking ritual on her like this," Amy says, solemnly. "She's too weak."

"Not like this, no." Then again, Danael had always had to make difficult choices where Nickie was concerned, hadn't she?

That much hadn't changed.

It is in everyone's best interest, Danael tells herself, that Nickie lives.

If she died, there is no telling what it could mean for the state of her soul or the current apocalypse. If either Lucifer or Michael got ahold of her, it was game over for all of them.

It isn't a selfish interest, Danael assures herself. It isn't.

In fact, if Nickie came into full power, they might actually stand a chance. *Humanity* might actually stand a chance. It was the best 'might' they were ever going to get.

She has to do it. She has to.

Amy is less convinced.

"I don't like it," the demon says as Danael finishes drawing the blood circle around a currently restrained and unconscious Nickie. They hadn't had to knock her out at least, her best friend having passed out shortly after her episode with Amy. "What if we're feeding exactly into what Lucifer wants?"

"Damned if we do, damned if we don't," Danael mutters, wiping the blood off her cut hand. Heading back over to the coffee table that was now adorned with ritual supplies, she turns back to Amy, "You're sure your blood will work as a replacement to the Hell essence?"

Amy stares at her. "I'm sure." And blinks. "Are *you* sure you're ready to force that blood down your best friend's throat?"

Danael pauses, staring into the flames of the recently lit candles in the corners of the table. What *was* Danael sure of anymore?

The world was ending. The world was ending and it was, at least in part, due to her unrelenting need to protect Hanael. The world was ending and they had no way to stop it.

Nickie was dying. Nickie was dying and it was, at least in part, due to her unrelenting need to protect Hanael. Nickie was dying and Danael had a way to stop it.

Danael couldn't save Hanael, but Danael *could* save Nickie. Danael could save Nickie and by some grace of the universe, Nickie might be able to save them all.

"None of us can afford to hang too tightly onto our morality right now," Danael finally says.

Amy doesn't offer a reply as he swipes a blade from the coffee table, cuts open his palm, and lets the crimson liquid drip into a new vial. The only sound for several long minutes being the *drip, drip, drip,* of blood and the quiet crackling of candles.

The foreboding ambience ends too quickly, and before Danael knows it, she is positioned on the outskirts of the circle – vial of blood in one hand and incantation in the other.

"Please forgive me," Danael says under her breath before laying a kiss to Nickie's forehead. Tilting said forehead back, Danael puts the vial to her lips and empties its contents.

Before Danael can turn her attention back to the incantation, Nickie's eyes snap open and Danael stumbles back.

Don't look at her, don't look at her, don't –

"What the fuck? Dani, let me go!"

Danael sucks in a breath and begins the incantation, "POILP A ALLAR C CNILA."

Nickie screams in pain and Danael flinches, giving a wave to Amy. From her peripheral, Danael can see him put a candle up to rope currently tied to either ends of the ritual bowls.

"DS I ULS TRIAN NOAN AG UML," Danael continues. "LAP A OLPIRT C ASCHA..."

The rope begins to sever. Nickie stops screaming long enough to shout out, "I'll never forgive you for this!"

Their eyes meet. Danael remembers the only other time Nickie had said those words to her. It was right after her overdose. Being each other's medical power of attorney, Danael made the request for involuntary commitment. It was approved.

Despite nine months of verbal spars and two spits to the face, Nickie had, finally, forgiven her.

Danael doesn't think she'll get so lucky this time around.

She finishes the incantation, "IL LANSH I LAP G."

The candles blow out, signaling the end of the ritual. Nickie stills, briefly, before she begins to seize. Danael is at her side just as quickly.

"Was this supposed to happen?" Amy hisses, tilting her head to the side as foam begins to leak out of her mouth.

"Probably," Danael says.

Amy curses and Danael grasps onto Nickie's hand in an effort to send what little angelic healing power she still had her best friend's way. It works, at least partly, as Nickie's body stills.

"Help me get her to the sofa," Danael says. Amy does, and once Nickie is deposited, the other two celestials mirror her on the opposite two recliners.

Danael isn't sure how long they sit like that. The prolonged silence feels tight against Danael's chest.

Or maybe that's the guilt.

Eventually, Amy rises from his place next to her with a tight, "I need a drink", before exiting to Hanael's wine cellar. Danael is also tempted, but she isn't sure if she could stomach it right now.

What if it didn't work? What if they had made things

worse? What if. What if. What if. It was a haunting motif as of late.

What if she had never made that deal to save Hanael? What if Hanael had never made the deal to save her? What if they had separated cleanly to begin with?

What if Danael wasn't the hero of this story at all?

It creeps into her mind then, like pitch black vines tightening around her psyche. All of the people she had been in her past lives. Not all of them good. Not even a handful, by Danael's calculations.

It was hard to be good in a world like this.

It also doesn't feel like an excuse.

As if the universe chooses that moment to cement her thoughts, Nickie's eyes flutter open.

Danael stills as Nickie sits up slowly, as if carefully choosing every inch of space she occupied. She cracks her neck, once, before her eyes settle on Danael.

There's something missing from them, Danael can already tell. Though she isn't sure at this point if there was hope for that to be a good thing or not.

"You always think you're doing the right thing, don't you?"

Decidedly not.

Nickie's expression is steeled, but Danael can see the barely contained fury under it. It reminds her of Lucifer.

"Dani the martyr. Dani the caretaker. Dani the hero." Nickie does bare her teeth then. "Except there are no heroes here. And even if there were – you wouldn't be one of them."

Danael doesn't have time to reply before Nickie vanishes. Though even if she had, all she would have had to say was, *"you're probably right."*

CHAPTER 24

HANAEL

It's not unconsciousness, Hanael decides, it's just darkness.

She stays there for a long while. How long a while? Hanael couldn't say. Time feels...fleeting. As if it exists but is just outside her grasp.

So too are the images that begin to flash in her peripheral when her mind can no longer comprehend her surroundings. She feels more than sees them. A life beyond this one. Memories, emotions, concepts – things that feel like they belong to her and don't.

There is a constant to them. A woman. Her eyes are a hardened brown and her lips move, but Hanael can't hear the words.

She doesn't hear the words for a long while.

When she does, they are a deafening, "WAKE UP!"

A blinding light follows. The memories return to her all at once. She remembers who she is, why she was here – and where was *here*, exactly?

Hanael's vision clears and she finds herself in a bright

yet almost entirely vacant room. The only addition being that of a small black table, two chairs, and chessboard.

Two bodies materialize on the chairs then: Lucifer and herself. Hanael is beginning to question the visual irony when she hears a female voice from beside her say, "Fitting."

Hanael doesn't startle. She only turns her head to look over the visage of Danael before saying, "It certainly is."

Hanael can feel Danael's eyes on her as she continues to watch her double and Lucifer play. Her double is, unsurprisingly, losing. Hanael doesn't understand the point of it: hadn't she already lost?

"You're not dead," Danael says. "At least not yet. Your mind is only separated."

"Separated?" Hanael asks, not really paying attention. Blood is dripping down the legs of the chessboard table.

"Yes. Lucifer is, well – calling it a 'lobotomy' might be a bit of a generous statement."

Hanael says nothing.

"I suppose that makes me your subconscious," Danael says, an inflection of teasing to her voice. Hanael only wishes it were the real thing.

"Are angels even supposed to have a subconscious?" Hanael asks.

"And since when have you ever followed the criteria of what angels are supposed to have?"

Because that had gotten her so far, hadn't it?

"Listen," Danael says, tone turning grave. "Lucifer doesn't know about the separation. Which puts you at an advantage. So, let's not waste the opportunity, yeah?"

A part of Hanael very much wants to. She is *so tired.* Tired of fighting losing battles and feeling the weight of her existence crush her. Only now realizing how long that weight had been there.

There is another part, however – the part that is standing next to her now – that remains undeterred.

And it always had been the best part of herself, hadn't it?

Finally, Hanael sighs and says, "What exactly is your plan here?"

Danael smiles before waving a hand towards one of the white, blank walls. A doorway slowly begins to take form, and beyond its arches lay the vastest library Hanael ever had the pleasure of seeing.

"Your memory is as good a place to start as any," Danael says, as she makes her way through the doorway. Hanael gives one final look over to the chessboard before following her.

The library is even larger on the inside.

Rows of bookcases and filing cabinets stretch across a seemingly endless low-lit space. Hanael walks, dazed, as she runs her fingers along some of the spines. There are no titles. Hanael frowns.

"You need to visualize what you're looking for," Danael says from behind her. Hanael turns around to face her.

"And what *are* we looking for?"

Danael shrugs. "Whatever might be of use against Lucifer. Or more specifically, the hold he currently has over your mind."

"A spell, then," Hanael guesses. The words are barely out of her mouth before there is an echo of pages turning and the bookcase in front of her is filled with visible titles.

'Healing rituals.'

'Unbinding spells.'

'Energetic attacks.'

Not specific enough. And how exactly was Hanael supposed to perform a spell? She was unconscious.

"It will need to be something we can perform from here. In your mindspace," Danael answers aloud.

"Is that possible?" Hanael asks.

"I suppose we're going to find out."

Hanael searches. And searches. And searches. Yet all she manages to accomplish is a further snuffing out of the minuscule hope she had left.

The passage of time is still a questionable entity; one that Danael can't provide any additional insight into. Hanael considers asking said subconscious for further help sorting current leads when she notices that she is alone in the library.

Hanael sighs. It seemed to be happening more frequently now. Danael would disappear, only to return looking far worse for wear to report any relevant information she had overheard from Lucifer. It's not a conscious effort on her part, and only a glaring reminder of how little time they had left.

This reminder is brought to an ugly head when Hanael notices that Danael still hasn't returned after several consecutive memory searches.

Something was wrong.

Hanael makes her way back towards the doorway and the previous white room. The first step she takes into it is met with a sticky *'slosh'* against her bare feet. Hanael looks down to see a bright crimson lining the floor.

Her eyes follow it to the chess table, where her double and Lucifer are playing. Her double is still losing, but the previous drip of blood down the table has turned into a steady stream.

Hanael swallows.

She was going to die, wasn't she?

Danael materializes beside her and it is the worst her subconscious has looked yet. Her under eyes are puffy and dark, a sharp contrast against her pale and clammy complexion. A thinly veiled horror in her expression pulls together the look.

Hanael very suddenly has the distinct feeling of someone walking over her grave.

"Lucifer is furious," Danael begins in a hoarse voice. "Amy has escaped. Michael is AWOL –" She shakes her head. "If you're going to do something, you need to do it *now*."

Hanael's gaze travels back to the chess table. What wasn't she seeing? Was this really how her story ended? Through a haze of smoke and misery?

Wordlessly, she approaches the bleeding chess table. Hanael's double makes her move. Lucifer makes his. Hanael makes another and Lucifer –

"He's cheating," Hanael realizes suddenly. "He keeps changing his moves. Touching the pieces without moving them."

"So?" Danael asks.

So. So, what? What did it matter? Lucifer is hardly the pillar of honesty. Pillar of loopholes, maybe –

The realization slams into Hanael so hard that now she is the one seated at the chess table. Perhaps she always was.

"It's a rigged game," Hanael breathes out. "It's always been a rigged game."

Danael smiles through her pain. "And how does one go about winning a rigged game?"

"You stop playing."

~

The triumph of Hanael's realization is short-lived. To stop playing Lucifer's game is to make herself an opponent that he no longer wanted to play with. Could no longer play with.

Free will was a funny thing. It was almost like a skill – acquired for angels and a natural talent for humans. It had its downsides, certainly, but the part of relevance here was the protection it offered against celestial manipulation.

"Are you sure you want to do this?" Danael asks. They are both back in the library as Hanael searches wild-eyed for the needed ritual. "You know what it will mean."

Of course Hanael doesn't want to do this. Much like one doesn't want to saw off their own limb when faced with the option to escape from captivity.

"If I don't, I'll die," Hanael says. "Danael will end up separated from me either way."

Eventually, Hanael finds the title she is looking for: 'Energy Reversals and Transmutations'. She slams the book down on a nearby desk and begins to read, "Celestial energy, if removed from its host source will invert back to its original form –"

"Void energy," Danael finishes. "Sounds like bad news for our resident Lightbringer."

"Bad news for any celestial," Hanael says. But good news for the apocalypse, and even better for her own liveli-hood. That is, if she timed it correctly...

"Has something like this ever been attempted?" Danael asks.

Doubtful. What celestial in their right mind would willingly detach from their own angelic energy? Their own other half?

"Lucky for us, you're not in your right mind," Danael says. "Now, how do we do this?"

∼

The ritual itself is relatively straightforward, the main ingredient being that of her own intent. Still, it is one she struggles to find.

Who would Hanael be without Danael? Even when the other angel's existence was erased from her memories, their connection hadn't been. A weak and hazy connection, no doubt, but it still existed.

This would sever it entirely.

"I suppose this is where we say our goodbyes," Danael says once they exit the library for the last time. The doubles of Lucifer and herself are long gone, replaced with a gushing stream of blood from the chess table.

It won't be long, Hanael thinks, until the pristine white room is an ocean of crimson.

"I suppose I will see you on the other side," Hanael says.

Danael smiles at her, sadly, before answering, "No. You won't."

Then she is gone and Hanael is alone.

She breathes in. Out. In. Out. In –

"OL LRASD A LANSH C IL DE ASCHA. TOOAT DE ZACAM, ZACAM. ZACAM, ZACAM, ZACAM. DE A AFFA C QAA."

Hanael loses track of how many times she repeats the incantation, focusing only on her will. Detachment. Survival. Revival.

Eventually, her environment falls away to that of the previous void.

Hanael startles, thinking the ritual had failed – *was she too late? Had she already died?* – until her eyes snap open and she is greeted by the sight of a golden mirror, sans her reflection.

Hanael repeats the incantation.

There is a slight jerk against her energy; unnoticeable had Hanael not been watching for it. When Hanael looks back up to the mirror, she sees Danael.

The reflection smiles sadly at Hanael. Understanding, forgiving, but no less devastated.

Hanael smashes the mirror.

There is no pain (that will come later, Hanael thinks, when the energy is physically removed from her) but there is loss. An anticipation of the emptiness that was to come when she completed the ritual.

It is a cold and frightening thing that almost makes Hanael regret performing the ritual.

Almost.

The ground is no longer solid, Hanael realizes suddenly. The viscous, tar-like substance engulfs her up to the ankles, knees, hips, breasts, neck –

Hanael takes a large breath.

She's going to need it.

Hanael exhales. Pain follows. Physical pain.

She was back in her body.

Hanael doesn't open her eyes immediately, instead choosing to scan her surroundings with her other senses.

Cold metal chains restrain her at the wrist and ankles.

The left side of her skull is moist from a recent head wound, though with thankfully minimal internal damage. To her left stands Lucifer, beside whatever hard surface he had strapped her to.

His energy is snarled and twisted. Hot with rage; equally hot with recklessness. It is much like how it had been during the Rebellion.

Which meant her plan would have a chance to go either very well or very badly.

Hanael opens her eyes. Lucifer's expression is as stoic as ever. With much restraint, she forces hers to mirror it.

"Speak," Lucifer says.

"What do you wish for me to say?" Hanael answers pleasantly.

His lips upturn, pleased. Wordlessly, he snaps his fingers and the restraints drop to the ground with a ringing *'clang'*. The urge to strangle him with them is a hard one to push down.

"Come," Lucifer beckons toward the exit of whichever prison cell they were currently in. Hanael's eyes are still adjusting to the muddled hue of greys. "We have much work to do."

Her vision clears as it focuses on him. She smiles. "Yes, we do."

CHAPTER 25
NICKIE

*A*t *least*, Nickie thinks hysterically, *she wasn't hallucinating Lucifer anymore.*

She stumbles, hands first, onto the rocky exterior of a cliff. The smell of sea water cuts through the air and Nickie takes several large gasps of it. When she manages to raise her head from her knees, it's to an overhead view of a vacant beach.

Nickie always had loved the beach. When's the last time she went?

She swallows. How much longer would they even exist?

Nickie forces herself to a standing position, only a few inches from the cliff's edge. She closes her eyes.

How did she get here?

She remembers being angry. Feeling like she couldn't look at Dani another second –

Nickie's fists clench as she forces in another breath.

She does feel better. More focused, less suicidal. Maybe a bit more homicidal, but no more so than the situation called for. And what *did* the situation call for?

Nickie's had enough. She knows that much.

Enough of this Truman Show level bullshit. Enough of being a plaything to her own fucking father. They wanted an Antichrist? Then she'd damn well give them one.

The teleportation takes some practice.

Nickie likens it to throwing darts. You needed a good aim, solid spatial awareness, just the right flick of the wrist – and voila!

Well, almost.

But hey – if Nickie had mastered darts, lock-picking, *and* the piano, she's sure she can master this. No doubt it would end up being the hustle of her career.

After the ninth snap of her fingers (and two very surprised old ladies), Nickie manages to materialize in front of a seemingly closed bar. Closed, except, the buzz under Nickie's skin tells her, for one demonic patron.

With a sigh, Nickie kicks open the door with her boot and enters the dim establishment. Didn't she promise herself she'd never stoop this low again?

"Hey princess!" Malphas is already pouring her a glass of bourbon. "Business or pleasure?"

Then again, who else to help pull off a hustle than a fellow hustler?

"Both," Nickie says, taking a seat next to him. "That is, if you define 'pleasure' as driving a blade through my father's chest."

Malpahs beams, sliding over her glass. "You know I do."

Nickie eyes the caramel liquid before raising them to meet the demon's. "What's it going to take for you to agree to do this my way?"

"What are you going to do to make it worth my while?"

Nickie knocks back half her glass. Liquid courage is still courage, right?

"An equal payoff," Nickie says. "We kill Lucifer and Michael and stop the apocalypse. I get to save the world and you get to rule Hell."

"And what makes you think I want to rule Hell?"

Nickie glares at him.

"You got me," he says, waving a hand. "Fine. You get Earth, I get Hell. But you follow my lead, you got that? That's the only way this is going to work. And you need to be convincing."

"Convincing?"

"Lucifer's only weakness is his ego. There is no part of him that ever thought you wouldn't be his good little Antichrist." Malphas smiles. "So, be his *good little Antichrist.*"

Nickie's hand tightens around her glass. She figured she'd have to do as much.

Malphas downs the rest of his before standing up and saying, "Are we ready to go, then?"

"Give me an hour."

"Fine," Malphas says with a roll of his shoulders. "Meet me back at the crossroads you entered into Hell the first time. I'll be waiting."

Malphas vanishes and the glass of Nickie's tumbler shatters under her grip.

It doesn't take long to find Amy, though Nickie kind of wishes it had. Maybe then she would have been able to talk herself out of seeing him.

It's a bad idea. Sappy shit like this never worked out in

anyone's favor, and yet –

Nickie trudges forward to the old oak tree where the demon was settled under. It's quiet here; solemn. An abandoned playground consumed by the sands of time and overgrowth of weeds.

Amy doesn't see her at first, probably too drunk to sense her presence. Nickie files the connotation of that away for later reflection.

When the demon does drag his eyes away from the bottle in his hands, they land on her. They both still. A blink later Amy is fumbling to his feet and Nickie is tentatively approaching him.

He stares at her, wide-eyed, before asking, "Are you... you?"

Nickie wrinkles her nose. "The hell is that supposed to mean?"

"Thank God," Amy says, dropping the bottle of scotch to the ground and closing the distance between them. "Nickie, I'm so sorry. I didn't want to do that to you, but – "

"You had no choice. I can relate."

A pause. "Nickie..." Amy's tone raises more than a few octaves. "Whatever you're planning on doing, please, *please* don't."

Yep. Definitely a bad idea.

"I need one person to believe in me right now, Amy," Nickie says, hating how desperate she sounded. "Just one. Excuse me for hoping that person might be *you*."

She turns around to leave, but Amy's grip on her wrist stops her.

"Wait," he says. "Just...tell me what's going on, okay? I promise I'll listen."

And so, Nickie does. Amy is less than enthused. But

Amy also isn't such an idiot that he won't take the only possible Hail Mary they have left.

"Have you talked to Dani about this?" Amy asks after at least twenty minutes of back-and-forth bickering.

"No. And you're not going to either."

"Why?"

"Because," Nickie says. "Her recent actions lead me to believe she's more than a bit unstable – "

"And you're *not*?"

"At least I have my priorities halfway out of my ass," Nickie says with a glare. "Listen, I can't afford a single liability right now, alright? You already told me Hanael's been brainwashed. God only knows how bad it'll be once I'm there. And if Dani has both me *and* Hanael to freak out over –"

Amy puts up a hand. "I get it, alright? I don't like it, but I get it. So, what do I tell her, then?"

"Tell her you saw me, I was pissed, and said I needed space. Tell her I'm okay and I'm myself but she better not look for me." Nickie looks down at her watch. "I need to get going."

"I'm tempted to join you."

"Michael will kill you on sight."

"I'm still tempted."

They lock eyes and something in Nickie's chest tightens against her will. Yep, yep, yep – this was *totally* a bad idea.

Then again, that was kind of her MO, wasn't it?

"Stay safe, okay?" Amy says after the silence starts to become awkward.

Nickie smiles a barely-there smile before answering, "Ditto." A snap of her fingers later and she's at the crossroad.

"That was more than an hour," Malphas says, visibly peeved.

"Time is an illusion that only rules lesser minds," Nickie answers pleasantly. *"Let's go."*

～

It's not like the first time. There's no high; only a vague magnetic pull that told her where in Hell she was. Nickie did feel good, though. Clear-headed. Focused.

Her rage is still coiled tightly under her skin, but in a willfully contained sort of way. It is, Nickie realizes for the first time, something she can use as weapon. Something that she can control and not the other way around.

The revelation is freeing. Enticing. Euphoric. Who needs drugs when revenge was going to feel this good?

"Follow my lead," Malphas says, breaking Nickie out of her perhaps premature self-assurance. They exit through a steel elevator and onto the Third Level, where apparently meetings and communications were held.

Emphasis on the apparently.

It's an utter clusterfuck of shouting and mismanaged demons. Somewhere in the mangled darkness, she loses track of Malphas, though the other demons don't pay her any more mind.

Welp. No better time to gain some good ol' fashioned intel, right?

Nickie maneuvers through the crowd, taking in the frustrated spits of indignance from the surrounding demons.

"Looks like Michael is AWOL."

"He shouldn't have been here to begin with! What was Lucifer thinking?"

"There's a question."

Nickie smiles to herself as she finds a quiet nook to watch the unrest from. This was good. Insurrection was always good for a takedown.

Her viewing party is cut short by the sudden silence of the demons. They all stand now, still and at attention. Nickie follows their eyes back to a steel elevator and can feel her lip twitch at the figure that walks out.

She closes them briefly to take a deep breath.

Showtime.

Lucifer's energy is coiled about as tightly as the demons had all been only seconds before. The echo of his wingtips ring out as he marches to the podium in the center of the room, the demons clearing the way as if they were in the line of an actual bulldozer.

Perhaps an accurate comparison, what with the look Lucifer currently wears.

It's a look that changes almost instantaneously, however, when the archangel's eyes land on her.

"My darling daughter," Lucifer beams, waving a hand for her to join him at the podium. "Finally, some good news. Come, come."

All eyes turn to her in a painfully slow succession. The demons pale and Nickie takes at least a little bit of pleasure in how they somehow seem to make room even more quickly for her.

It feels like Nickie is simultaneously walking death row and a runway. Though when she arrives at the podium, mere inches from her expectant father, Nickie knows her next words will decide which of the two it is.

Nickie turns her attention to the crowd of demons, raises her chin, and says, "Well, what are you waiting for? Bend the fucking knee."

They all drop. Lucifer laughs and wraps an arm around her shoulder before he begins listing off a round of updates, orders, and apocalypse timelines. Nickie listens and catalogues the information, all while trying very hard not to rip off the hand that remains firmly against her back.

It's all over thankfully soon enough, and the demons clear out just as fast. Malphas apparently clears out with them (the bastard), leaving only Nickie and Lucifer remaining on the podium.

"How are you feeling, my dear?"

"Good. Powerful," Nickie says, keeping her expression as neutral as possible. "And what are *my* orders?"

Lucifer laughs again. "My dear, you will be the one *giving* the orders, not the other way around." He smirks. "Which you obviously already have quite a knack for, no?"

"I do alright."

"In any case," Lucifer says, releasing his hand from her back. "The demons are at your disposal. Do as you see fit with them as well as the power Hell offers." He turns from her and ushers a hand out to a side hallway. "Hanael will escort you to our quarters. Make yourself at home. I have business to attend but will be back to make dinner."

On those parting words, Lucifer's form is soon replaced by Hanael's as the angel leads her back to the elevator. The doors close. Nickie eyes her a few moments before saying, "Thought you were brainwashed."

Hanael stiffens, eyes darting over Nickie's expression until the angel finally relaxes. "I thought the same of you."

"Guess we both play a good game," Nickie says as they exit the elevator into a smog of smoke. Which gives way to the most pretentious looking living room Nickie's ever seen.

Not that she had expected much different.

The piano is the only salvageable accessory, resting

center piece of a reading nook surrounded by several towering bookshelves. Nickie runs her fingertips over the lid as she hears Hanael approach from behind her.

"That's new," Hanael says. Nickie turns around to face her. "Seems Lucifer has done quite a bit of redecorating on your behalf while I was...otherwise occupied."

Otherwise occupied by what? Wrestling alligators?

"Do I even want to know what happened to you?" Nickie asks.

"Probably not," Hanael says. "It doesn't matter now, anyway. I assume we're on the same side?"

"If your side involves killing Michael and Lucifer, sure," Nickie says. "Though I'm all ears for suggestions. From what Malphas has told me, archangels don't tend to go down without a fight."

Hanael smiles faintly. "I do believe I might have one, yes."

CHAPTER 26
DANAEL

S omething is wrong.

It's a foreboding. Prickling under the skin of the back of her neck. Cold, threatening, loud.

Danael is tempted to laugh at it.

Which part, exactly, are her useless angelic senses attempting to warn her about now? The apocalypse? Hanael's safety? Nickie's? Or her own actions taken to try and preserve these?

Or perhaps, simply, Danael is unsure of what most to be afraid of.

She shudders, thinking of her recent encounter with Nickie. Still, she had looked for her. Which turned out to be a near impossible task without her full powers. All while Amy remained too busy drowning his rage and heartbreak in alcohol than to assist.

Funny, how similar he and Nickie were in those respects.

Danael does wonder about their connection. It was celestial, obviously (and no doubt heightened using Amy's blood in the ritual), though not the kind Danael was familiar with.

Then again, perhaps she wasn't the one to ask about healthy romantic attachments.

"Keep making that face too long and it'll get stuck like that."

Danael spins around from her position over the breakfast bar and plethora of tracking spells. She hadn't heard Amy come in. The demon looks only marginally less distraught than when he had left.

"You're one to talk," Danael says.

"That's what this is for," Amy says, tossing the empty bottle of scotch from his hand into the kitchen trashcan. It misses, shattering at Danael's feet. Amy curses.

Danael resigns not to comment.

"I talked to Nickie," Amy says next, once he's snapped his fingers and the glass has vanished. Danael's heart jumps to her throat.

"And?"

"*And*," Amy says, meeting her eyes. "She's okay. She's pissed, but she's okay. She's herself."

"She didn't seem like herself when she left here."

"Can you blame her?"

Danael bites hard into her lip. "What else did she say?"

"That she needed space," Amy says. "And not to go looking for her." The demon's gaze trails down to the scattered location spells on the counter. "A warning I would suggest we heed."

"It's the *apocalypse*," Danael says, a little crazed. Was she the only one who understood what that *meant* for Nickie? For all of them? "She shouldn't be on her own."

"I'm fairly certain she can take care of herself."

"That's what I'm worried about."

Amy grimaces, though not in a way that indicated disagreement. The demon turns his attention back to the counter as he shuffles the scattered paperwork and grimoires to the side, replacing them with two notebooks and adjacent pens.

"Ye of so little faith," Amy says, taking a seat at the breakfast stool beside her. "Let's worry about the aspects of this situation we *can* control."

"I wasn't aware there were any."

He smiles before snapping his fingers and an array of snacks appear on the counter in front of them. "That's why you have me."

They brainstorm, tentatively. The previous tension the Nickie situation had ignited has died down, but not enough. Still, Danael supposes it was better than doing nothing.

Or searching for a best friend that so clearly did not want to be found.

Six hours and copious amounts of shot down ideas later and the bottom of Danael's current notebook page looks something like this –

Kill Michael.

Kill Lucifer.

Enlist help from other celestials?

Reverse the apocalypse? How? Can Nickie do this? Revisit idea.

<u>*Alert the Heavenly Host of Michael's betrayal.*</u>

They were, obviously, not going to be able to play off Heaven's sympathy to stop the apocalypse. Their spite, however? Might form the outline of a workable plan.

Heaven did not take kindly to betrayals, regardless of the angel's status. The real challenge would be finding another angel both willing to entertain the idea of Michael's plotting and who was unafraid of the wrath that would follow such an accusation.

The choices are slim.

"Are there any other angels that hate Michael more than they fear him?" Danael asks. They are both back in the living room, separated by a plate of half-eaten chips and dip on the coffee table.

"How should I know?" Amy replies, reaching forward to grab another. "I've been gone as long as you have." He barely gets the chip into his mouth before a sickening look crosses the demon's face and he spits all of it out into a nearby wastebasket.

Danael is about to make a smart remark about his previous alcohol intake when a bitter feeling begins to rise up her own throat. Amy vanishes the remaining food from the table as Danael begins to gag.

Once the nauseating smell of salt and salsa leave the air, Danael fumbles for the remote to the TV. It turns on and the female news anchor looks similarly green-faced.

"For the past seven hours, reports have been coming in of country-wide, and what I have now been informed as world-wide, aversion to food. Sources are sparse, however, allegations are being made of a fast-acting airborne neuroendocrine chemical agent that was leaked from a Russian military base —"

Danael turns off the TV.

"The Black Horse," Amy says, needlessly. "Three down. One to go."

"Celestials shouldn't be affected by the Horseman, should they?" Danael wonders. "What does that even suggest?"

"Probably that we're running out of time." Amy sighs, weakly raising himself from the recliner opposite her. "I'd give it another twenty-four hours, at most, until the real fun begins. So! Let's go." He begins to pace. "Shitty ideas speed round edition."

"An angel of higher status might be our best bet for challenging Michael," Danael tries. "Perhaps another archangel?"

Amy seems to consider this. "Gabriel would be easy enough to summon, knowing his role in the apocalypse."

"And Gabriel never did care for Michael much."

Amy stops, clasping his hands together. "Great! Let's do it."

What? "Just like that?"

"Did you have any better ideas?"

Danael frowns, saying nothing. Amy leaves to go gather the needed ritual supplies while Danael is left staring out onto the now empty coffee table.

She *should* be looking for Nickie. Doing something – anything – besides pulling some inane idea out of her ass.

Though what was the alternative? Sit here and wait for the inevitable destruction of humanity? Even they would be the lucky ones; having quick, mortal deaths. Dying was easy. It was living that would be the hard part.

It always was.

Eventually, she lets out a defeated sigh as she stands. "Guess I'll be making the protection circle."

Danael steps away from the Enochian scripted blood circle which was now surrounded by lit candles. The energy of the awaiting magick is a quiet hum under her skin. Danael wonders if she will ever feel the white, hot electricity it used to be. Wonders more, if she wants to.

"We ready to rock and roll?"

Danael turns around to face Amy. She envies the optimism she sees.

"Are you sure the incantation will even work for you?" Danael had never heard of angelic magick being successfully executed by a demon.

"Only one way to find out," Amy says.

Wordlessly, Danael hands him a ripped-out piece of notebook paper. Amy takes the paper and on his next breath is reciting the incantation.

"OL UMD MIRC GABRIEL. OLPRIT C YAWEH. NIIS ASPT OL."

Danael stares, wide-eyed, at the demon's flawless pronunciation. Her eyes begin to sting, despite her best efforts. It had been *so long* since she's heard the language pass from another celestial's lips. It feels like a warm cocoon of light against her energy.

It feels like home, as much as Danael wishes it didn't.

The candles surrounding the sigil flare – up, up, up to the ceiling. Then down in one fell swoop. Danael's brief euphoria joins it.

Gabriel is livid.

"What is the meaning of this?" The archangel seethes, forcing his own energy against the magickal barrier, to no avail. He looks older than Danael remembers him. The once bright blue eyes are a dull shade of grey. Tension surrounds them and seems to encompass his entire body, forcing its way out to the living room around them.

Danael feels frozen. All rehearsed words have turned to ash in her mouth. Amy looks at her expectantly.

"Do you remember me?" They aren't the words Danael wants to say. What words does Danael want to say?

Gabriel's expression turns incredulous, then enraged. "You have some nerve, human! Release me at once or –"

"I am *not* human." Danael rumbles. The candles flare and Gabriel's eyes trail suspiciously over her energetic signature. Danael takes a deep breath, "My name is Danael. I am Hanael's twin flame. I was under Michael's command until...an arrangement was made for me to live on Earth. He erased the Host's memories of me."

Gabriel's eyebrows furrow briefly before tightening. "A convenient story, though unfortunately for you, not a very convincing one."

"Then tell me how I can improve it," Danael says. "Ask me something only another angel would know."

Gabriel's eyes trail her form again before he laments, "Fine. Why did my Creator flood the Earth?"

"Our Creator," Danael corrects. "Flooded the Earth because of Pagan worshipers. The other Gods were a threat to Him and so He eliminated their only source of power – their worshipers."

"*He* could have told you that," Gabriel says, eyes now trained on Amy. The demon only narrows his in return.

"Then ask me something Amy wouldn't know," Danael tries, pulling at strings. "Ask me something only an angel under Michael's command would know."

Gabriel stares at her again. His eyes are still steeled, but there is something else creeping into their corners. Debate. Confusion.

Unease.

"How did Michael react when he learned of Lucifer's rebellion?" Danael flinches before the words are entirely out of his mouth. It is not an easy memory to forget, though one everyone involved wishes they could.

"Betrayed," Danael starts slowly. Her throat feels like sandpaper. "In disbelief. You could see...the snap happening in Michael's psyche, his energy. You could feel Heaven's own energy twist and snarl around him. It was –" Danael shakes her head, before raising it again to meet Gabriel's gaze. "You can understand, I'm sure, that words will never do the memory justice."

Gabriel is silent. It's not a comfortable silence; both stuck back in the nightmare that was Michael's wrath. Had any of them ever really escaped it?

"Let's say you are telling the truth," Gabriel says. "Why tell me about it? What, exactly, were you trying to accomplish by summoning and *binding* me?"

Danael blinks, eyes trailing down to the blood-drawn sigil around him. She approaches it, despite Amy's vocal protests. With one draw of her foot, the line of blood is smeared, effectively breaking the circle.

Gabriel steps out of the circle to face her, their bodies only inches apart. Danael can taste the divinity on him.

"Michael is working with Lucifer," Danael says, braver than she feels. "Has been for some time. They started the apocalypse, among who knows what else."

Gabriel looks interested but unsurprised. He gives her a final once over before taking a step back and adjusting his overcoat.

"I'll look into it," he says.

In the next blink, he is gone. And had Danael braved the encounter alone, might be left wondering if it took place at all.

She still wonders.

"Well," Amy offers. "That went better than expected."

Had it? "We should still make preparations," Danael says. "In case this doesn't pan out."

"Way ahead of you," Amy says. With a snap of his fingers, a cardboard box appears on the coffee table, filled to the brim with occult paraphernalia. "Let's get to apocalypse-proofing this bad boy."

Danael chances a glance around Hanael's rental home. The protection sigils she created when she and Nickie first arrived are still fully functional. Though Amy is right – they'd be needing more.

A lot more.

Danael nods once, mentally preparing herself for war.

CHAPTER 27

NICKIE

Nickie's fingers hover over the piano keys. It's the first time she's sat at the instrument since arriving here eight days ago.

Eight days of precarious plotting with Hanael and Malphas. Eight days of familiarizing herself with Hell, Hell's power, and the father that wasn't.

Nickie wears the mask of dutiful heir almost too well. It's beginning to feel like it's getting glued to her face.

Her fingers clench and unclench several times before settling on "Lux Aeterna".

Soft music begins filling the air. Nickie closes her eyes, breathes in, and can almost taste the notes. If she tries really hard, she can imagine she's somewhere else. Somewhere that isn't Hell.

Does she want to be, though?

"That's beautiful."

Nickie's eyes snap open and over to an approaching Malphas, though she doesn't stop playing.

"I didn't know you could play."

Now, she stops playing.

"Lily taught me," Nickie says before forcefully shutting the lid. "You remember her, right? The innocent woman you killed?"

"Hardly innocent," Malphas says with a cock of his head. "And hardly relevant."

She could kill him. The thought feels different from the other times she's had it. *She could kill him and her own father would cheer her on.*

"Listen," Malphas says, taking a seat beside her on the bench. "We all make choices. And as a celestial, if those choices aren't in our own self-interest, well...what exactly is the point of them?"

He's so close – she could plunge her hand right into his chest. What kind of sound would that make?

"And what *exactly* is in your self-interest, Malphas? Killing off or driving insane everyone in my life that isn't you?"

He falters, only slightly, before smiling crookedly. The response, however, dies with the entrance of a familiar voice, "Am I interrupting something?"

"Nope," Nickie says before standing to face a disheveled Hanael, which she frowns at. The angel seemed to be looking worse with each passing day. They'd need to make their move soon if they wanted the remainder of Hanael's separation ritual to work.

"Any day now Lucifer will be instructing you to go back to Earth to usher in Death," Hanael begins, right to business as usual. "That's when we should make our move."

"When I'm on Earth?" Nickie asks. "No way. I want to be there."

"That would be unwise," Hanael says. Her eyes shift to Malphas briefly before she continues, "The spell will be directed at Morningstar energy. *Your* energy. We have no way of knowing if the Void would latch onto you as well."

Nickie grits her teeth. It wasn't ideal, but well – what was anymore? "Fine. Whatever. Just don't screw this up, alright?"

Hanael's lip twists upward in a polite feigning 'fuck you too, Nickie' before she exits back to Lucifer's elevator.

"Don't be too disappointed," Malphas says, standing to join her. "There's still plenty fun to be had. Come on –" He stalks toward the re-materialized elevator with a wave of his hand. "We still need to select a location for the deed to be done."

"Yeah, wow," Nickie says. "*So* much fun."

"And," he says with an inclination. "We might run into a few other demons for you to terrorize."

"And I can't just terrorize you, because..."

"Are you coming or not?"

Well, it's not like she had anything better to do, is it? Hell, she wouldn't even get to be present for the murder of her own father.

Nickie curses under her breath before following Malphas into the elevator.

The unrest among the demons had settled down exponentially since Nickie made her appearance. They make way for her now – parting like the Red Sea – and Nickie smiles to herself.

There's an annoying little voice in her head that warns her about her pride with that, but luckily that little voice had also been getting easier and easier to push down.

"Clear out!" Nickie booms out to the red, misty abyss of

the Ninth Level. Within seconds, a dozen or so armor-clad demons are filing out. Though two remain at the entrance.

Nickie steels her expression, approaching them.

"Are you deaf?" Nickie says. "What did I just say?"

"My Queen, I apologize, but we have direct orders from Lucifer to remain stationed here." The shorter of the two rambles off, as if hoping that talking faster might deter her wrath.

Nickie's finger twitches to the sword at her side – the fun, new shiny one Lucifer had given her – before Malphas' grip on her shoulder pulls her several feet back. She's about to redirect the sword into one of his fingers when her gaze follows his to a side hallway.

"Nicole!" Lucifer says, as cheerily as he always does when he greets her. "How nice to see you're familiarizing yourself with the Levels." His gaze hardens on Malphas and the demon drops his hand from her as if burned.

"Your demons are disobeying me," Nickie says before realizing her fuck up. Malphas' gaze trails to hers in poorly contained fury.

Maybe that annoying little voice served a purpose after all.

"Disobedience?" Lucifer asks, turning to the two demons in question. "How so?"

"Sir," The taller demon says, far more composed than the original. "The Queen asked us to leave our post, which would have been in direct violation of your previous orders. Shall we not be under the impression that you still hold the final orders?"

Nickie should have killed them both when she had the chance.

"Watch your tone, soldier," Lucifer says before turning back to Nickie and Malphas. "The security personnel is for your protection, Nicole." His eyes trail back to Malphas and Nickie can feel her heart begin to stutter in her chest. "A fact that Malphas would have been well aware of."

Fuck. Fuck. *Fuck*.

"Nicole wanted to practice her powers in privacy –" Malphas tries before being cut off.

"In privacy with *you*, you mean."

Think, think, think! How can she salvage this? Distraction? Diversion?

"Alright, I confess," Nickie begins slowly. "Malphas and I came here to have sex."

Because hey, when in doubt, kick your ex under the bus, right?

Malphas' eyes go bug-eyed just before Lucifer's hand wraps around his throat, further pushing them out of his skull. All while the two demons remain as unaffected as the Queen's Guards.

Then, there are sirens.

At first, Nickie startles, thinking it some kind of hellish lie detector. Thankfully, she is proven wrong when Lucifer shoves Malphas to the side and ushers Nickie forward.

"There is an intruder on the Eighth Level. Your next lesson in leadership awaits, my dear."

Nickie scurries forward while Lucifer gives Malphas one final glance that said this conversation was far from over. Which was fine. Malphas could suck it up. Saving face was all that mattered right now.

"Chin up, back straight – good. Remember what I told you."

"Yeah, yeah. Respect begins with confidence. Fill the room with your presence. I remember." Really. Where was this fatherly life advice when she was getting tormented in middle school?

Or by her mother.

Nickie wonders, not for the first time, if she's down here. Wonders if her screams are filling some nameless room that Nickie hasn't bothered to look for.

Nickie wonders if she cares.

Lucifer and Nickie continue along the upper-level route of the Eighth Level in silence. It's damp, dark, but nothing they couldn't easily navigate.

Then there's an echo of a *'splash'*– footsteps – and a hard shove against her back pushing her forward.

"Go," Lucifer says. "Approach the intruder. I will be right behind you."

Nickie swallows, her right hand gripping the handle of her sword at her holster. This was fine. She could do this, right? She could totally do this.

Nickie shuffles forward about ten feet before the dark environment gives way to a male form. Short, curly hair, and – what the hell was he wearing? Something from the eighteenth century?

"You are an intruder in my realm," Nickie says, words suddenly coming easy to her. "State your name and purpose of visit."

"Gabriel," he says as he looks her up and down. "I have come to confirm an accusation made against Michael."

"And what accusation would that be?" Lucifer says before she can, stepping to stand beside her. Nickie stiffens at the rage she feels pouring off his energy. "Not that Michael is any stranger to betrayal."

The air becomes uncomfortably thick, and Nickie can faintly taste metallic. She unsheathes her sword.

"That Michael has conspired with you on a number of

counts. Most notably to start the apocalypse for your own gain."

'Kill him.' Lucifer's voice suddenly broadcasts in her mind. Firm, non-negotiable. Nickie nearly drops her sword. *'The sword I gifted you will easily kill an archangel. Do it now.'*

It is as if she is playing 'Lux Aeterna' again. The notes are soft at first, quiet, and then they begin to blare as Lucifer manipulates the surrounding energy to restrain Gabriel.

Nickie is seeing and not seeing what comes next. The footsteps that march forward are hers and not hers. And the sword she lifts to Gabriel's throat feels heavier than physically possible.

Still, she slices the weapon cleanly across as easily as the 'C' note on her keyboard. Blood follows. A crescendo reaches.

Nickie steps back, perfectly still. All she sees is crimson.

On Gabriel, her fingers, her blade. Lucifer hands her a handkerchief and Nickie mechanically wipes the blood off before sheathing the weapon back to her side.

"I'm so proud of you," Lucifer says. The words sound like they're said under water.

Lucifer snaps his fingers and the body turns to grey, ashen dust. As if it never happened. Did it happen?

Nickie internally searches, desperately, for that annoying voice of reason. *Any* voice of reason. Anything telling her how wrong and horrible and guilty she should feel. But all she finds is silence.

Had her head ever been this quiet before?

"Come. Let us return. I have a spectacular dinner planned for us."

Nickie nods and follows him wordlessly back the way they came.

~

If Malphas senses something has happened, he doesn't mention it. Then again, Nickie doesn't give him much chance with how quickly she retreats to her bedroom to shower.

The water is practically scalding as Nickie slips under it. The blood washes off her hands almost too easily – the water running clear again in moments. An insignificant blip in her existence.

Maybe she *was* over-thinking this.

What does she have to feel guilty for, anyway? It had to be done. She couldn't risk breaking her cover with Lucifer. The *world* couldn't risk her breaking her cover with Lucifer.

Nickie thinks back to a conversation she, Malphas, and Dani had in their first year of community college.

They all decided to take Intro to Philosophy. Thought it might lead to some interesting debates. They weren't disappointed.

"Why can't there be a third choice?" Dani asks Nickie and Malphas in the dining hall, staring with pinched eyes down at their trolley problem worksheet. "Isn't the whole point of this class to 'think-outside-the-box'?"

"No," Nickie says. "The point is to learn how to make tough decisions. It's a numbers game." She shrugs. "The trolley's gotta go somewhere."

Dani had frowned. Malphas had grinned. And Nickie feels as unaffected then as she does now.

Stepping out of the shower, Nickie stares at the mirror, which was still obscured by steam. She makes a move to clear it before abruptly dropping her hand and exiting the bathroom toward her wardrobe.

Nickie thinks of Lucifer's mention of dinner and finally

decides to put on one of those 'leader-appropriate' suits he kept egging her on about.

It ends up fitting her better than expected.

Nickie flares the white collar before throwing on a pair of matching dress shoes and making her way back downstairs.

Nickie must have been getting ready longer than she thought, as when she arrives at the dining table, the plates and food have already been set out.

It's a large yet surprisingly simple meal. Bean stew, steaming lamb, fresh bread, and wine all ordain the long, circular table. Of which, Lucifer, Hanael, and Malphas are already seated at.

Nickie swallows. It's the first time since they've started plotting that they've all been together like this.

"You look exquisite, my dear," Lucifer says, pulling out the seat next to his. Nickie takes it, already pouring herself a generous serving of wine. God knows she'll be needing it.

"What's the occasion?" Malphas asks, bored. "I haven't been invited to a dinner like this since you demoted me to – what was my position again? Secondary security personnel?"

Nickie scoffs at the bitterness in his voice. Lucifer simply smiles at it before replying, "It has come to my attention that you have a...*unique* relationship with my daughter." Oh, god. "Of which, I would like to know the nature of. And how you plan to serve her." Oh, *god*.

Hanael sips her wine, gaze trailing between Nickie and Malphas. With a mentally absent look that Nickie doubts she has to fake at the moment.

Meanwhile, Malphas' own expression turns serious. And Nickie, frustratingly, can't tell if it's bullshit serious or seriously serious.

"I plan to serve her in every capacity I can," Malphas says. "I know what she is capable of. I want to see it. I want to see her on a throne, dripping in the blood of our enemies. I want to see her by my side, glorious in her destruction." He looks at her and Nickie struggles not to avert her gaze. "It's all I ever wanted for her."

Be careful what you wish for.

"Very well," Lucifer says, mildly pleased. "Perhaps Nicole will take this information under consideration when she is choosing her second."

Perhaps not.

"Now, back to the original purpose of our get together – I would like to both express my utmost joy in my daughter's current transition as well as announce we are reaching the finish line of Stage One. Nicole –" He turns to her and a very depraved part of Nickie wishes she could hold on to that look of fatherly pride. "Are you ready to usher in the Final Horseman?"

Nickie raises her wine glass. She's surprised her hand isn't shaking. *"Always ready for a little death."*

CHAPTER 28
HANAEL

Hanael watches the interaction over the dinner table with only mild interest as she sips her wine.

She had been wondering why Malphas hadn't approached her yet regarding her bluff to Nickie about needing to be absent from Hell during the ritual. Now, she supposes she has her answer.

Malphas seems to care about Nickie in the same way he had cared about Asbeel. With open eyes and an obsessed, twisted, fascination.

The demon no doubt saw what Hanael saw developing in Nickie. Except instead of fearing it, he embraced it. With far more eroticism that Hanael cared to hear about while eating.

In any case, Malphas wasn't stupid. He knew as well as Hanael what a liability Nickie might be to their plan. Lucifer had gotten his claws into her as easily as anything else. And if there was even the slightest chance Nickie might show sympathy for him...

Well, it wasn't a chance they could afford to take.

Malphas raises his wine class to clink with Nickie's but he's looking at Hanael. A smile curls at the corner of his lips as if he knows exactly what she's thinking.

Hanael raises her own glass, expression void.

She wonders how many of them Death won't take.

CHAPTER 29

DANAEL

anael stares grimly at the numerous protection wards and glamour sigils carved into the pale, blue walls of Hanael's living room. She and Amy had only been at apocalypse-proofing two hours before realizing they had both exhausted what little knowledge they had on the subject.

Danael never had been one for preemptive magick; that was always more Hanael's forte. And Amy, well – Amy was about as woefully out of practice in Heavenly warfare as Danael was.

The light of the full moon begins to peek through the bay window as Amy and Danael take a seat back on the recliner and loveseat. The night is eerily still. Neither can relax in their seat.

"How much do you think the wards will actually hold off?" Amy asks.

Danael doesn't answer. She wonders how Hanael and Nickie are faring. Maybe she should try and go searching for Nickie again? Or see if there was any way to contact Hanael –

A loud rattling from the front door jostles Danael's thoughts.

"Guess that answers that question," Amy says with a grimace as they both stand to face whatever threat waited on the other side.

Danael draws her sword and Amy positions himself in a guard stance, infernal magick dancing at his fingertips. There's a *'crash'*! The door swings open and Nickie stumbles in with a curse as she attempts to get the door back on its hinges.

"You couldn't *knock*?" Amy says, trying for exasperation but only managing to sound as relieved as Danael felt.

"Who knocks during the apocalypse?" Nickie bites back, giving up on the door. With a snap of her fingers, it's repaired. Just as quickly, Danael is in front of her.

Nickie looks...okay. Better than that. Though the black pantsuit does throw Danael for a momentary loop. As does the crushing hug Nickie initiates.

"I'm still pissed at you," Nickie murmurs in her ear. "But I understand why you did it." Her eyes meet Danael's and they are shining with something Danael doesn't recognize. "Needs must when the devil drives and all that."

Danael doesn't have a chance to ask what that means in this context before Amy takes her place. The hug they share is so intimate that Danael feels tempted to turn away to give them some privacy.

After parting, they share a look and Nickie turns back to Danael to say nervously, "So! Looks like I have a bit to fill you in on."

～

Danael wants to be mad, but also knows there's no place for it right now. Hanael was safe. Nickie was safe. Plotting with Malphas aside, that was all that mattered.

Still, there's something Nickie's not telling her. Not telling Amy either, by the crinkle the demon gets in his brow whenever Nickie sidesteps a question. But Danael supposes any progress at this point was better than nothing.

"Your protection wards suck," Nickie says, once the conversation has concluded. She eyes the walls with scrutiny before raising both hands, turning them over, and muttering an unfamiliar string of words under her breath. Danael's eyes grow wide as she sees her previous sigils twist and reform – cemented into the wood with a faint, red glow.

They aren't ones Danael is familiar with, but the power is pouring off them. Danael smiles, proudly, before having it fall at the look on Amy's face.

"Guess Lucifer hasn't wasted any time with his lessons," he says.

Nickie turns around, glaring. "And what? You'd rather we be defenseless?"

"I'd rather you quit lying!" Amy spits back. "I can *feel* you're withholding information, Nickie. What the hell aren't you telling us?"

"Oh, you can *feel it*, can you?"

"Enough!" Danael shouts, turning to Nickie with a frown. "Nickie, I'm so thankful and happy that you're here, but if there's something you're not telling us –"

Nickie's expression drops. She opens her mouth before promptly closing it. "Hold that thought," she says, putting up a hand. "We've got company."

No sooner do the words leave her mouth does a sudden

wave of energy shake the house, knocking all three celestials to the ground.

"It was those damn wards!" Amy says, dragging himself and Nickie to their feet. "It might as well have been an energetic beacon. And you didn't even try to mask it!"

For the first time since arriving, Nickie looks afraid. "Lucifer didn't teach me that."

"Of course not!"

"Guys –" Danael tries, feeling her energy coiling at the violent outbursts that knock against the wards, continuing to jostle the house. "Let's put it on ice, yeah? Nickie, do you know who's doing this?"

"Michael's people, probably," Nickie says, shaking herself back to a steeled expression. "He and Lucifer are on the outs. And whoever ushers in the last Horseman –"

"Sets the stage for the of the rest of the apocalypse," Amy finishes. "It really is the Rebellion Part Two." He forces a grin. "I kinda did call that one."

Memories of bloodshed and despair tickle at the back of Danael's mind. "Stand your ground, but stay on defense." Her sword tightens in her grip. "We don't know how many there are."

"Fuck that," Nickie says. "Let em' come. They'll be sorry."

"On that note," Amy says. "It was nice knowing you both. Or maybe not, considering our current –"

Another *'crash'*! Danael ducks as the entire wooden door flies past her head and into the wall behind them. There is a blur of color in her peripheral before pain explodes against the side of her head, knocking her to her knees.

Her ears are ringing and her vision is blurred. Somehow her sword still makes it into the foot in front of her.

The angelic intruder curses and the surprise is enough

for Danael to capitalize on. She's back on her feet – elbow to his back, knee to his stomach – and a shot of infernal energy from beside her sends the other angel flying into a breakfast bar chair, shattering it.

Her vision starts to clear. Nickie is beside her, gleeful. And Amy is beside Nickie, the opposite of that.

Danael isn't sure what she would label her own current emotional state.

There are four angels that Danael can see, including the one that is already making his way back to his feet. More probably coming. The four stand now, angelic energy coiling at the edge of their auras.

What were they waiting for?

"We're only here for the Nephilim," the angel she had attacked says. "Stand aside and we won't have any problems."

"Sure thing," Nickie says, tone dark.

Danael's stomach drops as her best friend waves a hand and she finds herself frozen in place. Her eyes dart to the side to find Amy in a similar hold.

"Come at me, bro!" Nickie shouts, holding her hands out in invitation.

There is a paralyzing moment where Danael thinks it will be the last words she hears from her best friend. Though that fear shifts when she sees the four angels try. Lead settles into her stomach as Nickie's sword expertly redecorates Hanael's living room to a shining shade of red.

Danael wants to feel some kind of way at the look of satisfaction on Nickie's face, but pushes it down. This was war and Nickie was acting accordingly. That's all it was. That's all survival ever was.

And really, what did she *think* was going to happen when she forced that blood down Nickie's throat?

He who wishes to fight must first count the cost.

The blur of movement calms and Nickie is standing front and center, four bodies slumped at her feet. Her gaze rises to meet Danael's, ready to release the hold, when another explosion of energy sends her best friend flying into the bookcase behind her.

The hold breaks and Danael stumbles forward as another angel materializes in front of her. Dark hair and grey, furious eyes.

He sends another shot of energy at Nickie before Danael can stop him. The bookcase topples over and Amy rushes to Nickie's side while Danael lunges for the assailant.

Her sword is drawn, ready to strike, before a high-pitched ringing cuts violently into her eardrums. Danael gasps, stumbles, and feels a pain explode in her spine.

Numbness quickly replaces it. Spreading from her back to her legs to her feet. Danael collapses.

It was killing a blow, she realizes fuzzily. She searches for some ounce of remaining angelic power to heal herself, finding none.

Iron overcomes her tastebuds. Danael feels like she needs to cough, but her body won't make the movement.

There's screaming coming from...somewhere. Another blast of energy. Nickie's yell of *'Get your hands off him!'* A harsher blast of energy.

Darkness dances at the corner of Danael's vision.

Nickie's face soon joins it.

There are hands on her then – Nickie's? The numbness vanishes. A white, hot pain takes its place. *Power* takes its place.

Her power.

The return only takes a second, but it feels like an eternity. An eternity of unlived lives, unspoken words, and unused power. A tornado settling into a familiar gust in her veins.

Danael coughs violently before jerking herself to a sitting position. "Nickie, how did you –"

She doubles back over. Angelic alarms are blaring in her mind, tearing at her energy – tearing at something Danael hadn't realized could be torn.

Her stomach swoops, dread clawing at her veins. As if she is standing at the precipice of a cliff, unsure of how far she is from the ledge. Or how high the drop.

He who wishes to fight must first count the cost.

Oh, Hanael. What did you do?

Danael's wings retract instinctually. Thoughts blur into emotions which blur into energy which materialize a portal to Hell. Somewhere in the distance, Nickie's protested shouting filters through the hazy atmosphere.

Danael pays no mind to it. No. Any qualms Danael might have had with breaking Hanael's deal are off the table. If Hanael's life wasn't already in immediate danger, it would be soon. And Danael would be damned if she lost any part of Hanael again.

The cost couldn't be this.

CHAPTER 30
NICKIE

"Shit," Nickie curses, eyes wide as the portal disappears in front of her, taking Dani along with it. "Shit!"

This was bad. This was so, *so* bad.

"You mind sharing with the class, now?" Amy grunts, swiping a layer of debris off his shoulder.

Nickie takes a deep breath. She isn't sure how to explain Hanael's plan without sounding like the bad guy. Isn't sure how long she has to do so before they're ambushed again.

Still, Nickie does her best. Though by the look on Amy's face, it isn't good enough.

"Then we go back to Hell," Amy says, aiming for neutrality and failing. "Stop Danael from interfering –"

"We *can't*," Nickie says. "The stupid Void thing will kill me, and my stupid dad will kill you. No bueno. We'll just have to stay here and hold down the fort."

Amy sighs, blinks, and finally meets Nickie's gaze. Though she sees none of the anger or disappointment or betrayal she was expecting. No. It's more like –

"You have no idea how scared I am for you, Nickie. No idea." He laughs raggedly and Nickie flinches. "The world is ending and I'm stuck simping over the women who's supposed to reign over its ruins."

Don't do it, don't do it, don't it –

Nickie kisses him.

It...wasn't what Nickie is expecting. What *was* Nickie expecting? Lust? Indifference? Regret?

It's none of those things. It's nothing like Nickie has ever experienced while kissing someone. It feels like... acceptance. Just...acceptance.

It feels like more than Nickie deserves.

"Mhhm," Amy breathes into her neck before laying another kiss over the surface. Nickie wonders if he can taste the blood on her skin. "And actions like this don't help my cause."

Hers either.

Nickie breaks the embrace, forcing a smirk. "And who says I want to help your cause?"

Amy laughs, less raggedly this time, but still pulling at Nickie's insides.

There's another rumble of energy that shakes the house. It knocks them both apart.

Amy looks at Nickie and Nickie looks at Amy.

Nickie *hopes* Dani won't fuck up their only chance at stopping at least her father. Their whole divide and conquer strategy would only work if the 'dividing' part took. The rest would be a game of Russian roulette with Michael's grief.

Thing is, though – hope had never gotten Nickie particularly far in the past. Which she's been thinking about; been thinking about since Hanael first presented their plan. It was a long shot and Nickie had never found much comfort in long shots.

She takes a deep breath, swallows, lets her eyes wander

to her blood-stained fingers.

If it comes down to it – and god, Nickie hopes it doesn't, as her eyes raise to meet Amy's – but if it comes down it, Nickie is choosing the one option that had always been the hardest for her. The option she had repeatedly skirted around and more recently, found forced upon her, despite her best efforts.

Nickie is choosing survival.

Nickie is choosing herself.

And maybe, if she's lucky, a fraction of humanity might be spared at her behest.

Another group of angels materialize in the living room. Amy's hand is in hers, squeezing once. They both get to work.

CHAPTER 31
HANAEL/DANAEL

I t's not ideal timing, when Hanael does decide to make her move.

News has been received of Michael's current brigade against Nickie, to which Lucifer promptly forms a retaliation for. The chosen soldiers take their orders and scamper off, while Lucifer instructs Hanael to join him in the Ninth Level.

This is where Hanael currently found herself, as Lucifer irately syphons magick from the bright, red walls while the two usual guards observe in stoic indifference.

The guards might be a problem.

"Nicole will be fine." Hanael wonders who Lucifer is trying to convince. "I am, however, already embarrassed on Michael's behalf. Wouldn't you agree, Hanael?"

Hanael struggles to not raise an eyebrow. Lucifer's voice is manic and his mannerisms are unkept; failing to reprocess the majority of magick he just syphoned into his own energy.

"Of course," Hanael says. "I am certain Michael's

brigade has already taken a heavy hit. Nickie is not the type to leave survivors."

A sliver of tension drops from Lucifer's shoulders as his hands continue to travel along the rocky exterior of the walls. Though it returns as a familiar male face rushes onto the scene.

"All hands on deck," Malphas says in a labored voice. "Michael's men are moving in quick and I've gotten word that he may have Death's Scythe in his possession."

An unreadable expression crosses Lucifer's face before he waves a hand in the direction of his guards.

"All three of you – go and join Unit Six. Hanael can remain Ninth Level guard for the time being."

Hanael's ears are ringing. Malphas gives her a wink before disappearing out of sight alongside the two guards. And just like that – Hanael's timing got a lot better.

Since Hanael first awakened from her torture, she has been mentally steeling herself for this moment. Or at least attempting to. Survival as a motivation could only get one so far, after all.

Hanael wonders what awaits her on the other side of this. What awaits all of them. Or if such a destination exists.

Perhaps it was in Samarra.

With a concentrated breath, Hanael begins gathering the dormant energy of the spell within herself. Lucifer, meanwhile, has gathered himself into what Hanael can only deem a constipated meditation.

She steps forward, one hand at the sheath of her sword, when Lucifer's eyes fly open.

"An intruder!" He shouts, eyes growing dark. "No doubt at Michael's behest."

Hanael feels it then, that familiar, albeit now weak, pull

of Danael's energy. Cool and crisp but sweet; like fresh rain over a field of lilies.

It hits Hanael then, that this is the last time she will feel that energy. Feel Danael. It's a devasting blow, and one she hadn't previously been able to afford to think about.

She still can't afford to think about it.

Hanael's hand is trembling as she pulls out her sword, incantation on the tip of her now numb tongue.

She did have an appointment to make, after all.

Danael's flight through Hell is more like a stumble, nausea gripping her at every turned corner.

Her connection to Hanael is weaker than it's ever been. A once strong rope that's been mercilessly sawed down to a barely tangible thread.

Danael gags as she touches down in the Ninth Level. She rights herself quickly, looks around, sees nothing. No demons, no Lucifer – only a familiar soft, red exterior glow and the hum of demonic energy. Danael wasn't fooled, though. If Hell was empty, she wouldn't be in this mess.

Posture stiff and coiled, Danael begins the trek down a winding hallway. Her feet *echo, echo, echo* against the granite. Hanael is not far off now, she knows. The grip on her sword tightens.

The energy shifts and Danael finds her feet stopping. She looks around, on guard, before the memory hits her.

The blood. On Hanael's dress, her sword, her hands. Devastation. Rage. Hopelessness. A begging cry to an uncaring God. *'Please help us –'*

Her knees weaken. The echo of residual energy is *strong* and it takes some real effort not to get lost in it entirely.

Danael's vision blurs for only a moment but it is apparently a moment too long.

A sharp pain pierces the back of Danael's shoulder. Her arm is twisted roughly behind her back, forcing her to the ground. The feeling of hard, cold granite meets her cheek as her blade *'clinks'* uselessly somewhere off in the distance.

Out of her peripheral, Danael can see Hanael. She stands only a few feet to Lucifer's right, stiff and emotionless.

Danael swallows. Was she already too late?

Danael swivels around to land a blow to Lucifer, but he catches it. Two loud *'cracks!'* later and Danael stifles a scream as her arm hangs limply at her side.

For a moment, Danael forgets herself. Forgets who she is and what led her to this exact place in time. It is in this moment that Danael is nothing more than a woman silently pleading with the love of her life to not be lost to her.

The love of her life who averts her gaze as Lucifer sinks his power like claws into her own.

Danael sobers but it's too late. God, it's *too late.*

How stupid is she? Danael had one chance, *one*, to get control of this situation and she didn't even think to use her power! The power she just got back! What was wrong with her?

"I tried to be reasonable," Lucifer says, releasing his hold on Danael's energy. She crumples to the ground. "I tried to make you understand." A kick; pain explodes in her lungs. "But you're just like Michael." He laughs and it is more unhinged than it was during his rebellion. Danael chokes, tasting iron, breath caught somewhere deep in her stomach.

Through her blurring vision, Danael can see Hanael.

Hanael, who is inching toward Lucifer with the kind of expression one wore when they were trying to convince themselves the horrible act they were about to commit was justified. It's an expression Danael has worn herself many times, in many different lives.

It's an expression that looks so utterly *wrong* on Hanael it makes Danael sick to her stomach.

"Look at you!" Lucifer continues. Danael tries, desperately, to summon any remaining magickal energy within herself. "Like Michael, so blinded by your heedless obsessions." Tries and fails. "Do you think you're so different?" That's all she ever did, wasn't it? God, she's failed everyone. Everything. "Look at where you are! Look at how your actions have served you!"

Her ears are ringing. Ringing and...something else. An incantation? Hanael –

There's a snap. A rip at the very core of her celestial energy. One Danael doesn't realize the true nature of until it is already over.

Snap.

That's all it is. Like a rubber band that had been stretched out one too many times. And it's too easy, too easy, too easy – to have just been broken like that. For Hanael to have been taken from her like that.

Danael gasps; vomit crawling up her throat. She pushes it down, forces her vision to clear. Her own body – her own *energy* – suddenly feels foreign. Empty. Sickening.

Much like Hanael's eyes look now, as she towers over Lucifer's contorting form.

Danael flies to her feet. There's a dark, formless energy engulfing the archangel. *Void energy*, a hysterical voice in the back of her mind corrects.

235

Danael sways on her feet. *Keep it together. Keep it together. Keep it –*

Hanael passes out and Danael is not there to catch her.

"Hanael?!" Danael screams, heart pounding in her ears as she darts to the angel's side. "No, no, no, no –"

She's not dead; can't be dead. Right? She's breathing. She's alive. But – god, there's *nothing*. Not a drop of angelic energy to be found.

This can't be happening.

Danael's glazed eyes trail back over to the coiling and snarling Void energy. She shudders, but it's not enough to move her to her feet.

Michael's incoming presence, however, is.

Adrenaline takes over and Danael quickly gets Hanael situated in her arms. Michael materializes in front of them and his expression makes Danael stumble back.

Devastation. Fury. No word will ever do it justice. Still, Danael utilizes his momentary stupor to fly them both out of sight.

Michael doesn't follow them but his energy does – the grief seeming to encompass all of Hell. The emotion intermingles with her own and Danael chokes back a sob.

Danael makes her way to the Twelfth Level in a blur, the weight of Hanael's body in her arms being her only respite. The portal back to Earth is in sight. A few more steps and –

The weight vanishes from Danael's arms.

No. Please no. *Please –*

Danael searches around wildly for any sign of Hanael. Nothing in sight, and there's no part of her that can energetically search for her other half anymore (*was* she still her other half?). It's a fool's errand to try.

Danael searches for Michael's presence instead. He's no

longer in Hell. *Right.* Focus on that. Hanael is somewhere and so long as that somewhere was not with Michael, she might stand a chance.

Squaring her shoulders, Danael forces her way through the portal. It takes the remainder of her frazzled energy to materialize back to Hanael's apartment, which means she has no recourse for what comes next.

The first thing Danael sees is blood. She recognizes it before anything else.

The next is Nickie's expression. First relieved at seeing Danael. Then contorted into shock, pain, denial – as Death's Scythe slices across her neck like butter.

Blood pools at the wound Nickie desperately grasps at. Someone screams. Devastation curls around the room like a vise.

There are no thoughts, just pain. Pain that tears into Danael's chest, bringing her to her knees. Pain that stings her eyes as she blinks away tears to see Michael standing over Nickie's slumped form.

Michael's grief is a mirror of her own. A smile crookedly stretches across his face before he disappears.

Gone. Gone. Gone. Oh, god. Nickie's really –

Focus on one thing. Just focus on one thing. One thing. Danael repeats the mantra like a prayer. The only one she has left. Until her breathing finally evens and Amy's sobs are the only audible noise in the otherwise silent house.

Focus on one thing.

Danael finds two.

The first is wrath. It flares in her veins; hot, coiled, promising war.

The next is Hanael.

Hanael. Where was Hanael?

CHAPTER 32
HANA

Once again, Hanael finds herself awakening to darkness. Not like the oblivion she had previously found herself in during Lucifer's sedation but –

Hanael blinks. Tries to draw on her celestial energy to light up her field of vision, but it doesn't take. Her chest tightens and the angel (Ex-angel? Fallen angel? Human?) is quickly reminded of recent events.

Thump, thump, thump, goes her heartbeat so hard in her chest it's painful. Had she had a heartbeat before now? Hanael forces her aching limbs to move and is horrified to find she can't.

Her hands shake violently as they search her surroundings. Dark. Wood. Underground? A box. A –

Hanael swallows. Her fingertips meet the area above her head to find an indentation of scratch marks. Somehow, even in the pitch-black surroundings, her vision manages to swim.

She's in a grave. She's in *Danael's grave.*

There's a scream in the back of her throat that Hanael

now realizes has been lodged there for a millennium. It escapes then, despite her best efforts to keep it down.

Hanael has never felt more alone.

Alone, desperate, exhausted, *scared* – there was no compartmentalizing her emotions now. They burrow into her like maggots feasting on a rotting corpse.

Which would be her own fate soon enough if she didn't act.

Hanael forces herself to breathe until it no longer catches in her throat. Forces herself to orient to her reality. She was not going to die down here. Not after everything she had endured.

If Danael had managed herself out of this situation, Hanael could too. Danael. She still needed to get back to Danael.

Hanael opens the coffin lid and swears she can hear Azrael laughing.

Hanael always thought she had a solid grasp on time. Time was measurable and constant. Time was predictable.

Only now that Hanael is forced to rely on her perception of time alone does she realize how fallible this knowledge is.

It must be less than two minutes, the time it takes her to break the surface of the graveyard. Has to be, lest she suffocate.

It feels like a lifetime.

It feels like more than Hanael will ever be able to manage.

When she collapses next to Danael's gravestone, eyes

straining against the afternoon sun, Hanael concludes, a little hysterically, *'it feels like humanity'.*

More pain than one ever thought their body could handle; that they ever thought possible. Barely mustering the willpower to push through this pain, with no certainty a worse fate didn't lie on the other side of it. All while your own thoughts torment you of what this worse fate may be.

There's a low groaning in the distance and Hanael's eyes fly back open. She's met by the sight of a hoard of staggering, dirt-covered people about twenty yards out.

Not people, Hanael realizes as she scrambles to her feet. *Corpses.*

Hanael gives a bitter glance to the hole she had risen from before making her own dirt-covered stagger towards the adjacent church. She has just gotten the back entrance closed and bolted before she can hear pounding on the other side. Though it's barely audible through the one in her own chest.

"Oh, my!"

Hanael startles, reaching for a sword she no longer has. The non-threatening visage of a middle-aged priest offers minimal reassurance.

"Oh, my," he repeats, slowly approaching, eyes blown wide at the door behind Hanael. "Are you alright? What's happened?"

"I'm –" Certainly not alright. Might never be alright again. "Alive. I'm not sure what's happening. There's...reanimated corpses –" She's stuttering. Can hardly breathe through her own words.

Where was Danael? What was happening?

Why does she feel so helpless?

Hanael slides down against the door, eyes stinging with tears she tries desperately to push down. She can't. And once the first sob racks her body, there's no stopping the rest.

"Miss? Miss!" Hanael feels a hand on her shoulder and flinches back, curling further into herself. She scrubs desperately at her eyes in an effort to stop the tears.

" – anything I can do to help? What is your name?"

Hanael blinks through the tears, dazed, before answering, "Hana."

In the event she survived tomorrow, Hana could no longer go by her angelic name. She needed to let go of at least that much if she had any hope of picking herself up off the floor.

"Hana. That's a beautiful name. Can I pray with you, Hana?"

Pray. Prayer. She could pray to Danael.

She *could have* prayed to Danael when she was six feet underground.

Hana swallows. Internally rambles off pleas and cries to Danael. All while grasping desperately at any remaining straws of her sanity.

The faint sound of wings reaches her senses only moments later. Hana raises her head to see the priest stumble back and Danael stumble towards her.

She's in Danael's arms and then...the pain is gone. The physical pain, at least. Hana looks down to find the graveyard grime gone, replaced with a clean, white sundress.

"You're okay. You're going to be okay." She's not. Neither of them is. And Hana's not sure she even appreciates the reassurance.

Hana doesn't have the time to examine that thought before they are both flown back to Hana's guesthouse. Hana's guesthouse that is covered in blood and corpses, one of which is Nickie's.

241

"Heaven," a male voice announces suddenly, manic. Hana turns to see Amy staggering towards Danael, covered in what Hana can only assume is Nickie's blood. "You can... go to Heaven now, right? There's still time. Quick trip. Grab her soul, pop it back in, and – "

"Amy," Danael says as Hana can feel the angel leading her over to a couch. "Nickie...Nickie's gone, alright? Please. Just stop."

"Fuck you!" Amy shouts back, eyes wild. "I'll storm the gates of Heaven *myself*. Seeing as you're too much of a coward to get anything done!"

Amy disappears in a puff of black smoke. Danael grimaces as she materializes Hana a glass of water, which the blonde eagerly downs.

A soft kiss is planted on Hana's forehead as Danael helps her to a lying position. She still feels so disorientated, mind spinning off axes she didn't know existed. Her body, though –

"Rest," Danael says and Hana does. It feels like the first sleep of Hana's existence.

Hana is woken to the sound of arguing.

"Then we open it! How hard can it be?"

"Nickie. Is. Dead, Amy! Azrael didn't come for her – her soul was *extinguished* by Death's Scythe."

Hana rises slowly from her position on the couch. Her vision clears to see Danael and Amy inches apart, each looking opposing degrees of devastated.

Amy laughs, cold and bitter. Hana looks closer and can see that his skin and clothes are charred.

"Nickie went to Hell for you," Amy says and Danael

stiffens. "Jumped in headfirst and you can't even entertain the –"

"Yes, and who was it that led her there?" Hana grimaces. "If you hadn't dragged her into this, she'd probably still be alive!"

Any remaining color drains from Amy's face. He laughs again tightly before shaking his head and disappearing for the final time. Hana lets out a breath.

The seat next to Hana dips as Danael joins her on the couch. They lock eyes. It's the first time that Hana has never been able to sense Danael's emotions. It's a hard feeling to wrap her mind around.

"I'm sorry," Hana says, despite knowing how little it's worth.

"There's no reason for you to be," Danael says, tucking a strand of hair behind Hana's ear. "You did what you had to. You're alive and Lucifer is dead. I'm going to take that for the win it is."

Hana stares at her. Memorizes her human features. Even without being able to see or sense anything else, Danael doesn't look any less beautiful.

"So," Hana says. "Some sort of zombie apocalypse, is it?"

"More or less," Danael replies. "And Hell is apparently locked from any ingoing or outgoing traffic. Both most likely Michael's doing."

"Where is he now?"

"I don't know."

Hana can feel her teeth clench as she sinks back into the couch. "And what are *we* going to do?"

"I don't know."

~

They bury Nickie's body in the dying rose garden out back. Death was everywhere now. The once beautiful and lovely woodland now a shriveling grey portraiture of what was to come.

Hana takes a deep breath and there is an aftertaste of ash.

"I should say something," Danael says. "That's what you're supposed to do, isn't it?"

"I wouldn't know," Hana says, staring off into the dying landscape. She wonders how much time they had before it was burning. "Though truthfully, I don't think anyone does."

"She was my best friend."

"I know."

"She didn't deserve this."

"I know."

Silence befalls them again. Hana shifts nervously under the weight of Danael's words. *Would Nickie still be alive if Danael hadn't come to her aid?*

Hana never thought any part of her would be relieved to be cut off from Danael's thoughts and yet –

"He's going to die for this," Danael says, shoulders squared and jaw set. "Even if I have to drag myself down with him."

Hana looks at her sadly. She wishes she could tell Danael that it wouldn't come to that; that Hana wouldn't *let it* come to that. Maybe in another life, another universe, she is able to.

Instead, Hana says, "I love you."

Danael's expression softens. She slips her hand into Hana's and replies, "I love you, too."

They stay there for another few minutes, hands intertwined. A sliver of light in a sea of death. It probably won't be enough light to save the world, probably never was. But as both women retreat back inside, Hana knows, it's enough for this moment.

And what are moments of happiness if not a world all their own?

ACT 3

CHAPTER 33
NICKIE

There's no white light at the end of the tunnel. Hell, there isn't even a tunnel. Then again, there's also no eternal damnation, so maybe Nickie should count her blessings.

There's really nothing here at all, wherever 'here' was. Nickie is only vaguely aware of her existence and the moments that led up to her death. Everything else is just blind, still, darkness.

She can't speak or see or hear. It should be terrifying. Nickie wonders why it's not terrifying.

Nickie wonders about a lot of things.

And boy, does she have a long time to wonder.

Days, weeks, months, years, millennia – Nickie isn't sure. Time doesn't exist here. Did it ever exist? What exists besides Nickie? Does Nickie exist?

Crack, crack, crack goes the pressure of the universe against her psyche. It's an easy egg to break.

What comes out should be terrifying. Nickie wonders why it's not terrifying.

What comes out is every horrible thought Nickie has

ever had. Every crippling emotion. Every trauma, fight, and regret. Everything comes out and Nickie is left to assign meaning to it until she realizes that...she can't.

They don't mean anything. They never did. Every single thing that has happened to Nickie was only a subjective moment in time. A label that she attached to earthly experiences to fit the mold of something she was only ever pretending to be.

A whiplash tears through Nickie's energy. It takes something with it, but Nickie isn't sure what. What's left in its place though – God, it's so much *better*.

It's orgasmic. Nickie screams out and realizes she has a voice. She screams and her body is on fire and her vision is white and –

She's eating an apple.

She's eating an apple from the same tree that Dani died under.

Except this time there's no tug of guilt or horror or mourning. There's no shadow lurking in the background. There's only Nickie and the best fucking apple she's ever eaten.

"Hello, my child."

Nickie gasps awake, hands flying to throat.

Skin. Skin. Closed skin. Scarred, but not bleeding. Not dying. Not dead.

Also not dressed.

Nickie's eyes stop their wild darting just long enough to survey her surroundings.

She's in Hell. The Ninth Level. In all its crimson, magickal glory. While her father's dead body lay only feet from her own. Which wouldn't be concerning except for what was *attached* to it.

Intermingled with the blood and lifeless, haunted expression on her father's face was some sort of...dark energy. No. Not dark. More like –

Oh, shit. Oh, fuck. Wasn't that the thing she was supposed to stay far, far away from?

Nickie swears the Void energy senses her thoughts. It rises and twists in a neat little line before slowly inching its way towards her.

Nickie is about to dart before noticing it stop. It twists again, snarls, and pushes forward. Still, there's like an invisible barrier stopping it from getting any further. The energy eventually gives up, melting into the ground directly below it.

"Okay? Cool. Bye!" Nickie gives a dramatic wave before wearily walking over the spot and approaching her father's body.

There's a lot Nickie would have liked to say to him, though she isn't sure exactly what. It's not like how it was with her mother. Nickie didn't have anything to grieve there aside from the fact she never really had a mother to begin with.

Nickie supposes it's more or less the same. With one added bonus.

"Thanks for the throne, dad," Nickie says. Her smile is all teeth as she pulls his sword from its sheath, snaps her fingers, and lights his body up in flames.

She walks away from the burning body, still naked, breathing in the scent of ash and flesh. The smile is right where she left it.

And, Nickie thinks, as she materializes a three-piece

suit and heels, heading towards the energetic pull of her demons, she'd be hard pressed to not let it stay there.

Malphas is trying to take over her throne because of course he is. Can't even take five minutes to grieve the loss of the Queen, huh? Tsk. Tsk.

All the demons are gathered in one of the meeting halls of the Third Level. Malphas has situated himself on a podium overlooking them and Nickie can feel her lip twitch.

"I realize this change will take some...adjustment. But we need to act quickly and action requires leadership," Malphas announces amongst a murmur of protest. Nickie approaches the podium, still energetically concealed from view.

"And what gives you the right to claim that title?" One demon shouts out. Focalor. Nickie suddenly finds herself aware of every demon's name, power, and rank.

"Exactly!" Another joins in. "You weren't even second in command! You were demoted!"

"Why can't we take a vote?"

"This isn't a democracy," Malphas spits. Nickie materializes a baseball bat. Baseball bats were always fun. "Nickie would have named me her second! Now if you can all stop —"

"Would I now," Nickie says, revealing herself. There's a cascade of gasps as Malphas spins around. He's met with the end of Nickie's bat.

The *'crack!'* of wood hitting skull silences the room. Nickie beams over a fading Malphas as she says, "Nice try... *princess.*"

Malphas loses consciousness and Nickie turns to face her demons.

"Now that that adorable display is over, let's get down to business, shall we? Valefor –" Nickie gives a wave. "Throw this traitor in prison where he belongs."

Valefor doesn't hesitate. He approaches the podium, gives a slight bow, and disappears in a plume of black smoke with Malphas in tow. Nickie continues, "I have been…indisposed for a period of time I can't recall." Like, at all. "Whoever has the most information regarding current statuses, step forward now. The rest of you disperse and we will reconvene shortly."

There's another round of brief murmuring before the army begins to make their exit. In their place remain a sultry, red-haired, female-presenting demon.

"Paimon," Nickie greets, tossing her now splintered bat to the side. "On top of things, as always." Her father always had nothing but good things to say about Paimon, particularly where loyalty was concerned.

Paimon smirks. "For you? Of course. Now, what do you wish to know?"

"How long was I indisposed?"

"I last saw you when you left for Earth to usher in the last Horseman. Roughly six hours ago."

Only…six hours? Nickie shakes her head. She needed to focus. Okay, six hours. Six hours Hell time equaled – wait.

"Has time in Hell returned to its normal operations?" Nickie asks.

"It had for a brief time." Paimon looks disturbed. "But now it seems all of Heaven, Hell and Earth are in sync."

Sounds promising. "I see I didn't miss much, then. Good. What else?"

"Lucifer has perished, which I'm sure you were already

aware of," Paimon says. "His cause of death is unknown but assumed to be the fault of Michael. Although some kind of...energy I'm unfamiliar with attached itself to his corpse –"

"I'm aware," Nickie says. "What else?"

Paimon blinks. "Michael disappeared from Hell shortly after Lucifer's demise. Presumably to take the apocalypse into his own hands. Though he...seems to have locked Hell from any ingoing or outgoing traffic –"

"*What?*"

"Apologies, my Queen. I certainly understand the inconvenience. Rest assured we have our best locksmith-savvy demons working towards a solution."

"They better be," Nickie says through clenched teeth. Breathe. Remember to breathe. Remember who has the control here. All the control. "Tell them they have twenty-four hours to figure it out. After that, every hour will be another body part I will *personally remove*."

Paimon smiles, then laughs. "I always did like you. Consider it done. Anything else?"

"No," Nickie says. "Once things have settled down, we'll have a proper coronation for myself. But for right now?" She smiles. "I have a date with a certain prisoner."

Malphas begins to stir from his place inside the cell. Nickie's been here a while; standing motionless a few feet from the bars. The current holding area is dark and damp and exactly how her father had left it.

Nickie thinks she might change that. Add a little more pizazz. Something that will actually make her demons afraid to be here.

An emotion Malphas would do well to be showing right about now.

"I've so missed our foreplay, princess." The grip on her father's sword tightens. "Is this the part where you punish me?"

A smile creeps up Nickie's face. She remains silent.

Malphas, up on his feet now, takes a step back as his eyes trail over her. Something sparkles in them.

"You look beautiful."

Nickie's smile widens. "I'm sure you will too with your spine ripped out through your throat."

"Harsh," Malphas says. "Kinky, but harsh. Now, why would you –"

"You tried to lead my demons," Nickie suddenly hisses out, face up to the bars. "Who the *fuck* do you think you are?"

Malphas staggers back, looking genuinely confused. The fucking nerve of the prick.

"I'm sorry?" Malphas says, raising his voice. "Hell was locked. How was I supposed to know you were still here? Even so, we had a deal. You get Earth, I get Hell. So, what's the issue?"

Nickie laughs. It bubbles up her throat like a champagne bottle being popped.

"The issue is," Nickie says as she materializes inside his cell, sword to his throat, "this is *my* fucking throne, Malphas. And if you were so much of an idiot to think I wouldn't claim it, well." She presses the weapon enough to encourage a trickle of crimson. "That sounds like a 'you' problem."

Malphas' eyes trail down to the weapon and back up to Nickie's eyes. There's that sparkle again. It's always been there, Nickie realizes. Something that only ever belonged to her. Something that she didn't entirely understand until now.

Malphas drops down to one knee. Nickie lowers her sword.

"No problem here," he says taking her hand, tracing his thumb over it. Nickie doesn't know why she doesn't pull away. "How can I prove my loyalty to you?"

Nickie sheaths her sword, takes a step back, examines him.

Malphas was a grade-A bullshitter. Always had been. It is, truthfully, why she had stayed with him for as long as she had. He was one of the few people she couldn't read and that interested her.

Though she's starting to see between the cracks now. What was it her father had told her about avid planning?

"How did you enjoy playing human?" Nickie asks. "When you pretended to be Dani's brother?"

Malphas quirks an eyebrow. "It was a necessary inconvenience. Why?"

"And there was no trace of your demonic power?" Nickie confirms. "Meaning, any energies directed at celestial forces wouldn't have an effect on you?

"Yes. That was the point. Again, *why*?"

Nickie takes two steps forward. Malphas is standing again, and now Nickie is almost against his chest. "It reasons then," She digs her fingernails into his shoulder. Malphas' eyes dilate. "That if you were to be human again, you might be able to bypass the current lockdown on Hell."

"It might," Malphas breathes out.

"Mhhm."

Malphas screams as she sinks her fingernails into his flesh. It's kind of like an energetic vacuum. Nickie turns on a switch and every ounce of Malphas' demonic essence is filed away in her own energy for later return.

Or not. Nickie supposes she'll have to see how useful he ends up being.

Malphas screams until Nickie releases her hold and he drops to the floor. He's unconscious on impact.

"Sleep tight. Don't let humanity bite." She smiles. "I know I won't."

With a wave of her hand, Nickie materializes to her father's quarters. Now her quarters.

Her quarters. Her army. Her throne. Her realm.

Yeah, Nickie was starting to like the sound of that.

CHAPTER 34
AMY

Amy doesn't remember his twin flame all that much. He knows that her name was Ariel, she was a skilled blacksmith, and attuned to the element of water. Friendly, cheerful, and then killed brutally by Michael when she failed to choose a side quickly enough in the Rebellion.

Amy had felt saddened by her death, of course, but nothing like what he feels right now.

Amy didn't know it was possible to feel like how he feels right now.

The forest around him is cold, quiet, and yet to be ravaged by the final Horseman. This is where Amy finally allows himself to collapse. And scream. And pound the ground until his fists bleed.

Fists which he won't be able to self-heal for a while what with his recent "storming Heaven" stunt.

Amy keeps pounding. At least, until a familiar voice stops him.

"You should have taken that deal, Amy."

Slowly, Amy raises his head to find Michael on the opposite side of the clearing. Amy's eye twitches.

"What?" Michael says, all teeth. "No heroic acts of revenge in the name of your beloved?"

Amy has never in his existence wanted so badly to bodily dismember someone. But Amy also isn't stupid. He had one shot to take his revenge and he'd make damn well sure it counted.

Amy makes his way to his feet and through gritted teeth asks, "And what would be the point of that?"

Michael smiles, clasping his hands together.

"I suppose you have a point. Shame. I did hope you would have a bit more fight in you for this conversation."

Awesome. What could it *possibly* be now?

"I thought it paramount to bring to your attention that those you've chosen to side with – Danael, Hanael – well." Michael's expression suddenly makes Amy nervous. "Perhaps you should start placing blame where it is due."

"Right," Amy says, fists balling and pushing down the turn in his stomach. "Because I don't remember Danael or Hanael being the ones to *slit Nickie's throat* –"

Keep your cool. Keep your cool. Keep your cool. *Sticks and stones can break your bones, but words can never –*

"No. But they **are** the reason you fell."

At first, Amy thinks he's heard him incorrectly. He must have...right?

"Excuse me?"

Michael smiles again, sharp as a knife. "In all things, nature demands a balance. Hanael didn't Fall when she was destined to. Therefore, *someone* had to take her place."

The cogs turn, turn, turn and finally *click*.

"It was nothing personal of course, on my end," Michael says. "I would have vastly preferred you to stay and fight alongside my army."

Amy laughs.

He laughs and he laughs and he laughs, because what is there left to do?

"Why not, right?" Amy says, spitting blood onto the ground from a healing scab in his mouth. From the expression on Michael's face, it's not the reaction he was expecting.

It's not the reaction Amy was expecting.

"What did you expect me to do with this information, huh?" Amy snarls, teeth now coated in blood. "Get angry? Get pissed? Turn against Hanael and Danael? Oh, I'm sure that's *exactly* what you were hoping for."

Amy staggers towards Michael in a rage. Michael only looks him up and down in growing disinterest.

"Actually, I was hoping we might discuss the possibility of another deal, but –"

"You can take your deals and shove them straight up your –"

"– cool if I take this, right?"

Blearily, Amy can feel someone rummaging through his jacket pockets, slipping something out. He doesn't know how long he's been in and out consciousness for. He's not sure if he cares.

His face hurts.

His face really fucking hurts.

There's a man in front of him.

Did the man punch him?

"Man, Michael did a number on you, huh?"

Michael. Michael punched him. So, who –

"Oh, pardon my manners. We haven't been formally introduced."

Amy's vision starts to clear just enough to give way to a stocky, blonde-haired man. He looks far too cheerful, given the state of the world.

"Name's Cain."

CHAPTER 35

DANAEL

Danel stares out the window of Hanael's bedroom, the echo of rain surrounding them. Crimson droplets pound down hard – on the patio, in the garden, on the roof. The previous dying landscape is now hidden beneath a blanket of blood.

They didn't have much time left.

They didn't have much of anything left.

Danael's gaze travels to a sleeping Hanael. The tension in her shoulders loosens ever so slightly at the steady rise and fall of the now human's chest.

Human. That would take some getting used to.

A crack of thunder fills the space and Danael rises from the bed, jaw tight.

Perhaps it was for the best, that Hanael wouldn't have to fight anymore; couldn't fight anymore. She had done her part and it was time for Danael to do hers.

Danael still struggles to decipher what that is. She hasn't gotten much farther than the image of Michael's evisceration playing on repeat in her mind.

Her now entirely unaccompanied mind.

It's...strange, being disconnected from Hanael in this way. Like a home you had shared with someone your entire life suddenly uprooted overnight. There's too much empty space and not enough of Danael's own belongings to fill it with. And the belongings she *does* have, well –

She could do better.

She needs to do better.

Danael makes her way out of Hanael's bedroom and back towards the kitchen. She's nearly at the breakfast bar when she hears the front door being rattled. Danael stops, draws her sword, and silently moves towards the noise.

A door slamming. Footsteps. The sound of a cabinet opening.

Danael turns the corner to find a human man standing at Hanael's liquor cabinet, helping himself to a glass of scotch. His back is turned to her and Danael is suddenly struck with the feeling she knows him.

Inching forward, sword still drawn, Danael inspects his aura. It's human, but seems almost too old to be so. Dark, corrupted, tortured. All reaching a peak on his forearm where there is a divinely branded sigil.

It's then that Danael realizes the man has turned around to face her.

"Cain," Danael says.

"Danael."

Danael sighs, sliding her sword back into her sheath. It wouldn't do her much good against Cain anyway. "Why are you here? How did you find us?"

Cain takes another swig of his drink before offering her a crumpled sticky note from the pocket of his blazer. It's the same sticky note Danael had given Amy that had Hanael's address on it.

"What did you do to Amy?" Danael asks, not sure she wants to hear the answer.

Cain takes a seat at the breakfast bar, drink still in hand. "I didn't have to do anything. Doesn't seem to have much to lose, that one."

Danael pushes down an internal grimace. Something makes her think Nickie wasn't the only one they had lost today.

"Why are you here, Cain?" Danael asks again.

"Does the name Mnemosyne mean anything to you?"

Danael startles. Between the apocalypse, Hanael, and everything in between, she hadn't had much time to process the deity who was responsible for her continuous memory losses between reincarnations. Not that she particularly cared to.

"*Why* are you *here*, Cain?"

"I'm *here* because you have a vested interest in saving the world. A world that I happen to be stuck on for the fore-seeable and non-foreseeable future." He stands, swirling the drink in his hand. "I'm sure you can see where our common goals align."

"And what does that have to do with Mnemosyne?"

"Mnemosyne is the Greek goddess of memories. Now, correct me if I'm wrong, but doesn't most of your current dilemma rest on the Host's lack of memories of your existence?"

"I don't know what you're suggesting," Danael says. "Even if the memory of my existence was returned, Michael is still practically untouchable. Especially now."

"Danael, Danael, Danael. Can't you feel it yet?" Cain raises his glass to the window, which was now caked in blood from the outside storm. "This isn't just about Michael. A war is brewing – a *Rebellion*. Lucifer lost with one-third of the angels, but what if you had more than angels?"

He can't possibly be suggesting –

"The Old Gods loathe us," Danael says. "Once Abrahamic religions took precedence, all other pantheons began to lose their worshippers; their power." No doubt even Mnemosyne was being forced to do Michael's bidding in the part she played with Danael.

"They won't have any power at all if humanity is destroyed."

Danael considers this. Angels and demons received their power from Heaven and Hell, respectively. Which meant they would retain their power regardless of the status of humanity. Other gods, however...

"Still," Danael says. "I think you are overestimating their willingness to join forces."

"You'd be surprised," Cain says. "I can't speak for the other pantheons, but the Greeks would be more than willing to lend a helping hand."

"And you know this, how, exactly?"

Cain shrugs, setting his drink down. "I had a fling with Clio back in the early eighteen hundreds." Danael raises her eyebrows. "Her mother, while unenthusiastic about our relations, was far from an enemy. It's how I found out about your reincarnation schtick to begin with."

Danael can feel her blood boiling. "And you're just now coming to me about this?"

"I rather thought you would have the situation under control by now."

Danael wants to punch him. She wants to break her knuckles against his face and then the wall, the window – every available service until the interior of Hanael's house is as raw and bloodstained as the exterior. Is as miserable as Danael's own insides.

The tiredness wins out, though.

God, she's so tired.

Giving a longing glance back towards Hanael's bedroom, Danael follows Cain into the living room.

Danael expects some kind of summoning. Maybe a prayer. Anything besides Cain taking out his cell phone, sending a text, and shoving it back in his pocket.

Mnemosyne appears moments later. It's the most anti-climactic thing Danael's seen all month.

Mnemosyne is just as Danael remembers her. Long, flowing red hair and high cheekbones currently upturned into a barely-there smile. More of a smile, Danael thinks, than she had ever seen on the goddess during her reoccurring trips to Hades.

"Danael," Mnemosyne greets. "What a pleasure it is to meet you in the land of the living for once."

Danael wearily shakes the goddess' outstretched hand before cutting right to the chase, "Pleasure and confusion. Are you genuinely here to help?"

"Indeed," Mnemosyne says. "We do, after all, have a common enemy. It would appear that the time is ripe for a deal."

Of course it was another deal. Of course. Danael sighs. "What are your terms?"

"I will return the memories of your existence to anyone they were wiped from. Furthermore, I will provide whatever resources I have at my disposal toward your cause." Mnemosyne pauses, as if thinking. "In return for this, all I ask is that you win. And ensure that all the Old Gods are given back the portion of land and power that Yahweh stole from us."

"And if I can't win?"

"Then we are all dead either way."

Danael winces. Her gaze finds its way back towards Hanael's bedroom. How was it that she felt like she had both everything and nothing to lose?

Danael turns back to Mnemosyne, forces a smile, and shakes the goddess' hand.

Hanael looks beautiful when she sleeps. Probably because she looks peaceful.

Danael's not sure the last time Hanael had looked peaceful.

A sick weight settles in Danael's stomach. Being here again with Hanael, in this moment, feels like facing the fallout of a nuclear blast before it's been detonated. Even if they win, they still lose.

Danael closes her eyes, digging her fingernails into her palms.

Michael's death is going to be painful. Danael is going to be there to watch the light leave his eyes if it's the last thing she does. And the way her luck was going, it probably would be.

Crossing the distance from the doorway to Hanael's bed, Danael takes a seat. Hanael shifts, mumbles, and ever so slowly, her eyes flutter open.

They fill with relief upon seeing Danael. Danael feels nauseous.

Hanael smiles half-heartedly before saying, "Watching

me while I sleep?"

"It's a very nice view."

Hanael laughs. It's a trying but broken laugh that does nothing for Danael's stomach.

"I have to go back to Heaven," Danael says, ripping the bandaid off.

Any relief that previously adorned Hanael's expression vanishes.

"To what end?" Hanael says, abruptly sitting up. "Danael, that's a *suicide* mission."

Hadn't it always been?

"I'll be fine," Danael lies. "I'll have help."

Danael begins to explain what said help involves. Hanael looks less than convinced.

"I have to do this," Danael says, taking her hand. Hanael looks down at it sadly.

"Well, I'm certainly in no position to be telling you what to do, am I?" Hanael says, though makes no effort to separate their hands. "I – just wish things were different."

Danael swallows. "So do I."

They sit like that for a long while, in the silence of their grief and regret. Until finally, Hanael breaks it, "Just try to be less reckless in your efforts than I was."

Danael kisses her. It feels surreal and foreign, but no less wonderful. Whatever else may come, Danael can at least have this moment to take with her.

They separate and Danael says, "Your efforts seem to have done just fine from where I'm standing. If anything," Danael lays a kiss to her knuckles, "I can only hope my own will be half as heroic."

"Sweet talking will you get you nowhere," Haneal huffs through her smile. Then it downturns. "Please, be careful."

Danael kisses her again before finally forcing herself to separate from the bed and Hanael.

"I'll do my damnedest, dear," Danael leaves with, and can at least take comfort in the fact it wasn't a lie.

Heaven is nothing like Danael remembers it. Danael isn't sure if that's from the current chaos or her own shattered perspective.

It's quiet. Far too quiet. The only vibrational frequency for miles is the bitter *'hum'* of celestial energy. No guards. No protection measures. No nothing.

This was bad.

Sword drawn, Danael begins to make her way from the First to Second Sphere. The actual structure of Heaven hasn't changed, so Danael can navigate it easily enough. The style, however – that has gotten an upgrade. An upgrade filled with white hallways, grey doors, and uncomfortable overhead lights. A nod to the human corporate workplace.

Fitting.

Danael approaches the end of the current hallway of the Second Sphere to find a grey door with a laminated label that reads "Soul Records Office". She turns the knob and enters. Still no one in sight.

It's a bare room, as Danael guessed most in Heaven still were. There was, after all, no need to have too many physically represented objects.

No, all Danael needed to do was focus on the soul in question and the answer would be provided. Sickeningly simplistic and it still takes Danael what feels like hours to bring the name 'Nicole Allbright' to the forefront of her mind.

Danael knows Amy didn't make it past the portal in his efforts to check on the status of Nickie's soul. A demon attempting to enter Heaven was the equivalent of diving headfirst into a high voltage electric gate.

Danael also knows she's wasting her time checking herself. Nickie was killed by Death's Scythe. There was no coming back from that.

Still, Danael checks.

Nickie isn't here.

Nickie isn't here because Michael killed her in spite. Many other people will also not be here because Michael will kill them in spite.

What was left to do than beat the bastard at his own game?

Danael squares her shoulder, swallows her grief, and exits the room, slamming the door behind her.

If Michael wanted a war, Danael would damn well give him one.

CHAPTER 36

ḨANA

Tick. Tock. Tick. Tock. Tick –

Hana narrows her eyes at the gold, filigree wall clock hanging in her living room.

She remembers the day she bought it, only days after Danael's resurrection. Hana had seen it on display in the window of A New Dawn and thought it would make a nice addition to her rental home. Perhaps even give her another much-needed chance to get in Nickie's good graces.

It had achieved neither.

Tock. Tick. Tock. Tick –

Danael has been gone three days now. Hana can't really recall what she's done in that time.

There are some scattered occult books on the desk in front of her. A notebook next to that which Hana had written nothing in. A glass of water – Oh. Yes, she needed to drink water.

Hana picks up the glass, hands shaking.

Tick. Tock. Tick. Tock. Tick. Tock. Tick. Tock. Tick. Tock. Tick. Tock. Tick. Tock. Tick. Tock.

Tick. Tock. Tick. Tock. Tick. Tock. Tick. Tock. Tick. Tock. Tick. Tock. Tick. Tock. Tick. Tock.

Tick. Tock. Tick. Tock. Tick. Tock. Tick. Tock. Tick —

The glass shatters, all its contents spilling onto the desk and soaking into what Hana knows are priceless grimoires. She watches, unfazed, as the blood from her hand slowly drips over the mess.

"You look like you could use a drink."

Hana's head rises to meet Cain's. She blinks once before wordlessly pulling out a shard from her palm and tossing it into a nearby trash bin.

"Or three." Cain shakes his head before making his way over to the liquor cabinet. Once he arrives, he splashes some vodka on a rag and tosses it in Hana's direction.

"Best keep that covered. Humans get these funny things called infections." He tsks, pouring two glasses. "You should have *seen* the 16th century —"

"I did," Hana says, wrapping her palm up with a wince. "I frequently visited Earth during that time, usually in guise as a nurse."

"Ah."

Hana sits up and wearily approaches Cain and the liquor cabinet. He hands her a tumbler and Hana stares at it.

It looks like Lucifer's tumbler.

Hana forces down the building nausea with the entire contents of the glass.

It takes very little time for Hana's vision to grow jilted and her body to collapse onto the nearby loveseat. It feels nice. It feels nice to not think about Danael.

"Careful there, lightweight," Cain says, and only vaguely can Hana sense him take a seat opposite of her.

"Death by alcohol poisoning is not the way you want to go, trust me."

Hana doesn't trust him. Isn't remotely amused by him.

Cain soon becomes bored with her unresponsiveness and leaves. Hana can't recall where he said he was going. Unconsciousness is beginning to pull at her vision when it is jolted back by the sound of the front door rattling.

She sobers quickly.

Hana stumbles into the kitchen where Danael had left their weapons. Human weapons that she hardly knows how to use. Her heart beats wildly as her eyes dart among the guns, ammo, and hand knives, before settling on one of the latter.

Doubtful, though, that any of them would do her much good going forward. Once again, she is the equivalent of a gazelle to a hungry lion.

Said lion's form comes into view from around the corner, though looks more akin to a startled cat.

"Whoa!" Amy hisses at her, putting his hands up. "Put that crap down! You're gonna hurt somebody."

Amy's presence should be more of a relief than it is. Her hand is shaking as she drops the weapon back down onto the counter. Metal clangs against marble and somewhere in the distance, the kitchen sink begins to run.

Hana turns to see Amy washing his hands. Amy, who Hana only now notices is covered head to toe in blood.

Hana's gaze causes his own to draw down to his body, as if only now noticing the blood wasn't only confined to his hands.

Amy turns off the sink, dries his hands, and turns around to face her.

"It's raining blood now," Amy says.

"I gathered."

Amy shifts under her gaze. He looks paler than when she last saw him.

"I'm sorry," Hana says at last. "About Nickie."

"I ran into Cain," Amy says as he pours himself a glass of water. Still, Hana sees an imperceptible flinch. "Gave him your address without – look, are you guys alright?"

"That's a rather asinine question," Hana says. "But we haven't been murdered yet by the immortal psychopath you sent our way, no."

Amy does visibly flinch that time.

"Why do you care? Didn't you tell us to go fuck ourselves?"

Amy slams his glass of water onto the breakfast bar and the noise echoes in the otherwise silent kitchen. Now Hana is the one flinching.

"Hell if I know," Amy says. "Maybe because Nickie cared. More likely because I want to see Michael dead as much as you both." He shifts, straightening his jacket. "I ran into the bastard. Right before I did Cain."

"What?" Hana gapes. "What did he say?"

"Less saying and more gloating. Son of a fucking bitch tried to offer me another deal. Told him where he could shove it."

"What was the deal?"

Amy stares at her. Seems to be searching her energy for something before –

"So. You didn't know either, then."

"Know *what*?"

Amy laughs, low and bitter. "You ever wonder how Michael was able to execute Danael's deal for you? How he was able to keep the balance between those that were marked to fall and those who weren't?"

Hana shakes her head. She wishes she hadn't gotten up from the couch.

Amy laughs again. "It was *me*. I took the place *you* should have had in Hell. I fell so you *didn't have to*."

Hana thinks those words should probably mean something to her. But she has no more guilt or grief left to give.

She says nothing, and neither does Amy. And for a moment she thinks they take comfort, at least a little, in the hell they've created for both themselves and each other.

The moment doesn't last.

The hairs on the back of Hana's neck rise as she follows Amy's wide-blown gaze to the doorway.

"Nickie?" Amy chokes out, stumbling forward.

It's not Nickie. Hana knows it's not Nickie before she even sees it. She only prays that Amy knows too.

"Amy," 'Nickie' says, too soft and too girlish. Amy freezes.

"You're not Nickie," Amy says, though still makes no move against the creature. Hana wants to scream.

There is a sickening *'crunch!'* as Nickie's head lolls to the side, broken. Her now angled eyes remain wide and alert and hungry.

"Shit –" The word doesn't make it out of Amy's mouth before the look-alike is pouncing on him. Still, *still*, he makes no significant moves against it.

Hana does.

She doesn't know when the knife returns to her hand or how she pushes through her heart trying to claw its way out of her throat. But now the weapon is in the creature's back and it's *screaming*.

Then, silence. The visage of Nickie gone, replaced by a black-haired female corpse.

"What was that?" The words don't sound like her own.

Amy stares at the unmoving body before slowly making his way back to his feet.

"Nothing good," he says. "I think – I think the zombies may be getting smarter. More evolved. Taking energy from their environment and...twisting it."

Hana flinches, remembering a similar creature from her time in Hell.

Glass shatters from the living room. A handful of weapons are shoved into Hana's hands as Amy roughly pushes her forward. They don't make it to the hallway before the twisted face of Danael fills her vision.

Hana beheads the imposter before its smile reaches its eyes. There's another banshee-like wail as Amy gapes at her and the form is replaced by another corpse.

The thought occurs to Hana (less hind-sighted this time) to pray to Danael. So, between labored breathes and a dash towards the basement, she tries.

Try being the key word.

The prayer goes out – and then straight back into Hana's skull. The words echo around painfully while somewhere in the background Amy curses and shoves her into the basement entrance.

"How the hell are they getting in?! This place is warded to the nines!" Amy curses as he locks the door behind them and they both stumble down the stairs.

It's a dead end.

That bodes well.

"Can you pray to Danael?" Hana asks, still in a daze.

"I'm a demon!" Amy hisses, beginning to pace. "And while apparently a wrongfully convicted one, still very much Not Holy Enough to send out a prayer."

"What are we going to do, then?" Hana says. "Did you bring us down here to die?"

There is a growing part of Hana that hopes for it. Is beginning to wonder if it would have been better if Nickie had lived instead of her. At least Nickie would be good for something.

"Excuse me?" Amy stops pacing, eyes baring into hers. "Would you rather have me leave you up there?"

"Yes!" Hana yells. "Nickie would still be alive if it weren't for me, you realize that, right?" The words are physically painful as they tremble off her lips and Hana wants them to stop. Stop, stop, stop! Everything just stop! "I should have died in Hell! At least then I won't have to watch the one person I've truly ever loved die in front of me!"

Amy continues to stare, expression falling from its snarl of tension. The basement door rattles above them, and they both know it won't hold for much longer.

"Welcome to my world," Amy says, voice hoarse. "I don't blame you for Nickie's death. I blame Michael." His eyes raise to the ceiling, shoulders tensing. "*Michael* is to blame for the apocalypse. *Michael* is to blame for the fucking undead freaks trying to kill us. And you'll bet your ass I'll spend my last dying breaths doing my damnedest to destroy him and everyone who follows him." His eyes meet hers. "And if you're not poised to do the same thing, well, I guess I overestimated your tenacity."

The basement door bursts open to reveal some 'familiar' faces and some not. All charging down the basement steps in a bloodthirsty haze.

The two yield what weapons they can against the creatures, but they're outnumbered. Hana stumbles to the floor less than thirty seconds into the fray and can only watch on helplessly as Amy fights a losing battle.

"How unoriginal," a voice echoes from somewhere in Hana's peripheral. And then there is blood.

On the floor, on the walls, on Hana. She forces her eyes closed and wills herself to breathe. Only when the room quiets does she open them to see Cain standing tall amongst a dozen mangled corpses. Standing across from him is a man that Hana knows but can't place a name to.

"Brother," the man – Abel – says cheerfully. He isn't able to let out a scream before his head falls to the floor and rolls right in front of Hana.

She feels ill. She feels so, so ill.

"Not exactly how I planned for this day to go, but I must say," Cain says, wiping the dripping blood off his knife with an equally bloody handkerchief. "It's put me in a supremely good mood."

"Well, how nice for you," Amy snarls, picking himself up off the ground.

"How nice for you," Cain says. "That I bothered to come at all."

"That's enough, boys."

All heads turn to see a red-headed, Mona Lisa-esque women descending the stairs. "Save your resentment for the real enemy."

Hana isn't terribly knowledgeable about the Greek pantheon aside from the vicious resentment they hold towards Abrahamic deities. Which makes Mnemosyne's appearance all the more surprising.

Danael had filled her in only briefly on her current 'deal' with the goddess. Hana had figured that's where Mnemosyne's efforts in their current battle ended.

"So…" Amy gives a motion toward the pot of earthy-scented boiling water on the stove. Mnemosyne had not wasted any time ushering them upstairs and making use of her own magick. Magick that seemed far more effective.

"It is a disorientation brew," Mnemosyne says. "As long as it simmers, the kathréftes fóvou will be unable to find your location."

"I'm sorry – the who now?"

Cain rolls his eyes at Amy while Hana's remain blank. She wishes she could care what was going on, but all she wants to do is take a shower and scrub her skin until it burns.

"Kathréftes fóvou," Mnemosyne repeats. "Fear mirrors. We have something similar in Hades, although Persephone is usually quick to contain them." She pauses. "Though you Abrahamic gods have no such fail safes, as the world can currently attest."

"We're not gods," Amy says.

"Perhaps that is your problem, no?"

Amy glares and Mnemosyne smiles. Before the demon can offer a response, the goddess disappears. Leaving only the scent of peppermint, rose, and sage in her wake.

"Well," Cain says. "Once again, you're welcome." And then he too, makes his exit.

As if nothing even happened. As if Hana isn't still covered in blood and shaking.

A silence falls between Amy and Hana before he sighs, struggles off his bloody jacket, drops it to the floor in front of her, and proceeds to the guest bathroom.

Hana stares at the item of clothing long after he's left.

The silence remains.

CHAPTER 37
NICKIE

Nickie isn't sure when her heart stops beating.

Maybe it was when she awoke in Hell those three days ago, no recollection of how she got from point A to point B.

Maybe it was when she tried to drown herself in the lake.

Maybe it never beat to begin with.

Maybe. Maybe. Maybe. Maybe. Maybe.

Nickie's fingers drift across the piano keys, another more nuanced rendition of "Lux Aeterna" playing. She plays better now. She does a lot of things better now.

"So, run me through this again."

Malphas is leaning against the piano. He looks relaxed; feigns it as well as he feigns anything else. The only difference is that now Nickie notices.

Nickie stops playing. "You'll go to Earth, find Dani, tell her I'm alive, and tell her to stop whatever stupid, self-sacrificing crap she's currently planning. We'll be taking care of Michael."

"We will?"

Nickie turns to look at him. She smiles and he doesn't.

"Right. Guess I'll just leave, then."

"Yes."

"By myself."

"Yes."

"With no backup or form of protection."

Nickie rises, crosses to her bookshelf, and tosses Malphas a turquoise, sigil-covered crystal. "Hang onto this. It'll protect you."

Malphas glowers, turns on his heel, and leaves.

Nickie smiles, sits back down on the piano bench, and plays.

"Status update, Paimon."

Nickie is seated with Paimon in one of the nicer office rooms of the Third Level. Nicer because Paimon is loyal to her, and loyalty is one of the few things Nickie can count on right now.

"We have found and contained the Void energy. At a... nominal loss to our army."

"How many?"

"Twelve." Oh, good. That's nothing. "Seir noted that the Void energy could break through the current hold on Hell, if crafted into a weapon." Paimon pauses, looking at Nickie with interest. "You would, however, be the only one that could wield it, seeing as the Void energy will not attach to you. We still don't know why that is."

Nickie does. "Guess that just means I was destined to be Queen."

Paimon grins. "A quite welcomed destiny, I would say."

"Not according to a good one third of my army." Which

Nickie had been expecting. Though at this time, no one was stupid enough to do any significant pushback. Not with Michael still to worry about.

"They will adjust," Paimon assures. "And if they don't, well." Paimon stands, gathers her folders, and turns towards the exit. "You're a smart girl, I'm sure you'll know where to cut the weak links."

The door closes behind Paimon and Nickie snaps her fingers, locking it.

Nickie used to be the weak link.

The addict.

The victim.

The failure.

Nickie breathes in deeply. Can smell the eternal torment of the souls from the Levels above her.

Maybe she'll change that. Give them all a chance for redemption. Maybe some tests to pass or loosen the sin threshold for damnation.

Maybe. Maybe. Maybe.

There are so many maybes now. Infinite possibilities. And once Michael is gone, there will be even more.

For the first time in Nickie's life, she is in control. She is in control and she will need to make damn well sure she doesn't lose it. Whatever that may take.

Nickie stiffens, looking down at her hands. She clenches and unclenches her right fist a few times, staring.

She shakes herself out of it.

Nope. No. Nah-ugh. She was *not* going to go there. Nickie refuses to bear any responsibility for what she is forced to do from this point onward.

She didn't ask for any of this. If all these supernatural fucks thought they could make her a pawn in their game, then it's their own damn fault for underestimating her ability to throw away the whole board.

Anyway, once this is all over, none of that will matter. She could fix things. She used to dream about that as a kid, before life beat it out of her. Doing something good, being something better. Now she actually has the power to do it. Make the world a better place and all that jazz.

As long as Dani was left alive and the Earth, Heaven, and Hell were somewhat salvageable, Nickie could work with that. She's worked with less.

This was war, and war was, after all, just a numbers game.

CHAPTER 38
DANAEL

Three days Danael had spent canvassing Heaven and she is no closer to an actual rebellion than when she first arrived. Not to say that she didn't have *any* support, but even the angels that loathed Michael's actions couldn't seem to overcome their fear of him enough to help with the cause.

Danael can't say she blames them.

That left Camael, Hadraniel, Jehoel, Muriel, and Ophaniel – all currently seated around a white table in their (for now) undiscovered planning room in the Eleventh Sphere. All here for no other reason than needing someone to believe in other than Michael.

Danael wishes there was a more promising third option.

Their surroundings are a white backdrop of nothingness. The energy is similar. The Eleventh and Twelfth Spheres hadn't been used for much since Yahweh left. The energy is far too dense for most angels to manipulate. And as per usual with most angels – if it didn't serve a purpose, it didn't serve to command any of their attention.

"Perhaps," Jehoel says, breaking up the cascade of voices. "We take our losses and leave. Another galaxy. Another universe. Why are we so intent on making Michael's temper tantrum our problem?"

"Because it *is* our problem," Muriel says from across the table. "All those humans will die if something is not done."

"So?" Jehoel says. "That's what humans do. What they've always done. It doesn't mean we have to join them."

"Then leave!" Danael shouts, standing up from her chair. "If you are not here to contribute to the fight then just leave."

Jehoel sinks back in his chair, silent. The entire table is silent now.

Danael wonders, in the silence, if Jehoel isn't right.

How much has she already done in vain? Already lost?

"Well, it is no wonder you haven't gotten anywhere if this is your idea of a productive meeting."

Danael turns around to find Mnemosyne approaching, long, red hair floating several inches behind her. The table has grown tenser, a group of distrustful eyes and clenched teeth leveled at the goddess.

"I take that to mean you have a better one?" Danael asks Mnemosyne, ignoring their demeanors. Old grudges had no place in a dying world.

"Simply an observation," Mnemosyne says. "I'm afraid any ideas I might have are limited to the small scope of knowledge I have of your kind. So, please." The goddess takes the last open seat on the table, despite the group's unkind looks. "Enlighten me."

Danael does. And once the other angels begin to relax to the idea of help, they do as well. Mnemosyne listens intently and patiently to a millennium worth of knowledge, though Danael can see the flash of pity.

Eventually, the recap concludes, and the room is once again silent. Mnemosyne seems to think carefully before she speaks again.

"Your past history is unfortunate," Mnemosyne says, voice level. "I will need time to take this information and gather the army and resources I need."

"How much time?" Danael asks.

"Undetermined. Rest assured, I will work as swiftly as possible."

Mnemosyne disappears and Danael winces. Vague plans are made to head to the battlefield.

Danael feels sick to her stomach giving the orders. She shouldn't be giving these orders. These orders are a death sentence.

How far does Danael expect her anger to carry her?

Danael wishes Nickie were here. Nickie had the kind of anger that could be weaponized as easily as the pull of a trigger, while Danael's own was left sitting like a messy backfire in her chest.

Perhaps, Danael thinks, Nickie could have been the leader this army needed. She had the character for it, the strength, the ability to make blood-stained sacrifices.

Danael wishes she had told her that.

Danael wishes she had told Nickie a lot of things.

Taking a breath, Danael takes flight back down to Earth.

Danael arrives back in Hanael's living room to be met by

the sight of shattered glass, an upturned loveseat, and several blood trails of indeterminate locations.

For a moment, Danael can't move. Her visions swims, blurred into nothing but glistening crimson.

"HANAEL?!" Danael screams. She's preparing herself for the worst. Hanael was all but human now. Why hadn't she thought more about what that meant? Why hadn't she taken more precautions? Why hadn't Hanael –

Another body slams into hers. When Danael looks up, the startled face of Hanael stares back.

Danael feels sick with relief.

She wonders how long it will last.

The embrace is immediate and Danael tries, desperately, to push down Jehoel's previous words of abandoning ship. Hanael's next words make it very hard to do so.

"It was the...zombies. If you could even call them that." Hanael shivers and Danael leads her to the recliner. The smell of sage, rose, and peppermint fills Danael's senses as she runs to the kitchen to grab Hanael a glass of water.

God, she looked pale.

"I tried praying to you," Hanael says after a large sip. "I'm...it didn't work."

"Are you okay?" Danael asks and cringes. What a stupid question.

"I'm...managing," Hanael says.

She's not. She's not and Danael is sick of pretending she's okay with it and it's only going to get worse and one day soon Danael is going to have to watch her –

"I think we should leave," Danael blurts out. "There are other universes, other galaxies. Ones without any version of Michael or Lucifer, I'm sure. If we start looking now, then maybe –"

"No."

Danael's stomach drops. "...No?"

Hanael squeezes Danael's hand and her stomach drops further. She seems to be thinking very carefully about her next words.

"I don't want to see the kind of person you turn into if you were to let the world burn even more for me, Danael. I can barely stand to see the way you look at me now."

"And what way is *that*?"

"Bad time?"

Both women swing their heads around at the familiar and very much unwelcome demon in the threshold of the living room.

Danael draws her sword and Malphas startles. Odd.

Actually, everything about the demon's presence was odd. His demeanor, his energy –

"Listen, ugh, I know you have no reason to believe me –"

"You think?" Danael says, taking a step forward. Malphas takes two back.

"Hey, wait! Listen, alright? Nickie is –"

Any remaining words fall off Malphas' lips as quickly as his head falls off his body. It rolls halfway to Danael's feet and Hanael makes a sick noise from behind her. All while Amy's eyes travel from one blood-soaked body part to another.

"That...wasn't a zombie?" Amy asks, befuddled. "That's – that can't actually be Malphas, right? Nothing can get in or out of Hell right now." His jaw clenches. "Believe me, I've tried."

"It didn't seem like Malphas," Danael says, sheathing her sword.

"So, it *was* a zombie?"

"Why are you here, Amy?"

287

The demon straightens his back. "What, no 'Thank you so much, Amy, for saving my girlfriend's ass?'".

Danael turns to Hanael. "Did he 'save your ass'?"

"Moderately. Though Cain did most of the heavy lifting."

"Yeah, because Cain's a maniac," Amy says, wiping the blood of his own sword. "Dude gets off on dismembering. I swear I saw him jerk-"

"Just –" Danael puts up her hands before motioning to the body. "Get rid of that, please."

"Why me?"

"Your kill, your cleanup."

Amy lets out a grumble but starts on the task regardless. While he does, Danael motions Hanael to follow her down the hall and into Hanael's bedroom. The door closes and a thick silence fills the space.

Hanael approaches the bed before taking a seat. Danael watches as the other woman stares blankly into the mirror on the desk across from her before asking, "How did you manage?"

"What?"

"The pain," Hanael says. "All those times you were human...how did you manage it?"

Danael sighs as she approaches the bed and takes a seat beside Hanael.

"I didn't," Danael says, placing one hand over Hanael's. "In some lives, I drank. Others, I took my anger out on those around me. Denial. Distraction." Hanael looks at her. "The ignorance made it easier, though." Did it? "A millennium of humanity-shaped shadows on the cave wall." Danael swallows as she sees despair flicker across Hanael's expression. The realization that Hanael's situation was the reverse of

Danael's. That she would have to live as a human with the knowledge of what it was like not to be one.

No words seem correct now. Nothing Danael can say will offer any kind of reassurance. Still, an "I'm so sorry, Hanael" falls out and the angel cringes again.

Hanael lets her back hit the mattress, staring at the ceiling. "I suppose I only have myself to blame."

Danael lowers her body beside Hanael's. The plain white vaulted ceiling stares back at her. Devoid of color. Devoid of meaning.

Danael wishes it meant something. Wishes the angled grooves and paint chips could paint her a picture of how to navigate what their existence now was.

"You survived," Danael says. "Survival always comes at a cost."

"But was it too high a one?"

"No." Danael turns on her side to look at Hanael. She tucks a strand of blonde hair behind her ear, hoping her expression isn't as desperate as she feels. "Are you sure you don't want to leave?"

"Yes."

"Even if it means we're fighting a losing battle?"

"We always were, Danael."

Hanael kisses her. Softly, but with intent. Danael's grip tightens at the back of her neck.

"Make me forget, please," Hanael says between breaths. "Just for a little while."

That, Danael could do.

Danael's eyes shoot open to the sound of shattering glass.

Several of Hanael's framed contemporary paintings have dropped to the ground, broken.

"Is that an earthquake?" Hanael asks, wrapping the sheet tight around her naked body.

The shaking stops and Danael stands up from the bed. She barely materializes her own bare body into jeans and a blazer before the door to Hanael's bedroom flies open. Amy enters in a disarray.

"Hate to break up your fun time, but ugh –" Amy's gaze travels from Hanael to Danael, turning severe. "Whatever Rebellion you're planning? Yeah. Might want to put a rush on that."

CHAPTER 39
NICKIE

They're so close.

Seir is almost done crafting a sword to contain the Void energy. Nickie's lost a few more demons to the task, but that was to be expected. Can't make an omelet without cracking a few eggs, right? Although the Void seemed particularly skilled at the cracking part.

Nickie rolls her shoulders, aiming a blade for a target some twenty feet away. She's currently in a training room on the Tenth Level. She remembers spending a lot of time with her father here when she first arrived. It was a good place to think.

Bullseye.

Nickie lowers her hand. It's like the Void energy just... extinguishes demonic and celestial life forces. The only thing Nickie knew to be able to do that was Death's Scythe and the sword her father gave her. Her eyes briefly flicker down to the latter on her waist.

Perhaps Nickie should be more concerned about it, she thinks, as she takes out another knife, but it's serving its purpose and for now, that's all Nickie needs. The rest could be put on the back burner.

Anyway, it certainly wouldn't hurt to have another weapon that would...encourage her demons to accept their new leadership.

Now all she was waiting on was Malphas.

There's a knock on the training room door and Nickie sighs, placing her blade down. She makes her way towards the door, passing a variety of targets, weapons, and equipment. She opens the door and on the other side is Gaap.

Like Paimon, the short, stocky demon had been agreeable in Nickie's transition to power. She's keeping a close count on those showing initial loyalty and treating them accordingly.

"Hello my Queen," Gaap greets, blinking twice. "I am here to inform you of Malphas' return to Hell."

Speak of the wanna-be devil.

"Perfect," Nickie says. "Where is he?"

Gaap shifts on his feet. "It seems that Malphas was killed shortly after you dispatched him to Earth." Nickie's jaw tightens. "My sincerest apologies, my Queen. He is currently on the Fourth Level, in his personal Hell. Shall I retrieve him?"

Of course. Of course the idiot had already gotten himself killed.

"No," Nickie says. "I'll be handling this. You're dismissed, Gaap."

Gaap scurries off and Nickie is left wondering what fresh hell will be greeting her in Malphas' own.

∽

The Fourth Level is, as always, seemingly infinite. Infinite halls, infinite doorways, infinite cells, infinite torture.

Nickie sniffs out Malphas' energetic signature easily enough, although if she had known what laid on the other side of his door, Nickie might have taken more time finding it.

It's her.

Well, it's her in an infinite loop of deaths.

The scene starts out with Malphas and her double arguing. Something, something, who's in charge of Hell, something. Their usual. Until there's a physical altercation, Malphas grabs Nickie's sword and...shoves it through her heart.

Bold.

"No," Malphas breaths, yanking the sword back out and attempting to stop the bleeding. Atrocious first aid care, truly. "No, no, no, no, no!" Malphas falls to his knees, *screaming*, with Nickie's corpse in his arms.

Then the scene starts again.

Nickie doesn't let it play out a third time.

She puts up her hands, feels across the sigil covered veil at the entrance, and pushes forward, breaking the illusion. The dead not-Nickie disappears from Malphas' arms and his head shoots up. His eyes land on Nickie.

Malphas is disorientated for a good couple of minutes. Nickie simply waits for him to come out of it.

"It wasn't Asbeel," Malphas mutters, beginning to show signs of consciousness. "Why wasn't it Asbeel?"

Nickie startles, but shakes herself out of it as she marches towards him.

"Why are you dead? Did you even have time to get the message delivered to Dani?"

Malphas starts muttering again and Nickie grabs his

293

head to force him to look at her. His brown eyes are blown wide, and his mouth parts open as he stares at her. Gears are turning, turning, turning –

Whatever Nickie was about to say exits the stratosphere as his mouth collides into hers.

Malphas has never kissed her like this. So deep and desperate and hungry. His body presses into hers like he's trying to conjoin them and Nickie...Nickie makes no effort to stop him.

Actually, Nickie does the opposite.

Because really, what's the harm here? A little pre-battle hate sex never hurt anyone. Might even boost the ol' morale.

"I love you," Malphas breathes into her neck, hand going up her shirt to cup her breast. Nickie lets her back arch. "You have no idea how much I fucking love you." A kiss. "How much I've missed you." Then another. "How much I *need* you."

Nickie moans. The idea of having Malphas so compliant – so perfectly under her thumb – turned her on more than the actual sex.

Go figure.

"Do you, now?" Nickie says, digging her fingernails into his back. "Why don't you show me?"

Malphas doesn't disappoint. Then again, as Nickie's starting to admit to herself, he never did.

They somehow end up in an actual bed, as opposed to whatever available surface was nearest to them.

It's refreshing, Nickie thinks, as she rises from the mattress. Nickie can see Malphas watching her from the corner of her eye. She smirks before snapping her fingers to materialize a fresh suit. Malphas groans, about to protest, before dust begins to flitter down from the pillared ceiling.

Then there's a wave of...something. Nickie loses her balance, cursing, as she catches herself on the bed frame. Malphas isn't so lucky, his body falling to the floor with a *'thud'*.

"What the hell was that?" Malphas grumbles, dragging himself back up to a standing position.

Nickie feels inclined to make a well-timed belittling comment, but she can feel a calmness settle over her. A readying, electrifying calmness.

Another finger snap later and Nickie has traded her suit for some sleek, black, skintight, full body battle-wear. She admires herself in the mirror as Malphas approaches from behind, still in is boxers.

"Ah. I assume it's go time?" He asks.

Nickie turns to face him. At least her smile was belittling. "What do you think?"

"I think I'm looking forward to seeing you on the battlefield," he says. "Especially in *that*."

"What makes you think you're coming?"

"Because you're not stupid. You know you'll need all the help you can get."

Nickie smiles, slipping on her gloves. "You'd need your magick for that."

"And it's about time you give it back to me."

She fastens her utility belt, letting her eyes trail up and down Malphas' form.

"Maybe," Nickie says. "Though I'd still like you to beg for it."

"Haven't I spent enough time on my knees today?"

Nickie takes several steps forward until they are chest-to-chest. "Beg. For. It." Her eyes are amused, but not that amused.

So, he does. And Nickie laughs.

Malphas glowers.

"Cute," Nickie says. "But I already gave it back to you when you were...previously on your knees."

Nickie turns her back on him and begins gathering essential weapons and making mental checklists. She can feel Malphas' eyes burning a hole in her back but knows he won't do anything. Knows that now more than ever.

"Gather my demons to the open meeting area on the Third Level," Nickie orders. "Tell them we are preparing to depart for battle. I'll be convening with Paimon about the status of our weapon shortly."

Nickie then exits the bedroom without a single glance back.

∼

The sword is perfect.

Cold, smooth metal meets a textured, serpentine grip with a single jewel on the shoulder. Black, simple, and all Nickie's.

Nickie slides it into a sheath at her hip before beginning the trek with Paimon to the Third Level. Power pulsates from her side with each step. She's all smiles.

From what little information Malphas was able to relay, Dani, Hanael, and Amy were alive and kicking. Good enough. It might be better that no one knows she's coming, anyway. Then there's no possible way for Michael to know.

The poor bastard won't know what hit him.

Nickie approaches the podium in the Third Level, remembering the day she did the same thing towards her father. Except now, her back is straighter, her smile is more vicious, and she stands alone.

Oh, happy day.

"For those of you who don't know, Seir, with the help of his team, has crafted a weapon that I will use to break through the current lockdown on Hell." All her demons stand at attention in silence. "Once we walk through that barrier, we are at *war*."

"And for any of you wondering," Malphas enters, walking down the aisle and taking a seat in the front. The front seats were reserved for her currently most loyal supporters. "Yes, Nicole is the only one who can yield this weapon."

There are a handful of demons who give side-eyes and Nickie makes careful notes of which.

"Meaning," Nickie says, raising her voice. "I will yield my weapon with the utmost viciousness against all who oppose us. Oppose *me*." A pause. "And I fully expect all of you to do the same. Is that understood?"

She's gained a few more supporters with that statement, she can tell. Whether out of fear of her or the prospect of being able to unapologetically tear into Michael's army, she doesn't know. But hey – support was support was support.

"Let's have a little contest, shall we?" Nickie says. "The top ten demons with the most kills will put themselves in the start of the running for my second in command and top generals." Now, *that* gets their attention. Confusion, excitement, and rage pass through the crowd in equal measure.

"That's right." Nickie walks back down the podium, eying each row of demons as she passes them. There's about 400 in total. The remaining 200 aren't present, designated to remain in Hell as strategic backup and guards. "Gone are the days of assigned ranks. Anyone has the power to move up, if you're willing to work for it."

One very stupid demon, Barbatos, decides to shout out then, "And if by work for it, you mean with our dicks, right?" He points a gangly finger towards Malphas. "Guess that's how Malphas moved back up!"

The only noise in the area is Malphas shooting up from his chair and storming down the aisle to where Nickie is standing. She puts up a hand and he freezes.

Four, three, two –

Purson, a petite, spunky blonde, shoves her blade through the back of Barbatos skull into his left eye. Blood streams down his face as he screams. There's a burst of movement and drawn weapons before several other demons work to restrain him.

"Well," Nickie says, brushing off a piece of dust from her shoulder. "You know what to do."

Purson and two other male demons drag Barbatos off to the cells. None of them have the weapons to actually kill each other, which is good. She needs to keep her numbers up. Any traitors will just have to take a little time-out.

"Are we good here?" Nickie says, reaching the end of the aisle and drawing her sword.

There's a cascade of *yes's* and Nickie nods.

"Then let's go kick some angelic ass."

CHAPTER 40
HANA

Hana has slipped back on her nightgown when she feels Danael's lips press fleetingly against hers. A gust of wind later and the angel is gone, leaving only an aggrieved Amy in the doorway.

"Just," Amy makes a vague motion in her direction, covering his eyes. "Get yourself together, yeah? I'll meet you in the living room."

Hana does not, in fact, 'get herself together', only trailing behind Amy as he makes his way out of the bedroom. Cain is waiting for them, an enchanted machete in each hand, looking far too giddy than he has any right to be.

"Guess we're in the endgame now," Cain says, throwing a machete to Amy. Amy barely catches it. "Where's our star rebel?"

"Danael?" Amy asks. "Back to Heaven, I can only assume. Gathering the troops and all that." He turns to Hana. "Did Danael say anything to you before she left?"

"No," Hana replies. And maybe that's for the best.

"Right," Amy says. "I guess we're waiting on her signal, then?"

Hana shrugs, looking down at her bare feet.

Amy grinds his teeth. Cain quirks up an eyebrow.

"Here," Cain says, holding up his phone for Amy. "Ring Mnemosyne for an update. I'd like to go over some weapon-handlers' basics with Hanael."

Amy looks at Hana and then back to Cain. The demon eventually lets out a grunt, grabs Cain's phone, and heads over to the now fully weapon-stocked kitchen.

Cain stares at her for far longer than Hana feels comfortable with.

"You won't last long in battle," Cain says.

Hana startles back.

"Thought at least someone should be honest with you," Cain says, taking a seat. He crosses one leg over another, looking so...unbothered. Hana hates him for it. She hates him and she wants to crawl back into bed and *not* hear whatever is about to come out of his mouth.

"Listen," he says. "I get it. Life sucks and all that." A beat. "Death is...very intimidating. Or so I'm told."

"Is this conversation going somewhere?"

"If you want it to," Cain says. He pulls up his sleeve to reveal his Mark. "In favor of time, I'll make this brief."

Hana feels a foreboding crawl up her skin.

"I can transfer my Mark to a...willing donor," Cain begins. "Quite frankly, I've been trying to get rid of it for centuries. I've made friends in Hell. So, once I die, I'm rather set. No hell loops, just an exciting, new chapter."

Cogs are turning in Hana's head. Painful, slow, nause-ating cogs.

"Easy switcheroo," Cain continues. "You get my Mark, I get to leave this god-forsaken planet before it gets any worse, and you – " He's smiling. Hana doesn't know how he's smiling. "You get to protect your precious Danael and whatever's left of Earth."

Ringing. Ringing. Ringing. A deafening ringing as Hana's vision tilts to one side.

"You, after all," Cain says. "Have far more to lose in death than myself." *No, no, no, no, no, no.* This can't be happening. It can't, it can't, it can't, it just *can't.* "Where is it, do you think, someone in your position would go when they expire?"

"STOP!" Hana screams. So loud, apparently, it sends Amy hurtling back into the room.

"What the hell is going on here?!"

Cain stands up abruptly. "Think about it," he says, before handing Hana a slip of paper and making his exit. Like a ghost. A ghost. A ghost. A ghost. *Was* he a ghost?

Was she?

Amy approaches Hana, putting a tentative hand on her shoulder. Hana shoves the paper in her nightgown pocket without thinking.

"Did he hurt you?"

Did he?

"No," Hana says. "I'm just –" At my breaking point. Out of options. Feel like I'm still in Hell. "Tired."

Amy frowns. "You should eat something. Get in some warmer clothes. I'll keep you updated."

Hana rises without another word to her bedroom. She feels like she's floating there – into the shower, out of the shower, into jeans and a sweater, towards the mirror on her dresser.

It's Danael's visage that finally clears the fog as it appears in the reflection. But only for a moment.

Danael's expression is morphed into one Hana hoped

she'd never have to see again. It's the same expression the angel wore before her first deal with Michael all those millennia ago. It's an expression that only meant one thing.

Danael smiles, painfully, as she comes from behind, wrapping her arms around Hana and laying a kiss to her shoulder.

"Goodbye, Hanael."

Hana's vision blurs and she is dragged into unconsciousness. It's a familiar feeling now, that darkness. Somewhere in its depths, she can hear Lucifer laughing.

CHAPTER 41
DANAEL

"Where is Hanael?" Danael freezes as she enters the living room. She is dressed head to toe in the best battle-gear she could find – black, padded combat pants, a loaded weapon holster, and heavy angelic gold-plated chest armor.

"Hanael," Danael begins slowly. "Is resting. She's in no shape to take part in this fight. We're going to go ahead without her."

Amy's eyes narrow. "Resting, huh?"

Still, Amy doesn't elaborate. Neither does Danael. There's no point.

"Oh, good," Cain says, breaking the silence as he enters the room. "I take it we're getting to the fun part?"

"Michael's made his first move," Danael says. "Mnemosyne is readying to meet us on the battlefield with whatever other Gods she can manage."

"Where?" Cain asks, already throwing the remaining weapons into the lined-up duffle bags.

"On the outskirts of Roselake. In the forest clearing, near the two bigger lakes."

That's all that's said before Amy and Danael begin to follow suit in gathering, loading, and making any last-minute enchantments to their weapons. Danael forces her focus to remain lasered on the task at hand.

She, truly, has no more regret to spare.

About twenty minutes later and they're at the front door. Danael takes one final glance towards Hanael's bedroom before slamming the door closed behind them.

The effects of the apocalypse are at their peak. What used to be green and lush is now grey and petrified. Fog can be seen drifting over the two lakes that now housed a bubbling, crimson liquid. Even the air is unclean; the scent of rot wafting somewhere in the distance.

Danael gags. When was the last time she had been outside?

As Danael, Amy, and Cain make their way into the center of the clearing, they are approached by an unfamiliar woman – strong features, olive skin, and a parliament of owls circling above her.

"I am Athena. And I am here to offer my forces towards your cause."

Athena gives a wave and a group of Greek figures emerge from the forest, including Mnemosyne.

Another leader steps forward. This one a stocky, dark-skinned man holding a staff.

"I am Montu. And I am here to offer my forces towards your cause."

And so it goes. Various leaders from various pantheons lead their army onto a battlefield that should have never been a battlefield. Into a situation that started and was going to end with Danael.

Because she *was* going to end it. One way or another.

As if Michael could hear her thoughts, he materializes. An army of battle-clad angels stands at attention behind him.

It's such a surreal sight. The round, clearing of forest almost split down the middle. They're not evenly matched. Not even close. Danael has maybe one-third the number of bodies Michael has. *Maybe.*

Danael wonders, somewhere behind all the rage and adrenaline and regret, in what universe she is on the other side of that forest. Where would she be if she hadn't made that deal with Michael? If Hanael had never been a staple in her existence?

Where would she *want* to be?

"It's a creative attempt, I'll give you that much," Michael says, offering a vague motion to the army now situated behind Danael. "Though one whose, like most efforts of yours, will only end in your undoing."

Danael is gritting her teeth so hard they feel like they're going to shatter. "I guess we'll have to see, won't we?"

Michael smiles and Danael hopes she'll get the opportunity to cut it off.

Michael gives his mark to his army and Danael gives hers. Weapons raise. Orders are shouted in tandem.

They fight.

And blood paints the grey clearing.

Twelve of her angels are dead, bodies mangled from foot traffic of the ongoing fight. Danael isn't sure how many she started out with. Three hundred? Four hundred? How many had Michael?

Is it…ever going to matter?

There's an explosion from behind her and Danael flattens to the ground. The battle energy surges past her and lights a nearby tree aflame. Danael watches it burn.

At least the gods were holding their own. No casualties as of yet. A fact that Michael was becoming increasingly agitated over.

Good. Maybe she could use that to her advantage.

Danael attempts to help herself off the ground before doubling back over with a curse. Every single joint and bone feel like they're on the verge of breaking. She isn't used to expending her magick like this – doesn't think she ever has, even during Lucifer's Rebellion.

A hand touches her shoulder and Danael tries to jolt forward and only manages to cry out in pain.

"It is only me," a soft, feminine voice says. *Feronia*

Feronia had been one of the primary healers for Danael's army. The goddess refused to fight herself but had been incredibly helpful thus far in reducing casualties.

A cold sensation flows through Danael's shoulder to her neck, chest, and down the rest of her body. Feronia helps Danael to a standing position and Danael doesn't have time to thank her before the goddess disappears.

And an angel from Michael's army takes her place.

It's instinct now, to shove her blade into the angel's chest. Danael knows his name. Knows that they used to have occasional meetings together. He was pleasant, all things considered.

Danael yanks out her sword and watches, emotionless, as the black-haired angel collapses to the ground in a pool of his own blood. It trickles down until it meets another pool, and another –

Danael forces a breath. If she was going to make a move against Michael, she needed to do it now, before her energy was completely depleted.

Amongst the shouting, explosions, and clanking of swords, Danael's eyes trail to Athena. The goddess has landed another one of her arrows in its intended angelic target while her army of owls flutter wildly around her.

"I need a distraction," Danael says breathlessly as she stumbles towards her. She barely avoids another blast of battle energy. "I'm going to take a shot at Michael, but he's too heavily guarded."

"I can do that," Athena says, dimpled cheeks rising into a smile. "Paidiá! Pigaíno! Apeleftheróste tin tréla ston echthró mas!"

Athena's owls let out a fierce *'hoot!'* before assorting themselves mid-air and taking aim for Michael's current brigade of angels. There's several shocked cries as the owls begin their attack, causing a visible opening.

Danael takes her shot, sigil-covered blade slicing into Michael's right side. She raises it again, but a sharp pain and audible *'crack'* leaves the weapon falling to the ground. Danael cries out, cradling the broken arm as she sees Michael ready a blast of energy.

Danael swallows the pain and follows suit.

The blast of opposing energies sends them both tumbling to the ground, where Danael's good hand finds a rock and swings it to the side of Michael's face. He falls back flat, dropping his own weapon – *Death's Scythe* – several feet away. Danael eyes it through ringing ears and a hunger she didn't know she possessed.

It's the weapon he killed Nickie with. The only weapon

on this battlefield that would be guaranteed to kill an archangel in one blow. It's only a few feet away. She can get it. God, she *has to get it.*

As Danael crawls towards the weapon, it feels like things are moving in slow motion. Like she's in a dream; caught in quicksand with no way to move any faster.

Just as Danael reaches out her hand to grab the handle, another wraps around her ankle and pulls her backwards. Dread tears at her as she begins kicking desperately, like a child.

One of her feet eventually makes contact with Michael's face. Utilizing the last ounce of adrenaline she has, Danael makes another dash towards the scythe. So close, so close, so close –

Pain explodes against the side of her skull, and before Danael's body even hits the ground, she knows – she's lost.

Her only consolation is that Hanael isn't here to see it.

"You know, I could have killed you long ago, Danael," Michael says. "But I wanted you to see it. See this." Michael waves a hand out to the battlefield and Danael stares with vacant eyes.

Athena is dead. Montu is dead. Mnemosyne is dead. Feronia is dead. Camael, Hadraniel, Jehoel, Muriel, and Ophaniel are all dead. Cain is dead. Danael's not sure where Amy is...

Wait. Cain? How is Cain –

There's a crushing pain in Danael's chest as Michael presses his boot into it. Consciousness begins to fade as every breath feels like a hot iron pressed into her lungs.

"And in your last moments, who will you have to blame? Truly, Danael. Because we both know I can only take credit for so much."

Danael isn't sure if the words come from Michael or her own mind.

Assurance. What a fickle, fickle thing.

Danael was sure every action she made up until this point in time was the correct one. Or at least, the best she could do with the information she had.

Now, she's not sure. Not sure if there was fault with her actions or if it would matter if there was.

If Danael's chest wasn't on fire, she would laugh.

She's come full circle.

The battlefield fades to darkness.

CHAPTER 42
NICKIE

E very second of Nickie's existence had been leading up to this moment. And boy oh boy, was it a hell of a moment.

This amount of blood and violence should make her sick. It should make her curl up on the cold, now dead grass, and vomit.

Instead, she stands tall and beaming and so, *so* hungry.

The black of her sword seems to sparkle under her grip. As if it can feel how ecstatic she is, *how ready*, and is as starving for blood as her.

Nickie cocks her head to one side, raises her sword, and just like that, her army descends upon Michael's. The look on the archangel's face is priceless.

There are, however, other – entities? gods? – that throw Nickie for a loop. A few of her demons are set to attack before Nickie raises her left arm, calling them off. They seemed to be working in Dani's favor and shit – *Dani*.

Not looking good, not looking good.

Nickie cuts her sword across an angel's neck that was unlucky enough to block her view from Dani. Its head falls several feet away and two angels stumble back from it, eyes wide and darting around.

Being invisible made the killing less fun, but was a necessary evil if she planned on truly catching Michael unaware.

Necessary evil. She should put that on a wall calendar.

Ha. Ha. Ha. Ha. Ha. Ha. Ha. Ha. Ha. Ha. Ha. Ha. Ha.

Ha. Ha. Ha. Ha. Ha. Ha. Ha. Ha. Ha. Ha.

Ha. Ha. Ha. Ha. Ha. Ha. Ha.

Ha. Ha. Ha. Ha.

Ha –

Wait.

What is she doing? Why is she just standing around?

Nickie stares at Dani. Her best friend is bloody, injured, and nearly unconscious. Michael stands over her and suddenly...Nickie understands him.

The look in his eyes is no doubt the same that's in her own right now. That hunger for power. The insatiable need to take and take and take until there is nothing left.

It's the same hunger that was in her father's eyes. The same hunger that started every war known to man. The same hunger that God, almighty himself, probably felt on the regular.

Nickie's best friend is bloody, injured, and nearly unconscious and Nickie...doesn't want to help her.

Nickie *can't* help her.

Something happens then, and Nickie will spend the rest of her existence telling herself that the actions that followed were heroic and sacrificial. That she didn't have a choice. That the trolley had to run its course.

Maybe it's true. Maybe it isn't. Nickie isn't sure it matters.

What Nickie *is* sure of is what happened when she died.

It comes to her in a flash. One bleep in the universe that will completely shift Nickie's own.

It doesn't matter if they kill Michael because *Michael didn't start the apocalypse.* Dani did. It was *Dani's* release of power that broke the first seal. It was *Dani's* deal to save Hanael that started the cogs of this entire mess.

Michael knows this. Michael will not kill Dani because of this. Because the only way for the apocalypse to stop is for Dani's life force to be extinguished.

"Consider it a divine, mission, my child."

Maybe it was. Maybe it wasn't. Nickie knows it doesn't matter.

Nickie's body feels heavy and disconnected from itself as she makes her way over to Michael and Dani. Every step feels like a step she is taking away from her humanity.

When Nickie arrives behind Michael, sword raised, she isn't sure how much is left.

She needs to see Dani's face; needs Dani to see hers. Nickie needs it to be burned into her skull. It's the only way this is going to work.

"I'm so sorry, Dani."

"Nickie?"

Nickie shoves the sword through Michael's spine. It glides effortlessly through his midsection and into Dani's.

Somewhere in the distance, Hanael is screaming.

Nickie isn't screaming. She isn't crying. Nickie doesn't feel anything.

Because this was all she needed. Just that...look. Of shock and betrayal and horror on Dani's face as the light fades from her eyes.

That's all she needs to turn it all off.

CHAPTER 43
THE QUEEN OF HELL

Dani's eyes close and a burst of blinding light follows. Nickie's eyes close and she allows the warmth to wash over her. When she opens them, the skies are clear and the battlefield is silent.

Nickie's mind is also silent.

It's so silent it's funny. It makes Nickie laugh.

She laughs and laughs and laughs until she is bent over her knees and wiping the tears from her eyes.

She eventually straightens her body and dusts herself off. It's still silent. There are expressions of varying degrees of rage, confusion, and horror from all the supernatural onlookers.

Nickie smiles at them, pulling out her sword from the two dead bodies. The bloodied weapon pops out with a *"squelch"* before Nickie slides it back in its sheath.

"Guess I'm the main character now," Nickie says.

And doesn't that have a nice ring to it?

.

ACKNOWLEDGMENTS

Foremost, the author would like to express the utmost gratitude for her readers, and those who willingly chose to pick up this novel, despite the warning signs.

Just kidding! Kinda.

Really though. It means the world to me, as a debut indie author, and someone who poured her heart and soul into into this novel, to have anyone as interested to read it as I was to write it!

My goal, with all of my writing, is to create a unique, cerebral, and cathartic experience for the readers. The characters are often bastards. The author is also kind of a bastard. See: my deepest apologies for that ending, and the progression of Dani and Hana's story overall.

I did warn you it wasn't a love story.

I didn't want it to end like that, truly. I wrestled with the ending for over a year. But the characters, as characters do, had taken on a life of their own. They made their decisions, and I was just left to document the fallout.

The story is far from over, though. It just has a new MC. Then again...maybe it was Nickie's story all along.

Did you love Rise and Fall? Hate it? Need therapy from it? I'd love to hear about it! (Note that the author is not responsible for any therapy bills.)

Please leave a review! It helps more than you know.

See you next time.

ABOUT THE AUTHOR

Krista Cooper-Schmidt is novelist, screenwriter, and actor. With a deep love for learning and humanity, Krista aims to create art that is introspective, cathartic, and character-led. She has a bachelor's degree in psychology that she often draws on to bring the most believable characters to the page and screen. Krista lives in Arizona with her wife, their reptiles, and a plethora of books and plants.

instagram.com/krista_writes_666

tiktok.com/@krista_writes_666

STAY IN TOUCH!

www.ingramcontent.com/pod-product-compliance
Lightning Source LLC
Chambersburg PA
CBHW050011120726
47903CB00006B/1724